"In *Wasted Years*, John Harvey deftly weaves past and present, blending the strands of character and story to form the kind of rich tapestry that lifts the police procedural into the realm of mainstream novel."
—Sue Grafton

"Nobody writes police procedurals better than John Harvey. Nobody. Harvey is out of the American gumshoe school: his coppers, including the overweight, jazz-loving Resnick, are plodders not poets, but they know their jobs. *Wasted Years* takes us back and forth in time, weaving contrapuntal melodies involving Resnick and his fellow coppers and drawing us gradually toward an atonal finale that crackles with all the dissonant power of a piano solo by Resnick's hero, Thelonious Monk. Just as Monk made beautiful music from jagged chords and tentatively played notes, so Harvey prods and pokes at the detritus of wasted lives, finding not just despair but also the still-smoldering sparks of human feelings."
—Bill Ott, *Booklist* (boxed and starred)

"Harvey's economy of prose is a given, as is his ability to pull together the many composite parts—the interlocking crimes, the boozing, infidelity, and Resnick's very human bunch of underlings—that make a Charlie Resnick mystery such satisfying reading. No wasted time here."
—*Publishers Weekly* (starred)

"In *Wasted Years*, the fifth police procedural in a haunting series set in the industrial wasteland of Nottingham, Harvey switches time frames like song keys to tell a story about the cold hopes and lost chances that breed crime in the red-brick provinces."
—Marilyn Stasio, *The New York Times Book Review*

"Harvey reminds me of Graham Greene, a stylist who tells you everything you need to know while keeping the prose clean and simple."
—Elmore Leonard

JOHN HARVEY'S
CHARLIE RESNICK CRIME NOVELS

Lonely Hearts ✗

Rough Treatment ✗

Cutting Edge ✗

Off Minor ✗

Wasted Years ✗

Cold Light

Living Proof

Easy Meat ✗

Still Waters

Last Rites

✗ Available in Owl paperback editions

WASTED YEARS

WASTED

YEARS

JOHN HARVEY

A MARIAN WOOD / OWL BOOK
HENRY HOLT AND COMPANY   NEW YORK

Henry Holt and Company, Inc.
Publishers since 1866
115 West 18th Street
New York, New York 10011

The lines on page 308 are from "Ghost of a Chance"
and those on page 311 are from "Temps Greatest Vol II,"
both by John Harvey and published in *Ghosts of a Chance*
(Huddersfield, England: Smith/Doorstop, 1992).

Library of Congress Cataloging-in-Publication Data
Harvey, John.
Wasted years: a Resnick novel / John Harvey.
p.   cm.
ISBN 0-8050-5499-5
I. Title.
PR6058.A6989W37   1993   93-247
                                                  CIP

Henry Holt books are available for special promotions and
premiums. For details contact: Director, Special Markets.

First published in hardcover in 1993 by
Henry Holt and Company, Inc.

First Owl Books Edition 1999

A Marian Wood / Owl Book

Printed in the United States of America
All first editions are printed on acid-free paper.∞

10   9   8   7   6   5   4   3   2   1

Although this novel is set in a real city, it is a work of fiction and its events and characters exist only on its pages and in the author's imagination.

1969

1

"Don't forget the Boat, Charlie. Half-eight, nine. Okay?"

Resnick turned at the sound of Ben Riley's voice, picking out his face without difficulty, the only one amongst the crush of supporters hard against the fence not jeering, calling abuse. Two minutes from the end of an apparent nil-nil draw, a war of attrition played out in the no-man's land of late-season mud, the ball had skidded out towards the wing and the few blades of grass remaining on the pitch. The winger, shaking off one challenge, sprinted thirty yards before cutting in. At the edge of the area, uncertain whether to pass or shoot, a defender felled him from behind, sliding in, feet up, to leave his stud marks high inside the winger's thigh. The free kick, mishit, spun off an outstretched boot and crossed the line into the net. One-nil. Fifty or so visiting fans charged their opponents' end, sharpened coins bright in tight fists.

Resnick had lost his helmet in the first scuffle, something wet sticking to his hair he hoped was spittle, nothing more. They were trying to pull the troublemakers out of the crowd, the worst of them, diving in amongst the flailing feet and words, punched and kicked, not caring, get your hands on one and drag him clear, show you meant business.

He had one now in a headlock, blue and white scarf, bomber jacket, jeans. Doc Martens with steel toe caps that had caught Resnick's ankle more than once.

"Better be there, Charlie."

The last of the players had left the pitch, those in the crowd who'd come with their kids were pushing them towards the exits. "Get down here and give a hand," Resnick called above the noise. "I'll be away sooner."

"No chance." Ben Riley laughed. "Off duty. 'Sides, you're doing okay. Overtime, i'n't it? Come in handy later, buy me a pint."

The youth wriggled his head out from under Resnick's arm and ran on to the pitch. His feet had already started to slither when Resnick's tackle sent him sprawling, the pair of them headlong and thick with mud.

"Right state you've got yourself in there, lad," Resnick's sergeant said to him outside the ground, vans filling up with those arrested, shuttling them to the station to be booked. "Have your work cut out getting that clean. Early shift tomorrow, aren't you?"

Resnick walked along the riverbank towards the bridge, the football ground at his back. The last straggle of fans moved grudgingly aside to let him pass, muttering, avoiding his eyes. Oarsmen were lifting their boat from the water and carrying it towards the nearest of the two rowing clubs that stood back from the path, side by side. Later that evening the buildings would be transformed by flashing lights and speakers pushed almost to distortion. "The Boat, Charlie. Half-eight, nine." Resnick thought he might be lucky to get there at all.

Resnick's landlady had his uniform jacket off his back almost before he was through the front door. "Let me have them trousers, duck, and jump into't bath. Water's hot. I'll have this lot like new by morning, not to fret. Trouble at match, again, I s'pose. Ship lot of 'em off into't army, best thing for 'em. Nice bit of fish tonight, keeping warm in oven."

Resnick handed her his trousers round the bathroom door. Fifty-eight years old and with three lads of her own escaped out into the world—two down the pit, one in Australia—she lavished mushy peas, strong tea and what passed for common sense on her lodger with steely determination. Each night for the past six months, Resnick's planned announcement of his intention to move had foundered upon the directness of her stare. Her need of him. Him and next door's cat she tempted in with scraps, the budgie moulting in its parlour cage.

He finished running the cold and lowered himself into the water. There was a bruise the size and shade of a large orange on his calf, another on his upper arm; he winced as he rubbed soap across his ribs. Careful, the tips of his fingers traced a ridge of dried blood through his hair. Once his transfer to CID came through, that would see an end to all this, alternate Saturdays as punch bag and kicking pole. Object of derision and hate. Once his transfer came through he could go to Mrs. Chambers, clear conscience, and explain. Find a flat on his own, somewhere he could relax, ask people back, liberate his record collection from the tea chest where it languished. How long now since he had heard Paul Gonsalves taking chorus after chorus in front of Duke's band at Newport, the slow fall of Ella's voice in "Every Time We Say Goodbye"?

Resnick walked along Arkwright Street, away from the city, the muffled bass patterns audible before he stepped onto the bridge. In shadows close by the river, young men made one-handed assaults upon girls' clothing, metal clasps and elastic, glow of cigarettes cupped between their fingers. A Hammond organ surged as Resnick handed over his money, stepped inside. Thick with bodies, the room swam with the scent of sweat and tobacco and the possibilities of sex. The sweet odour of dope which he willed himself not to recognise. On the stage, a seven-piece band was playing "Green Onions." In those days, they were always playing "Green Onions."

"Charlie! Here. Over here."

Ben Riley was over by the wall, one hand resting against it, arm extended past the head of a girl with mascara eyes and a plum mouth. Not a minute over seventeen.

"Charlie, this is Lesley. Reckons as how she's here every week, on the bus from Ilkeston, but I told her, got to be having us on. Here that often, we'd've seen her for sure. Eh, Charlie?"

Ben Riley winked and Lesley glanced at Resnick's face and then away, a glass of rum and black held close against her waist.

"Lesley's got a mate, haven't you, Lesley? Carole. Off dancing with some bloke right now, but she'll be back any minute." Ben winked again. "What d'you reckon, Lesley? Think she'll go for Charlie, here? Your mate Carole?"

Lesley giggled.

The band took a break.

Carole turned out to be stooped, self-consciously tall, a narrow-faced girl with fair hair and a soft voice that was lost almost as soon as it left her body.

"Can't win 'em all," Ben Riley said, squashed up against Resnick in the crush for the bar. "Maybe she's got hidden talents."

Resnick shook his head. "It doesn't matter," he said. "I'm not interested."

"Come on. Don't be such a— Two pints, love, rum and black and a lager top."

"You carry on," Resnick said. "I'll catch up with you tomorrow."

Ben handed him one of the pints and the rum and black-currant. "All right, you have Lesley. We'll do a swop. Another couple of these and they won't notice anyhow."

Resnick sighed and pushed his way back to where the two girls were waiting. "Here you go," Ben said cheerily, "reinforcements."

"We'll have to be going soon," Lesley said. "Our last bus."

"No, 's'all right." Ben grinned. "You don't have to worry about that. We'll see you right."

Resnick handed over the drink and stepped away. "To-morrow then, Ben. Okay?" He nodded at the girls and moved off into the crowd.

"What's up with him?" he heard Lesley ask.

He was moving too fast to hear Ben Riley's reply, and besides, by then the band was back on the stage.

Nursing his pint, Resnick found a space up close but out of range of the dancers—he'd ducked flailing arms enough for one day as it was. The tenor player squirted out a quick spiralling phrase and set to readjusting his reed. A jazzman by nature, Resnick reckoned: given a mid-tempo blues and the chance to stretch out, he was worth careful listening. Now, though, it was a quick run through "Time Is Tight," a change of riff, a spotlight—"Put your hands together for the fabulous . . ."—the horns hit three notes hard and the singer launched into "Tell Mama" as if her life, or the next thirty minutes, depended upon it.

Ruth Strange.

Ruthie.

Resnick had seen her before, this band and that, one club or another. A small woman with a rash of auburn hair, cheekbones that threatened to pierce the skin where they touched. She wore a black sweater, sleeves pushed back to the elbow, black skirt, black tights, red heeled shoes. One hand gripped the mike stand when she sang, the other punched or tore or windmilled through the air. A voice that seemed to come from some other—larger, older—body altogether.

Before the applause for her first song had begun to fade, she had signalled to the keyboard player, closed her eyes, thrown back her head, beaten in the tempo with an open hand against her thigh.

Slow blues in three flats.

Wedged into the middle of the floor, Ben Riley and the stoop-shouldered girl stood with their arms around each other, scarcely moving.

Wasted years . . . Ruth sang, raw-edged.

"Sure you don't want to dance?" Lesley's voice close by Resnick's shoulder.

"No, thanks. Really."

A suit-yourself shrug and she was turning away.

> *Every night I spend waiting,*
> *All those dreams and wasted tears,*
> *Every minute, every second, babe,*
> *The worst of all my fears,*
> *When you walk back through my door again,*
> *All you'll have for me are empty arms,*
> *And empty promises,*
> *And ten more, ten more, oh baby,*
> *Ten more wasted years.*

The band driving hard behind her, the final note torn and ugly, a wrench of pain. Arms loose now by her side, she stood, head bowed. Applause. Resnick finished his pint and checked his watch. Early shift. Ben Riley no longer in sight. He left his plastic glass on the corner of the bar, rather than have it splintered underfoot. A final glance over his shoulder as he moved towards the door.

"Hey!" A woman's voice, sharp and aggrieved.

"I'm sorry."

"I should think so, too."

"I was just—"

"Leaving. Yes, I can see. And I was coming in."

"I didn't mean . . ."

"Difference was, I was looking where I was going."

"Look, I said I'm sorry. I don't know what else—"

"To say. No, I don't suppose you do. Walking all over my feet like that. It's a wonder I didn't go flying back down the stairs. And don't stand there grinning."

Resnick bit his lip and looked at her seriously: not tall, around the same age as himself, mid-twenties, not pretty, anger bringing brightness to her eyes, a glow to her skin. Her shoe, where he had trodden on it, was scuffed; her tights were torn.

He reached towards his pocket. "Maybe I could buy you . . . ?"

"A new pair of tights? Don't bother."

"I was thinking more of a drink."

"What?" Eyes widening. "And pour it down my front."

"Elaine," a voice said off to the side and Resnick realised for the first time that she was not alone.

"All right," she said, withering Resnick with one more look as she squeezed past. "Coming."

Outside on the bank, the water looked dark. Buses moved in slow convoy across the bridge, heading towards the lights of the city. Gravel crunched lightly underfoot. "Elaine," Resnick said quietly, testing the name on his tongue. It would be more than four years before he would say it to her face.

1992

2

"Espresso, Inspector?"

"Please."

"Full, yes?"

Resnick nodded and unfolded the early edition of the local paper, thumbing through the pages in search of hard news, knowing he wouldn't like what he found. Fifteen-year-old youth wounded by four girls in knife attack; old woman of eighty-three robbed and raped; Asian shopkeeper driven from estate by racist taunts and threats of violence. In the magistrate's court, a man explaining why he pushed a petrol bomb through his neighbour's letter box—"Night and day they had this music playing, night and day. I asked them to turn it down but they never took no notice. Something inside me just snapped."

Setting the newspaper aside, Resnick sipped the strong coffee and, for a moment, closed his eyes.

The Italian coffee stall was located amongst the market stalls on the upper level of one of the city's two shopping centres. Vegetables, fruit and flowers, fish and meat and bread, Afro-Caribbean and Asian specialities; the two Polish delicatessen stalls where Resnick did much of his shopping, replying to greetings offered in his family's language with the flattened vowels of the English Midlands. His stubborn use of English was not a slight, merely a way of saying I was born here, this city, this is where I was brought up. These streets. Eyes open, Resnick scanned the other customers sitting round the U-shaped stall: middle-aged shoppers whose varicose veins were giving them gyp; mums with kids who couldn't make up their minds which flavour milkshake and would never sit still; old men with rheumy eyes who sat for hours over the same strong tea; the photography student from the Poly who drank two cappuccinos back to back and whose fingers smelt of chemicals; the solicitor who could eat a doughnut without getting as much as a granule of sugar on the skirt of her power suit; the tramp who waited till someone bought him a drink, then skulked off by the photo machine to finish it, legs visible through the rags of his trousers. These people.

Angled across from where Resnick was sitting, Suzanne Olds licked her finger ends clean with the fastidious delicacy of one of his cats. Lifting her leather briefcase from the floor, she slid from her stool and approached. The last time they had spoken, one of the solicitor's clients had been up on five charges under Sections 18 and 47 of the Offences Against the Person Act, shuffling alibis like a dog-eared pack of cards.

"Inspector."

"Ms. Olds."

"I was at dinner with a new colleague of yours a few nights ago. Helen Siddons. Very bright. Sharp." Suzanne Olds smiled. "Aware of the issues."

"I thought crime was the issue: solving it, preventing it."

Suzanne Olds laughed. "Come off it, Inspector, you're not as naive as that."

Resnick watched her walk away, incongruously elegant and somewhat intimidating as she passed between local grown spinach and pink and white shell suits, the latter greatly reduced, council clothing vouchers welcomed. He had met Helen Siddons a number of times since she joined the local force; transferred from Sussex, detective inspector at twenty-nine, eighteen months and she would have moved on. A graduate with a degree in law, she was being propelled by the Home Office along a fast track towards the highest ranks. She should be looking at assistant chief constable by the time she was forty. Resnick could see how well she and Suzanne Olds would have got along; serious conversations between courses about the sexism endemic in the force, racism, the errors—careless or malicious—in police evidence which had led to conviction after conviction being so publicly overturned.

Why was it, when he agreed, at heart, with most of the beliefs women like Helen Siddons and Suzanne Olds held, he found it so hard to give them his support? Was it simply that he found them a threat? Or the almost certain feeling that the support of men like himself, career coppers for more than twenty years, would not be welcomed?

"Another?" asked the stall owner, whisking his cup into the air.

Tempted, Resnick checked his watch and shook his head. "Got to be off. Important meeting. Maybe see you later. Cheers."

And he ambled away, shoulders hunched, a wave at the man from the fish stall forever on at him about giving a bit of a talk to the Church Fellowship, a bulky man in a shiny suit that had been beautifully tailored by his uncle more than fifteen years before—for somebody else and not for him.

Reg Cossall was standing on the steps of the central police station, swopping tales of arson with the senior officer from the fire station alongside.

"Hey up, Charlie," Cossall said, falling into step with Resnick as he pushed through the front door. "Heard the latest?"

Resnick was sure he was going to, any minute.

"They only reckon Grafton's going to get Tom Parker's spot. Can you believe that? Malcolm bloody Grafton a chief inspector. Over the likes of you and me."

Resnick grunted noncommittally and started on the stairs.

"Tell you what, Charlie. That bastard's done so much sucking up, must have a gullet like anyone else's large intestine. Not to mention wearing through three sets of knee-caps."

Resnick opened the door and waved Cossall through ahead of him. Most of the other officers were already present, a round dozen, inspector and above. Maps marked with coloured pins and tape hung from the walls; memos and computer printouts lay in plastic wallets on tables of walnut veneer. The overhead projector was in place, screen pulled down. Jack Skelton, Resnick's superintendent and heading up this particular task force, stubbed out one of his rare cigarettes, poured a glass of water from the jug, cleared his throat and called the meeting to order.

"Operation Kingfisher, let's see what we've got." Eighteen months previously, five men, masked and wearing track suits, had forced their way into a bank in Old Basford right on closing time. The two remaining customers had been told to lie on the floor, the cashiers bound and gagged. One of the weapons the gang had been carrying, a shotgun with sawn-off barrels, had been placed against the assistant manager's head. They had got away with close to forty thousand pounds, changing cars three times in making their escape.

Driving in to open a newly refurbished supermarket at Top Valley five months later, the manageress had her Orion forced off the road and a pistol flourished in her face. Only after she had facilitated the opening of the safe was the gun withdrawn from sight. All the manageress could tell the police about the person threatening her was that he was of average height and wearing a Mickey Mouse mask.

Mickey was on hand when the Mansfield branch of the Abbey National was held up one busy Saturday. It was Goofy, though, who placed a suitcase beside the protective screens on the counter and informed the nearest cashier that it contained a bomb. None of the staff felt like testing the possibility that it was just a bluff. Nor did they appreciate suggestions that the whole thing was a publicity stunt on behalf of Euro Disney.

The most recent robbery, three weeks ago now, took place in the inner city, Lenton Boulevard, just as the sub–post office was opening for the day. The door was locked from the inside and, while a line of grumbling customers grew along the pavement, the staff were tied to one another, shut inside a cupboard and warned that if they tried to get out or raise the alarm, shots would be fired through the door.

Four robberies: close on half a million pounds.

Five men: all wearing gloves, instantly disposable clothing, masks. All armed.

Between three and five cars, stolen days in advance, used on each occasion.

Threats of violence, so far not carried out.

Some of the stolen money had surfaced in places as far apart as Penzance and Berwick-on-Tweed; most of it, it was assumed, had already been laundered abroad for a fat commission.

Operation Kingfisher had been set up after the second incident, between thirty-five and fifty officers had been involved. All of the information gathered had been entered by civilian operatives on to disc and checked against the Home Office's central computer. Possible links were being followed up in Leeds, Glasgow, Wolverhampton. Known criminals implicated in similar raids were being tracked down and interviewed. Comparisons with similar robberies in Paris and Marseilles were being made. Flight manifests at East Midlands and Birmingham airports had been checked.

Sooner or later, somebody would make a mistake; so far, no one had. Resnick hoped it wouldn't be some building society clerk or bank teller acting out of bravery or panic, a misplaced sense of loyalty to his employers.

"You know what, don't you, Charlie?" Cossall said as they were leaving, best part of two hours later.

"What's that, then, Reg?"

"What this lot reminds us of. That bloody business— when was it?—ten years ago."

But Resnick didn't want to be reminded. Not then or ever. Refusing Cossall's offer of a quick pint in the Peacock, he slipped into a pub on High Pavement he rarely used and where he was unlikely to be known. *That bloody business ten years ago.* Never one to drink in the middle of the day, Resnick surprised himself with two large vodkas, one sharp after the other, the tonic he had bought to dilute them still open and unused when he pushed his way back on to the street.

3

Peter Hewitt farmed several hundred acres in what had once been known as Rutland—the smallest county in England. To those families whose roots had taken long before local government rationalisation, it still was. To them, Hewitt was an outsider, welcomed guardedly. He represented new blood, new stock, new ideas.

Hewitt had not always been a farmer. Brought up, as farm children always were, to take his share of the work from an early age, he had turned his back on the land at seventeen and gone to sea. As an officer in the Royal Navy, he had served in the Falklands Campaign, a lieutenant commander on H.M.S. *Argonaut.* Along with other vessels, his ship had come under heavy hostile fire in Falkland Sound: her fellow frigate, the *Ardent,* had been sunk with the loss of over twenty lives; the *Argonaut* had been more fortunate, she had remained afloat and only two of her crew had died.

Only.

The word teased Hewitt cruelly still.

He thought of the parents of these men when they heard the news; thought of chance and misfortune, stability and flow, the sea and the land. As soon as he was able, he left the navy.

Hewitt's father had retired; rather, the recession and rheumatoid arthritis had retired him. Now he lived quietly in a cottage in Northamptonshire, grew vegetables, kept goats, grew lonely. Peter had bought a farm near him but not too near; his intention had always been to go his own way. He had given this a great deal of thought and it seemed right that his methods and means should be as organic as good business sense and the land would allow.

In addition to the acreage given over to crops, Hewitt kept a herd of Friesan cows and had several contracts to provide organic milk. His wife, Pip, ran a profitable farm shop. Together, they encouraged local groups and schools to visit the farm so that they could explain their methods. Spread the word. Hewitt found himself increasingly in demand as a speaker in various parts of the country, occasionally in Holland or even France.

This work, as an ambassador for organic farming, he took seriously, just as he did his time as a school governor, his stint as a J.P. If you take something from the community, he told friends less convinced, you have a duty to put something back. It was the way he felt about the land. It was why he had accepted the invitation to be on the Board of Visitors at the local prison without hesitation. Part of his duties there was to serve on the Local Review Committee, whose recommendations were forwarded to the parole board.

This was why he was driving in today, beneath low skies, to interview a long-stay prisoner whose application for parole was due for review. *Showing a callous disregard for the safety of others, you were prepared to threaten and use violence in the pursuit of personal gain.* Hewitt had read the judge's summing-up before leaving the house. The man he was going to see had been found guilty on five separate counts and sentenced to fifteen years. The nature of the offences, the use of violence, meant there would be no automatic release once two-thirds of that sentence had been served. After ten years, however, there was the question of discretionary parole.

Hewitt slowed as the side road leading to the prison came in sight, checked his rearview mirror, changed lanes, signalled his intention clearly.

The moment he walked through the twin doors and heard them close behind him, Peter Hewitt felt something leave his body. He would not regain it until some hours later, pacing the fields of his farm, marvelling over visible horizons.

"Good one for you today, sir," the warder remarked. "Very nice fellow, I'm sure."

Prior was sitting in a room without view or natural light: plain wooden table, metal chairs with cloth seat and back. He scarcely glanced up as the door opened.

"One thing we didn't succeed in teaching him," the warder said. "Manners."

"Thank you," Hewitt said. "We shall be fine."

As the door was being closed, Hewitt introduced himself and offered his hand. Sitting, he took out the packet of cigarettes he had bought that morning at the village shop and slid them across the table. Box of matches, too.

Prior said thanks and helped himself, lit up and looked at his visitor squarely for the first time.

"You understand, of course, the importance of this interview?" Hewitt asked.

Something of a smile floated at the back of Prior's eyes. "Oh, yes," he said.

Prison had stripped weight away from him, made him strong. It was that way for some, a few; those it didn't institutionalise or weaken, break down. The ten years had greyed Prior's skin to putty, but it was tight, the muscles of his legs and arms, chest and back were strong: the eyes were still alive. Sit-ups, push-ups, stretches, curls. Concentration. Save for one occasion, whenever he had been tempted to lash out, respond, overreact, he had thought about this moment, this meeting. He had kept himself largely to himself, waiting for this: the possibility of release.

"Before I can make a positive recommendation," Hewitt was saying, "I have to be convinced in my own mind that you have no intention of offending again."

Prior held his gaze. "No problem, then, is there?"

Hewitt blinked, shifted the position of his chair. "The offences you committed . . ."

"Long time ago. Different life." Prior released smoke through his nose. "Wouldn't happen again."

"It did then."

"What I think," Prior said, "people change."

Hewitt leaned forward, leaned back.

"You believe that, don't you?" Prior said.

"Yes. Yes, as a matter of fact I do."

"Well, then . . ." This time the smile was unbridled. "There you go."

"Have you thought," Hewitt asked after some moments, "about work, finding a job?"

"Used to be a chippie . . ."

"Carpenter?"

"Joiner, yes. That's my trade."

"Good, good. I'm sure your probation officer will try to find something for you. After all, having a skill, a real skill, it's what so many men in your position sadly lack."

Way this is going, Prior thought, better than I could have hoped.

"You've friends on the outside?"

"A few."

"That might be willing to help you find work?"

"They might."

"And you've a wife."

"No."

"Surely you're married?"

"Legally, maybe, but no. Not anymore. Not really."

"Ten years, it's a lot to withstand. It takes a very special woman . . ."

"Oh, she was that, all right."

"Was? She isn't . . . ?"

"I haven't seen her. Don't know where she is."

"I'm sorry."

Prior shook his head. "One of those things. Can't put in the sort of time I have, expect everything to stay the same."

Hewitt was thinking what he would do if for any reason Pip left him. A partnership, that was how he referred to it when he was making his after-dinner speeches, a partnership in which my wife is the strongest part.

"What I want to do," Prior was saying, "start my life over again, do things right, before it's too late."

"Of course, I understand." Second chances, second lives, they were very much what Peter Hewitt was about. One of the two men killed on board the *Argonaut* had been celebrating his eighteenth birthday that day. No second chances in his life. Hewitt hated the waste, the brave waste.

"Exactly," he said again. "I do understand."

Prior looked into his face directly, held his gaze. "Good," he said several seconds later. "Good. Because too much of my life has been wasted. There are things I want to do while I still have the time."

4

Darren knew about prisons. YOIs anyway. Young Offender Institutions. Places like Glen Parva, where, if you didn't find a way of topping yourself in the first few months, chances were you learned enough to graduate into the big time.

Glen Parva: that's where he'd met Keith. Walked into his cell, free time, thinking to scrounge a snout, and there was Keith, all five five of him, struggling to loop his towel round one end of the upturned bed.

"What the fuck d'you think you're up to?" Darren had yelled. One thing for certain, what Keith hadn't been doing, devoting himself to spring cleaning.

Keith's only answer had been to hide the towel behind his back and blub: tears like some six-year-old caught offing sweets from the corner shop.

"You don't want to do that," Darren had said, sitting on Keith's bunk. "Give these bastards the satisfaction of cutting you down. How much longer you got to do, anyway?"

"Couple of months."

"You'll get through that."

Keith hung his head. "I won't."

Darren looked at him, pathetic little bugger, sticky-out ears and soft skin and hands like a child's. No wonder they'd been at him again in the showers, gang banging him most likely, smearing smuggled-in lipstick round his mouth before making him suck them off.

"'S'okay," Darren had said, "I'll look out for you. Anyone tries anything, let them know they got to deal with me."

Keith was looking at him in wonder. "Why d'you want to do that?" he asked.

Darren had seen this film once, staying at his sister's, Sutton-in-Ashfield, western it'd been. This soldier, cavalry, spurs and sabre and yellow stripes, big deal, he saves the life of some Indian chief and after that the Indian follows him everywhere, waiting for the chance to do the same for him. Some kind of crazy blood brothers. Shit! That wasn't what it was like with Keith and him. Reason Darren hung around with Keith after they were released, nothing to do with that old bollocks. What he put up with Keith for, there wasn't nothing Keith didn't know about cars. No car he couldn't nick.

Crossing towards the parade of shops, lunchtime, Darren looked at his watch: one fifty-four. If Keith was late, he'd take his legs off at the knees. Laughing aloud: poor sod was any shorter he'd be underground.

Keith had cased the multi-storey from top to bottom, nice Orion worth making off with, owner obligingly leaving the parking ticket sticking out of the ashtray. All Keith had to do at the exit was hand over a quid—cars came, this was cheap at the price.

What he hadn't reckoned on was road works on the ring road, single-lane traffic and there he was, trapped behind some geriatric in a Morris Minor—nice motor, though, well looked after, likely worth more now than when it was new.

Keith knew full-well Darren would be less than happy. No way he was going to make it on time now. Working the horn wasn't going to make a scrap of difference. Boring, aside from anything else, not even a radio to listen to. Almost the first thing he'd noticed, sizing up the car, some bastard'd already had the radio away, torn wires all over the place, owner too tight to get it replaced.

The road suddenly widened and Keith stood on the accelerator. Too close to two for comfort: Darren wasn't going to be worth speaking to.

It had been a pizza place last time Darren had been there. Deep dish or thin 'n' crispy. Hawaiian a speciality. Darren had made the mistake of having one once. Pineapple chunks that stuck in your throat like gobbets of vomit: ground beef and gristle a dog wouldn't cock its leg to piss on.

Before that, what? A Chinese chippie. Paki sweet shop. When he was a kid, one of them baker's where they sold stale cobs in bags of three, half price, the morning after—cheese and onion or turkey breast or haslet with a touch of Branston pickle.

Across the street the Co-op offices had been bulldozed flat to make way for a spanking new DIY superstore—three floors of wallpaper, fake Formica and self-assembly kitchen units that fell apart faster than you could screw them together. Darren had got a job there once, sixteen, humping great boxes about the back, ten quid and calluses at the end of the day, no tax, no questions asked. That had been before he had the good fortune to get himself nicked and sent away: before he had learned there were easier ways to make a living.

Now there were signs plastered across the superstore windows—EVERYTHING AT HALF-PRICE, MUST GO, CLOSING DOWN. The pizza place was boarded up: fly posters for Soul

II Soul and Springsteen and The Fabulous Supremes LIVE at Ritzy's torn and graffitied over. In the doorway, cardboard boxes and a nest of rags: somebody's home.

Out of the remaining six shops set back from the street, only three were still in business. A newsagent's with metal grilles at its windows, a sign—NO MORE THAN TWO SCHOOL-CHILDREN AT ANY ONE TIME—taped to its door. A factory textile shop, direct from the makers to you, cut out the middleman, sold tea towels and shirts with little to tell the difference between them. Between those two, a sub-office of the Amber Valley Building Society, closed for lunch between twelve forty-five and two.

It was now almost a quarter past.

Darren looked across at the door, Open sign hanging down; half a mind to go in on his own, get the business done. But then what? Legging it down the main road, sack on his back?

He was flexing the fingers of his right hand when the blue Orion slipped into sight and eased towards the kerb, Keith's face just visible in the lower half of the windscreen.

"What happened to you? Go by McDonald's for a Big Mac and a chocolate shake?"

"Chicken McNugget."

Darren had hold of the front of Keith's T-shirt, like to choke him, before he realised it was a joke.

"Anyone go in yet?" Keith asked, once Darren had let him go.

Darren shook his head. They had watched the office carefully the past three days; not once had they had a customer between reopening after lunch and twenty minutes past the hour. It was now two-seventeen.

"Why don't I dump the car?" Keith suggested. "Try again tomorrow."

"Like fuck we will!"

Keith shrugged, not about to argue. He knew that tone

in Darren's voice all too well; had seen him break a glass in a youth's face once, just for asking him was he sure he didn't have a light?

"The talking," Darren said. They were crossing the patch of bricked-off earth in front of the shops, stepping between the dog turds.

"What about it?"

"Leave it to me."

Keith nodded: as if he needed telling.

Lorna willed herself not to turn her head towards the clock, up there on the wall between the aerial photograph of the High Peak and a poster advertising High-Yield Tessa returns. This was the part of the day that always dragged, right from when she got back after having her packet of Slimma chicken and vegetable soup for lunch, two pieces of Swedish crisp-bread with just a scraping of extra low-fat margarine, from there through to tea, four or four-fifteen, Marjorie fretting over the kettle, leaving the tea bag in too long, shaking a tin of custard creams under her nose no matter how many times Lorna pursed her lips and waved them away.

Marjorie back there now with Becca, practically fawning over her, turned Lorna's stomach, that's what it did. Becca in her smart little grey suit with its high collar and tapered skirt she wasn't above sliding up her skinny legs whenever the area manager happened to pop in. Three years of elocution lessons and a Polytechnic degree in Modern Languages and they'd made her acting branch manager about as soon as she'd finished her training. Two years older than Lorna, nothing more.

"It's still confidential, of course, but Mr. Spindler says I'll be moving on to one of the main branches within the year."

She'd heard her one day, telling Marjorie as if she was

doing her a big favour, letting her in on a secret, and Marjorie, all soggy-eyed, "Oh, Becca! How lovely!"

Never mind the way Spindler treated Marjorie herself, patronising bastard. "Well, Marjorie, keeping these two youngsters in order, are we?" Seventeen years she'd worked there, Marjorie, passed over every chance of promotion there was, all the while pretending that it hadn't happened.

Not me, Lorna thought, that's not what's going to happen to me. Eighteen months tops and I'm putting in for a transfer, and if I don't get it, I'm straight off to the Halifax, the Abbey National, the Leeds. And I don't care who knows it.

Twenty-three minutes past two. There—I looked.

Oh, well.

Lorna eased her back against the padded chair and turned the pages of last week's *Bella,* which was resting on her knees. In the raised area behind her, she could hear Becca and Marjorie at their desks: Becca going on about her holiday in Orlando, Marjorie retelling the story of her sister's ovarian cyst, the size of a small baby—Sunday mornings going round car boot sales for a shawl and a secondhand cot before she realised the truth.

The door opened slowly and Lorna's eyes flicked back towards the clock. Twenty-five past. Old Mr. Foreman in his carpet slippers and his zip not properly fastened, paying in fifteen pounds and withdrawing five—"Did you see such-and-such last night? Bloody tripe! Don't know why those people get paid."

She closed her magazine and slid it beneath the ledger.

Darren stood just inside the door, Keith behind him. Already he could feel his heart pumping. Three women, one at the front, behind the only cashier's window in use, the others further back, neither of them looking round, paying any attention. The girl at the window, though, round glasses, staring at him through big round glasses, surprised. Well, he'd give her something to be surprised about.

"The door," he said to Keith, moving forward.

"Uh?"

"Watch the door."

Lorna sat readying her smile, a new customer, probably nothing more than an enquiry, how d'you go about opening an account?

"Lorna Solomon?" Darren smiled, reading her name off the engraved plate at the side of the window.

He wasn't bad-looking when he smiled.

"Yes," she said. "How may I help you?"

Darren laughed, more of a chuckle than a laugh. He opened the front of the loose leather jacket he was wearing and pulled out a bin bag, black. "Here," he said, passing it through to her. "Fill that."

Behind the blue-framed glasses, Lorna blinked.

It had to be a joke, a wind-up, someone kidding her for a bet, a dare.

"Do it," Darren said. "Don't make no fuss. Do it now, eh?"

It wasn't a dare.

Lorna's gaze shifted towards the second youth, far shorter, over by the door. Neither of them older than she was herself.

"Don't keep me waiting," Darren said, his voice a little louder.

"Miss Solomon," came Becca's toffee-nosed voice from behind. "Is something the matter?"

"This gentleman has a query, Miss Astley," Lorna said, turning her head. "Perhaps you should deal with it yourself."

"What the fuck're you playing at?" said Darren, face thrust close against the screen.

"What's going on?" said Keith, stepping away from the door.

Trim legs on the short flight of steps, Becca saw the plastic bag in Lorna's hand, read, uncertainly, the expression on her face, saw the movement of the young man behind.

Becca threw poise and elocution to the winds and screamed.

Darren pulled the hammer clear of his coat and smashed it against the centre of the screen.

Fumbling with his passbook, trying to free it from its plastic cover, Harry Foreman came through the door, whistling through his half-dozen remaining teeth the theme from "Limelight." Always one of his favourites. That Mantovani, couldn't be beat.

"Keith, where the hell did he come from?"

Keith wasn't certain: about anything.

"Here . . ." said Harry.

The third time Darren hit the screen, it splintered, top to bottom.

Lorna crouched beneath the counter, shielding her eyes. Becca ran back up the steps, turned and ran back down.

"Here . . ." said Harry Foreman as Keith grabbed hold of his bony arms and pushed him back against the wall.

Marjorie eased her way across the rear of the office towards the telephone.

"Stuff the money in that bag," yelled Darren, "and quick!"

But Lorna didn't seem to be listening. Inch by inch, she was sliding her hand towards the alarm.

"Take your hands off of me," Harry said, ducking his balding head towards Keith's face. "Don't think I'm going to be pushed around by the likes of you."

Darren knocked away a section of screen and vaulted onto the counter. Becca stopped screaming and cried instead. "Hello," said Marjorie quietly into the receiver she was shielding behind her size-sixteen dress, "I want to talk to the police."

Lorna squinted up at Darren's black jeans, the worn soles of his Nike trainers, fear and fury on his face, and pressed her thumb against the button hard.

"Darren!" called Keith. "The alarm!"

"Fucking genius!" Darren said. "That's you." He aimed a kick at Lorna's head and missed, swung wildly with the hammer and liberated several inches of varnished chipboard from the countertop.

Harry Foreman stuck out a leg and Keith half-tripped, staggered wildly before breaking open the skin above his left eye on the corner of the wall beside the door.

"What's this?" Darren said, jumping down. "Home fucking Guard?"

"Don't think I'm frightened of you," Harry said.

Darren swung the hammer two-handed and cracked it against the side of his head, just in front of the ear. Before the old man had finished falling, Darren was out of the door.

In front of him, Keith was skating across several yards of mud as if they were glass. An Asian face peered round the newsagent's door, then pulled back from sight. Further up the street, a mother pushed two children under two in a pram. As Darren cursed him, Keith's fingers fumbled with the keys. His head felt as if it had been split open and blood was trickling into the corner of his eye.

Darren snatched the keys from him and pulled open the car door. "What the hell d'you lock it for?" he asked, pushing Keith inside.

"Leave it unlocked outside here," said Keith. "Some clever bastard'll have it away."

He turned the key in the ignition and the engine fired first time; scraping the gears, he revved hard and swung the wheel. The first police siren could be heard no more than half a mile away.

"Watch the pram!" Darren called as Keith hit the kerb and skidded up over the pavement, evading the pram but striking the mother, rear bumper swiping her legs and knocking her off her feet. Swerving wildly, Darren rounded a lamppost, squealed back onto the road and accelerated away.

"Next time," Darren said as Keith threw the car into a right-hand turn and headed the wrong way up a one-way street, "make sure you're not fucking late!"

5

"Bloody mess, Charlie, that's what it was. Beginning to end." Skelton hung his overcoat behind the door, automatically smoothing the shoulders along with his hands. He and Malcolm Grafton had been comparing notes over a couple of glasses of a nice Valdepeñas when his bleeper had sounded the alert. "Bunch of professionals is one thing, but this—couple of cowboys without a brain between them. . . ."

Distaste showed clearly on the superintendent's face as he settled behind his desk, careful first to unbutton the jacket of his double-breasted suit, a soft grey wool-mix smelling faintly of the dry cleaner's.

"Walk in off the street and ten minutes later there's an old boy fighting for his life in intensive care, one woman with a suspected broken leg and another under sedation for shock."

Sitting across from Skelton, Resnick nodded. He had spoken to the doctor at the hospital himself; Harry Foreman's condition was touch and go. The injured mother's two children were being looked after by the Social Services Emergency Duty Team until contact could be made with either the estranged father or the grandmother, living out at Heanor.

"Week before last," Skelton was saying, "went to this seminar at Loughborough, Department of Criminology. Pair today would have given them a field day. Deprived area. Disadvantaged youth. Striking at a building society because it symbolises the property-owning class that is still presented as the desirable norm."

Resnick looked past Skelton's head towards the window, the red brick of factory buildings that had either been left to crumble or were slowly being turned into architect-designed flats with central saunas and swimming pools that no one had the money to rent or buy. Out there, the norm was mornings at the job centre, signing on, filling in forms for housing benefits; afternoons amongst the bright lights and plastic plants of the shopping centres, trying to keep warm. Whatever language the professor might have couched it in, Resnick thought, as far as he was concerned the economic theories about the causes of crime held more water than most.

More so than those of the Secretary of State for Education, who had recently blamed the increasing crime rate on the Church's failure to preach the perils of hellfire and damnation. Over half the churches in Resnick's patch had been pulled down or deconsecrated and turned into sports centres; of the rest, at least two had been set on fire themselves.

"Banks and building societies," Skelton said, "hundred percent increase in robberies in the last two years. Mostly armed." He pinched the bridge of his nose between forefinger and thumb. "As we know all too well. At least those two today only went in with a hammer."

"I don't suppose Harry Foreman'll be thankful for that," Resnick said.

"If it had been a gun," Skelton said, "he might not have been so keen to get involved."

"And if he had?" Resnick asked.

Skelton shook his head, dismissing the thought. "Members of the public, situations like that, best keeping their heads down, eyes open. No place for heroes."

Do that, Resnick thought, not going to be a great help as witnesses, aside from remembering the colour of their own shoes.

"Interviews proceeding, Charlie? Your team."

"Yes, sir."

"Keep me up to date. Anything that looks like a positive ID. Should be in a better position when we get prints in tomorrow."

Resnick was on his feet.

Skelton lifted a memo from his desk. "Two calls already from the local union rep, Banking, Insurance and Finance. Requests an urgent appointment. Why aren't we doing more to protect his members?"

He sighed and straightened the family photographs on his desk and Resnick, sensing his own stomach about to rumble, managed to keep it under control until he was on the other side of the door.

The CID room was in chaos. Four days before, the station's heating system had gone on the blink and, despite having the central boiler overhauled, there were still parts of the building to which no heat had returned. This was one of them. Cold enough, in Mark Divine's words, to freeze a witch's tit.

Some of the desks had been hauled out into the corridor, others piled on top of one another while the source of the trouble was tracked down. Several lengths of floorboard had been prised up and now rested precariously against a well-marked street map of the city. Pieces of piping lay on most available surfaces and a workman in grey overalls lay on his stomach, hammering cheerfully while his mate sipped cold tea and laboured over the previous day's quick crossword.

"Is it always like this?" Lorna asked, the tempo of the hammering increasing.

Kevin Naylor, interviewing her about the robbery, shook his head and smiled. "Not always."

"You are busy, though? Plenty to do."

"Oh, yes. Pretty busy."

Lorna crossed her legs: soft, between hammer blows, the faintest swoosh of nylon over nylon. "You're lucky," she said.

Naylor looked at her: how come?

"What happened today, first bit of excitement in weeks. Months. Since before Christmas." She leaned forward just a little. "What it was, this chap come in, red nose and top hat, tinsel all over it, collecting for charity. Children in Need, one of them. Anyway, there he was shaking his bucket under Marjorie's nose and he keeled right over. Started kicking his legs, nineteen to the dozen against the floor, having some kind of a fit. Marjorie put her Bic in his mouth, stop him swallowing his tongue, and he bit right through it."

Naylor was still looking at her, questioning now, and she stared right back at him, eyes unwavering behind her glasses. "The pen, not his tongue."

"Our Kev," Divine said quietly, leaning over Lynn Kellogg as she sat questioning Marjorie Carmichael, "on to a good thing there. Dip his wick before the night's out."

Lynn scowled and refused to turn her head to as much as look at him, while close beside her Marjorie pretended that she hadn't heard.

"All right, Marjorie," Lynn said as Divine walked off chuckling, "why don't we try and concentrate on the hair?"

They had been sitting for close to half an hour, turning the sections of a spiral-bound book back and forth. Facial types: heads divided into three. A game, the object of which was to match up the most likely combination. She had had one similar as a girl, Lynn remembered, but that had been the whole body, top to bottom, a picture-book blonde for whom you chose from different sets of clothes. "Oh, Lynnie," her mother had exclaimed, "just look at you. You can't put them colours together, pink and green." "Why not?" Lynn had asked. "Because they just don't go. Anyone tell you that." And she had stopped briefly to brush Lynn's straight dark hair with her fingers, stroke her cheek with the palm of an oven-warm hand.

"There," Marjorie said, pointing. "I'm sure that's right."

Lynn looked at the high forehead, generous mass of curly hair.

"Isn't that the one I picked before?"

"No. Not exactly."

"Oh, dear. I am sorry." Marjorie turned towards Lynn, disappointed, wanting so much to please.

"Don't worry," Lynn said, smiling faintly. "It's not easy." Shifting a little in her seat, more cramped than usual, telling herself that women Marjorie's size were prone to problems with perspiration, it wasn't really her fault.

"You weren't frightened, then?" Kevin Naylor was saying.

"Not at first," Lorna said. "It didn't seem real. You know, the way he come over to the counter, taking his time. Posing, almost. I didn't think he was serious. . . ."

"No."

"Then, later . . ." She was trying not to make it too obvious, the way she was angling her head, trying to look at Naylor's left hand, tucked under his notebook, not certain whether she'd seen a wedding ring or not. "Later, when he started going a bit wild, I suppose I was frightened then. Well, anyone would be."

"Of course."

"Anyone in their right mind."

Kevin Naylor nodded.

"I mean, look at what happened to poor Mr. Foreman."

"He was trying to stop them, was he, from getting away?"

"I don't know. I suppose so. Tell the truth, I didn't really see. I was still behind the counter, ducked down out of the way." She smiled and he moved his hand and there it was—damn!—thick and gold and looking as if it could do with a bit of a shine. Third finger, left hand.

"You didn't actually see, then, what happened? Which one of them hit him?"

"Had to be him, didn't it? The one who did all the talking. I mean, he was the one with the hammer. The other one, the little bloke, he just stood there like a spare part, never done a thing."

"Do you think either of the others would have seen— the manageress, for instance—do you think they would have seen the blow being struck?"

"I don't know, I doubt it. I mean, Marjorie might, ask her. But Becca . . ."

"That's the manageress?"

Lorna sucked in her cheeks and put on an accent. "Rebecca Astley. Little Miss Hoity-Toity. Real mardy, she was. Scraightin' and carrying on."

"Lots of people panic, situations like that."

"Even so."

"You were the one sounded the alarm, though."

"That's right."

"Not easy, thinking what to do."

"Thanks."

"No, I mean it."

For a second, Lorna touched her hand to the frame of her glasses. "So noisy in here, isn't it? Hardly hear yourself think."

Naylor glanced over his shoulder and saw Divine grinning right back at him. "Been like this for a couple days," he said.

"There isn't anywhere else . . ." She waited until he was looking at her again. "There's nowhere quieter we could go? You know. Somewhere else?"

"Yes," Naylor said, standing, feeling himself starting to go red. "We could try."

Lorna was on her feet already, noticing the way he was blushing and not caring, thinking it sweet. So what if he did wear a ring, that didn't have to mean so much, did it? Not these days?

"What'd I tell you?" Divine called above the sound of hammering. "Over the side and no messing."

"Your trouble," Lynn Kellogg sang back. "Judge everyone by your own standards. Least, you would if you had any."

Divine was still laughing when Resnick came into the room. "Busy, I see, Mark?"

"Yes, boss."

"Best take a rest, then. Tea break."

"No, you're all right. . . ."

"Get yourself over to the deli, fetch me a couple of sandwiches. Ham and cheese and a chicken mayonnaise and salad. Mustard on both. Right?"

Divine took the proffered five-pound note and headed for the door.

"How's it going?" Resnick asked, pausing alongside Lynn and Marjorie.

"Slowly," Lynn replied. And feeling Marjorie's sagging disappointment, added, "But I think we're getting there."

"Good."

Resnick opened the door to the partitioned section that formed his own office and willed the phone not to ring until Divine had come back with his sandwiches, at least until he had got as far as sitting down. He had his second wish by as much as five seconds. Graham Millington was calling in from somewhere between Stapleford and Sandiacre, where what might have been the getaway car had been found abandoned.

"If wrapped around a 'Keep Left' sign constitutes being abandoned," Millington added.

"Hang fire," Resnick said into the phone. "I'll be right out."

"Got mysen a packet of crisps." Divine grinned when Resnick intercepted him on the stairs.

"Your money, not mine," said Resnick, taking hold of the bag containing his sandwiches, pocketing his change. "Come on, you're driving. I'll eat these as we go."

6

Graham Millington had been Resnick's sergeant for a little over five years and was beginning to think that six would be too long. Not that he had anything against his immediate superior, far from it. When some of the others started grumbling into their pints and calling Resnick for being too soft by half, too airy-fairy in his ideas, Millington always squashed them with a firm word. Any reflections he might have about Resnick's appearance—surely someone of his rank and salary could afford at least one decent suit that seemed to fit, one white shirt with all of its buttons intact?—or his eating habits—if Millington saw him fumbling his way through one more overstuffed sandwich, he might just go out and buy his boss a voucher for the nearest Berni Inn, prawn cocktail, nice bit of steak and Black Forest gateau to finish, that was what you called a meal—like the loyal sergeant he strove to be, Millington kept them to himself.

No, it wasn't six years in Resnick's shadow that weighed heavily upon him, it was the prospect of six years beneath anybody.

Especially when a vacancy had come up and before Millington had been able to dust off his CV or fill in his application form, they'd whisked that woman in without her feet touching the ground this side of landing.

"Tough luck," Resnick had commiserated. "She's on her way to a top APCO post and there's nothing you or I can do about it."

"Another time," Skelton had said, scarcely stopping to speak. "You're still a young man."

Not, Millington had replied soundlessly to the super's back, for much bloody longer.

"Assert yourself more, Graham," his wife had said. "Let them know if you don't get promotion next time, you'll put in for a transfer."

In his more paranoid moments, Millington imagined Jolly Jack Skelton writing him a glowing reference and offering to pack his bags, shipping him east to Cleethorpes with an engraved tankard and a digital watch that would stop the second he crossed the Lincolnshire border.

"Not inspector by the time you're forty," Reg Cossall had said, "might as well curl up your toes and crawl into the body bag."

"You know what they say about water," Malcolm Grafton had smirked, "finding its own level."

Maybe his wife was right, the thing to do was march into Skelton's office with an ultimatum and if the result was moving somewhere else, well, why not? Except, for all her talk, he knew the last thing his wife wanted to do was move from where they'd settled. The local WEA group had just voted her onto the steering committee, the amateur dramatic and choral society had promised her something big in next season's *Iolanthe* and she was just getting to grips with the new border they'd put in alongside the caryopteris. And that was without level-two Russian.

He reangled the interior mirror and checked his moustache. Annoying the way those little hairs at the top kept poking themselves into his nostrils. He was using his fingernails to tweak one or two away when Divine brought the unmarked Ford to a halt behind him and Resnick climbed out of the passenger seat, brushing the last of his sandwich down the front of his raincoat.

"Right across there," said Millington, pointing towards the intersection. "Tow truck's on its way."

Directions had scarcely been necessary. The stolen car had three wheels on the pavement, one several inches above the surface of the road. The street sign seemed to have bent to meet it, scoring a deep groove through the roof and buckling the near-side rear door, shattering the window.

"What makes you think it's the one we're looking for?" Resnick asked.

Millington gestured towards the motor supplies shop along the street. "Bloke in there, heard the crash and saw two white youths haring up that side road, round the back of that building. One tall, he thinks maybe curly hair, the other either a runt or just a kid."

"Any other description?"

"Taller of the two had this loose coat on, apparently. Brown, possibly grey, anorak type of thing. Jeans, the pair of them. Couldn't give us a lot else."

Resnick shrugged. "Other witnesses?"

"Not so far."

"Cut along and knock on a few shop doors," Resnick said to Divine. "Before they all lock up for the night. Someone else must have heard what happened. Take a statement from the bloke Graham spoke to; might come up with a little more this time."

Divine nodded and hurried away.

"Checked the registration," Millington said. "Reported stolen from that car park out at Bulwell, sometime between twelve and two."

"Doesn't sound as if they bothered with gloves at the robbery," Resnick said. "If this is down to them, likely be prints on the car as well."

"I'll make sure they go careful shifting it, see it gets checked thoroughly soon as it gets back."

Resnick had stepped away and was staring down the narrowing street. "Ought to be a reason they came this way."

"Throw us off the scent?"

Resnick shook his head. "Everything we know about them this far, that kind of thinking seems a bit out of their league."

"Heading for home, then?"

"Could be."

"Run it through the computer. Likely got a bit of form anyway. Live round here, shouldn't be too difficult to find."

Resnick pushed his hands down into his pockets. Evenings like this, the temperature dropped as soon as the light began to fade. "Hope you're right, Graham. Quick result here'd be a good thing. Concentrate our energies where they're more needed."

"Back among the big boys."

Resnick nodded. "It needs sorting, Graham. Before somebody gets killed."

7

The way Keith felt about his old man, one of those old jossers get on the bus in the morning and suddenly you're staring out the window, hoping against hope they won't lurch over, sit down next to you. Clothes that reek of cider and cheap port wine. Open their mouths to speak and the next you know, they're dribbling uncontrollably.

An exaggeration, of course, but not much of one. The way his dad had gone since the divorce, starting his drinking earlier and earlier in the day, not finishing till the money or the energy to lift the bottle failed him. Last time Keith had called at the house, two in the morning, unannounced, his father was curled asleep on the kitchen floor, arms cradled round the legs of an upright chair.

It hadn't always been like that. As a young kid, Keith remembered his dad getting smartened up of an evening, loading his gear into the van, swinging Keith round by his arms till he screamed with excitement. Early hours of the morning, Keith would wake to the sound of car doors slamming in the street outside, called farewells, his dad's footsteps, less than steady, on the stairs, his mother's warning voice. "Don't wake the boy."

His father would sleep till two or three, wander down for a sausage and egg sandwich and pots of tea. Wash, shave, do it all again.

He had been drinking, Keith realised, even then; more, probably, than had been clear at the time. Clear to Keith, at least, though he could still hear his mother's shrill sermons echoing up and down the narrow house. And as the work had dried up, the bottles and the cans had appeared on every surface, lined the chair where his dad would sit, not watching the TV. "One thing," he would say, over and over, "one thing, Keith, I regret—you never knew me when I was big, really big. Then you might've felt different."

Keith fished the key from his pocket and turned it in the lock. Found the light switch without thinking. Strange how long this had been home.

"Keith, that you?"

No, it was Mick Jagger, Charlie Watts'd finally decided to jack it in, old Mick couldn't think of anyone better to take his place.

Around when Keith had been twelve and thirteen and you didn't have to be a genius to see how far things had fallen apart, that was the kind of guff his dad would sit him down, make him listen to. How he could have played with the Stones, back in the early days, Eel Pie Island, before Mick started on the eye makeup, all that poncing about. Back when they were playing real music.

Playing the blues.

"Keith?"

"Yeh, it's me. Who d'you think?"

All the bands his old man could have played with if things had only fallen right: the Yardbirds before Jeff Beck, John Mayall's Blues Breakers, Graham Bond, Zoot Money's Big Roll Band. The night he should have depped for Mickey

Waller with the Steampacket, some big festival—instead of sitting behind the drums, his dad had popped too many pills and spent the set in the St. John's Ambulance tent throwing up.

"Keith, you're coming down here, fetch us a beer."

As far as Keith knew, his father's only substantiated nights of near-glory had been back in 'sixty-four when he gigged with Jimmy Powell and the Five Dimensions, joining them in Nottingham when they were on the Mecca circuit and sticking it out until they were hired to back Chuck Berry on his British tour. First rehearsal, Chuck stopped short in the middle of his duck walk and asked who the motherfucker was trying to play the drums. That was it: beginning and end of his old man's big career. For sale, one pair of Zildjian cymbals, one mohair suit, scarcely worn.

"Keith, I thought I asked you to—"

"Here. Catch."

The can bounced out of Reg Rylands's hands and rolled across the basement floor.

"What you doing down here?" Keith asked, snapping open the Carlsberg he'd fetched for himself.

"Oh, you know, pottering around."

Keith grunted and snapped open his can.

"What's that you've done to your eye?"

"That?" Keith said, gingerly touching the swelling, the bruise. "That's nothing."

The house was two-storey, flat-fronted, an end-terrace in the Meadows—one of those streets the planners overlooked when they ordered in the bulldozers on their way to a new Jerusalem. Keith had been born here, brought up; his mum had moved out when she divorced, lived now in a semi in Gedling with a painter and decorator and Keith's five-year-old stepbrother, Jason. Keith's father had stayed put, letting out first one room, then another, sharing the house with an ever-changing mixture of plasterers and general labourers and drinking mates who dossed down for free whenever their Social Security ran out.

"What's this?" Keith asked, pointing at the Z-bed opened out along the wall. "You sleeping down here now?"

"Just for a bit. Coz's got my room." He drank some lager. "You remember Cozzie. Some woman with him this time. Tart."

Keith didn't know any Cozzie, but he could guess what he would look like: tattoos across his knuckles and scabs down his face. "Hope he's paying you."

"Course."

Which meant that he was not.

"So what you doing here?"

Keith shrugged. "Come to see you, didn't I?"

"You weren't thinking of staying?"

"Thought I might."

"What's wrong with your mum's?"

"Nothing."

"Haven't had a row?"

"No more'n usual."

"So?"

"Change, that's all. Couple of nights."

"You're not in trouble?"

"No."

"You sure?"

"Yes."

"'Cause if it's anything like before . . ."

Keith hurled his half-full lager can at the floor and stormed towards the door.

"No, Keith, Keith, hold on, hold on. I'm sorry, right?"

Keith stopped, feet on the cellar steps.

"You want to stay, that's fine. Got a mattress I can bring down here, you take the bed." Keith turned and came back inside. "Just for tonight. Bloke up top, moving out next couple of days. I'll explain. Give him a nudge. It'll work out, you see. Here . . ." He bent down and picked up the Carlsberg and handed it back to his son. "Like old times, eh?"

"Yeh."

"Might go out later, couple of pints. What d'you think?"

Keith sat down on the Z-bed and it rattled and squeaked. In an old chest opposite, fronts missing from two of the drawers, were his father's clothes—those that weren't draped anyhow across a succession of cardboard boxes or hanging from the back of the cellar door. A pile of shoes from which it might be difficult to find a decent pair. Bundles of old newspapers and magazines, yellowing copies of the *NME*. An old Ferguson record player with only one speaker: a radio without a back. Two snare drums, not on stands, but lying side by side, skins patched and slack. A pair of wire brushes, bent and tangled at the ends.

"Yeh," Keith said. "Yes, sure. Drink'd be fine." He looked quickly at his father from the corner of his good eye. "You might have to pay."

8

Resnick had arrived back at the station in time to find three uniformed officers hauling a seventeen-stone West Indian up the steps and backwards through the double doors.

"Argument with a taxi driver, sir. Reckoned he was charging him over the odds. Jumped on the roof and dented it. Stuck his boot through the rear windscreen. Driver tried to pull him down and got a kick in the head for his trouble."

Resnick held one of the doors open as, finally, they succeeded in lifting him inside. A good bollocking from the custody sergeant, a night in a cold cell and an agreement to pay restitution to the cab driver and that would likely be the end to it. Summary justice: there no longer seemed to be a lot of it about. Back when Resnick and his friend Ben Riley had been walking the beat, so much could be settled with a warning look, a word, the right intervention at the right time. All too often now, the first sign of police intervention brought about an immediate escalation of trouble. A violent response. Unthinking.

A wpc, out of uniform, on her way home from the cinema, stops near a fiercely quarrelling couple, the man shouting at the top of his voice, the woman yelling back through her tears. When the police officer goes closer, asking them to calm down, asking the woman if she is all right, the pair of them rounds on her, the woman spitting in her face.

A young constable, six months on the job, steps between two groups of youths, squaring up to one another on the upper floor of the Broad Marsh centre. Set upon, forced back towards the top of the escalator, he calls for help, which only comes when he has tumbled to the bottom. Three cracked ribs, a dislocated pelvis, he would suffer intermittently from severe back pain for the rest of his life.

"Call for you, sir," said Naylor, passing Resnick on the stairs. "D.I. Cossall. Left the message on your desk."

"Thanks, Kevin."

"Couple of us going over the road for a pint if—"

"Yes, maybe. Later."

Resnick squeezed past the furniture that had been moved out into the corridor and pushed open the door to the CID room. Loose boards were still stacked against the wall, and from the temperature nothing had been achieved by setting the heating to rights. A lamp burned over Lynn Kellogg's desk, her coat still hung from the rack in the corner, but there was no sign of her. Divine would be in the pub already, getting them in.

Scarcely a time in the last months Resnick had walked into that office and his eyes had not flicked towards the far wall where Dipak Patel used to sit. Now there was a space, a gap in the floor, lengths of piping running through shadow. Coldness. What was it Millington had said about Patel and death? Scatter rose petals and sit around wailing where he comes from, don't they?

Well, wailing there had certainly been, that cold Saturday when the wind had whipped off the Bradford hills and cut across Resnick's back like a stick. Flowers, too. Roses. Patel's father had shaken his hand gravely, thanked Resnick for attending, never looked him in the eye. Never understood. No. What was there to understand?

"Don't," Patel's girlfriend had begged that evening in the city centre. "Please don't get involved."

"I have to," Patel had said.

Moments later, the blade with which one youth had been attacking another was turned on him. Another fucking Paki. Another fucking Saturday night. Blood from the artery spread wide and the best you could say, the only good thing, the only consolation you could find, it had not taken Patel long to die.

"Sir?" Lynn Kellogg said quietly.

Resnick had failed to hear her come in behind him.

"You all right?"

He turned his head and looked at her, slowly nodded.

"I sometimes think," she said, "that he's, well, that he's still here."

"Yes."

"But he isn't. . . . He's . . ."

For the briefest of moments, Resnick put his hand on her shoulder and she rested her cheek sideways against it and closed her eyes and Resnick's breathing seemed unnaturally loud in the darkening room. And then she got her bag and her coat and said good night and Resnick said see you in the morning and after the door had closed he went into his office and read the note.

Reg Cossall was standing at the bar, more leaning, face round and broken-veined and wreathed in smoke. Angled above his head the highlights of a women's soccer match were being played out, rise and fall of the commentator's voice barely audible beneath the whir of the cash register, blur of voices.

Other faces Resnick recognised, greetings offered and shared.

"Message got through to you, then?"

Resnick bought him a pint of Kimberley and a large Bells, shaking his head at the offer of ice. For himself, a ginger ale.

"Not drinking, Charlie?"

"Not tonight."

"Bad news, then, is it?"

"Likely. You tell me."

One word had been written on the slip of paper, other than the details of where and when Cossall wanted to meet.

Prior.

"Up for parole, Charlie. Two-thirds of his sentence down the pan."

Resnick glanced up at the screen. A woman with fair hair pinned close to her head was writhing on the ground, tackled from behind. Some things changed, some remained the same.

"He'll not get it," Resnick said. "He'll be turned down."

"Not what I've heard. Not this time."

"Offences like his. Violence . . ."

"Not automatic, but like I say . . ."

Resnick swallowed down the ginger ale and before the glass had been set back on the bar, Cossall had beckoned the barman, ordered him a vodka, double. The bank of video games beside the entrance jingled and hummed. From the adjoining bar, the click of pool balls and a jukebox recyling The Jam.

"How long, Charlie? Ten years?"

"Nearer eleven."

"I have no doubt that the reaction of the public to these offences of which you have been convicted is one of the gravest horror and disgust. Motivated solely by greed and with an absolute lack of compunction towards anybody who stood in your way, prepared to threaten and use violence with a callous disregard for the safety of others, you and the men convicted

with you terrorised sections of the community in the pursuit of personal gain. As the undisputed ringleader of these men, I have no alternative other than to punish you with the full force of law at my disposal."

The public had been so disgusted that sales of the Sunday paper to whom one of his accomplices sold his story showed an increase of twenty-three percent. Prior's mother, convalescing in a nursing home after a stroke, was interviewed by both major television news programmes and a photograph that showed him as a child, receiving his school's annual prize for good citizenship and endeavour, was widely syndicated. A prostitute, who claimed to have been his lover, auctioned her kiss-and-tell exposé to five bidders.

"You think he'll come back here?"

"Would you?"

"No," Cossall said, chasing his whisky with a long swallow of beer, "but then I'm not a nutter."

"That what you think he is?"

"Don't you?"

Face to face in the garage, the two of them, himself and Prior, both near to breathless, the garage doors partly open, the car ready to go. Resnick had followed him through the house, the side door from the kitchen, Prior's hands disappearing behind the open boot of the car and when next Resnick saw them, they were holding the shotgun steady, angled towards his chest and face.

Outside were voices, torches, shouts of enquiry, warning. All Resnick saw was the narrowing of Prior's eyes, the tensing of the forefinger of his right hand. There were things he had been trained to say in this situation but he said none of them.

The tension in Prior's eyes had relaxed a little as he brought the shotgun up towards his own body and for a moment Resnick thought he was going to rest the barrels beneath his own chin, take his life. Instead he had reversed the weapon fully and handed it across the roof of the car for Resnick to take hold of, stock first.

"No," Resnick said. "He's not that."

"Happen you're right." Cossall shrugged. "'Sides, maybe all that time inside taught him a lesson. Back out a changed man, anxious to become a useful member of society. That what you reckon, Charlie, eh?"

"Get you another, Reg? I'm going to be on my way."

Cossall shook his head, opened his hand over the top of his pint glass. "Shouldn't be too difficult to find out where he's likely to head for, what his intentions are. That's if it happens. Still, best forewarned, eh? Make plans."

"Thanks, Reg." Resnick offered his hand. "Owe you one."

"Yes," Cossall growled. "You and the rest of the sodding world."

Over his head one of the teams had just scored what looked a lovely goal, only to have it disallowed.

Pip Hewitt came into the kitchen after speaking to her mother on the phone, to find her husband, Peter, sitting at the broad oak table, account books open near him, drinking black tea laced with rum.

"You're worried, aren't you?" she said, resting an arm along his shoulder. "Losing that last milk order."

Hewitt squeezed her hand. "It's not that."

She pulled round one of the chairs and sat close beside him.

"The parole review committee's meeting tomorrow and—"

"If you can't go, phone them. After all the work you've put in, they should understand."

Hewitt drank from the thick stoneware mug, holding it out first to his wife, who smiled and refused. "One of the men I interviewed—Prior—he's serving fifteen years, armed robbery. . . ."

"Was anybody hurt?"

Hewitt nodded. "The last raid before they were caught, a security guard . . ."

"Shot?"

"Paralysed down one side."

Pip Hewitt's eyes reflected the shock and pain. "And this man . . ."

"Prior."

"He was responsible? He shot him?"

"He says no, claims it was one of the others. Two weapons were discharged, but the police were never able to establish who fired which gun. Not without a shadow of a doubt. The shotgun Prior had with him when he was arrested, ballistic reports don't match it up with the injuries to the guard."

Pip took the mug from between her husband's hands and slowly sipped the laced tea.

"I wish I knew what to do," Hewitt said.

She gave his hand a squeeze. "You take everything so seriously."

"It is serious."

"I know."

"What's left of a man's life . . ."

"Darling . . ." Still holding Hewitt's hand, she got to her feet. "Finish your tea, come to bed, let's have an early night. You'll do the right thing. You always do."

9

Music. Darren had never understood what all the fuss was about. Loud or soft, fast or slow—how much else did you need to know? Keith, now, if he wasn't out hot-wiring some car, he was walking around with his Walkman on, tinny little sound leaking out, mouthing the words as it went along. Rap. Who gave a rat's arse about rap? Keith, for one. Outlaw. Gang Starr. X-Clan. Caveman. Least the names were okay, cool. What had he been playing the other day? Arrested Development. Darren laughed: Keith to a T.

Outside Michael Issacs's nightclub, he gave himself a quick once-over in the glass: chinos, white shirt pulled out loose above the waist, sleeves rolled back, silhouette of hair tinged purple in the light.

The dance floor was three-quarters full, blokes leaning back against the downstairs bar, suits some of them, carelessly watching him as he climbed the stairs.

As the DJ upped the tempo, Darren leaned over the balcony, nursing a lager top, checking out the talent. Two black blokes getting all the attention down below, buckling their legs and doing all that fancy stuff with their hands, kung fu sign language in overdrive.

There, over by the steps, big girl with reddish hair, a blue top which jiggled when she moved. Black trousers, loose at the hip. She might do the trick.

Darren shifted his position to get a better look.

According to the news, that old idiot he'd whacked was still hanging on. Arsehole! Why couldn't he mind his own business? Keep his hands to himself? Still fighting the tossing war. Saved this country for the likes of you. Yes, well, right, Grandad. Thanks very fucking much!

Sodding Keith today, as much good as a johnny with a hole at both ends. If he was going to get anywhere, he'd have to find a better partner than that. Late with car, forgetting to guard the door.

A youth in a suit jostled Darren's elbow and Darren straightened, giving him a look, and the youth mumbled something to the slag he was with and the two of them wandered away.

One thing Darren had to give Keith—once his nerves had steadied, he'd got them out of there like there was no tomorrow. Three police cars after them at one point and still Keith had lost them. Everything going great until he'd misjudged that turn going down towards Sandiacre. Legging it then, they'd been: till they'd found that van on Longmoor Lane. Some lamebrain who'd nipped into the paper shop for a *Post* and a packet of fags, left the sidelights on, indicator flashing, keys in the fucking steering column!

Back from there, through Long Eaton and into the city.

The tempo slowed and Darren figured it was time to head downstairs, see what was what at close hand.

That range, she was a lot bigger than he'd first thought, not that there was anything wrong with that. Some of them so skinny, he might as well have been back inside, putting it to some youth in the shower while a mate kept watch for the screws.

Face that wasn't about to win any prizes.

Her mate, the one she was dancing with, she was a lot

prettier and knew it. Aware that Darren was standing there now and watching them, thinking he had to be watching her. Toss of the head and yes, here comes the tongue, wetting both her lips.

Saying something about him, heads close together, laughing under the music. When the record changed again, they hesitated, then started to leave the floor.

As he intercepted them, the good-looking one smiled at Darren with her eyes and he gave her a quick grin back, moving past her, hand reaching out to touch her mate on the arm.

"Come on. Can't be packing up already."

Leading her back onto the floor, out into the middle where it was more crowded, a few minutes halfheartedly dancing round her, before hauling her close, didn't matter about the music now, whatever was happening was slow inside Darren's head. Press of her breasts against his chest, fingers of her hand against his back, his own cupping the curve of her arse, sliding up and down. Flesh there in plenty, knickers no more than a strip of material at either side.

"Where we going?" she said, almost to the door.

There had been the usual quick consultation with her friend, trip to the loo, queuing for her coat, Darren looking at himself reflected in the poster on the wall, not letting his impatience show.

"Back to my place."

"I can't stop long."

He looked at her, questioning.

"My mum, she'd worry."

Darren looked back towards the interior. "Say you're staying with a mate."

"I can't."

"That's okay," Darren said, moving towards the exit. "'S not far."

Out on the street he suddenly stopped. "Wait here," he said. "Be right back."

Surprised, she watched him as he walked back inside, mass of curly hair outlined against violet light.

There were two men at the urinals when he went in and he stood in line, taking his time until, laughing, they went back outside. Neither of the toilets seemed to be occupied.

Less than a minute later the music went loud and then quiet. The youth who came and stood one place down from Darren was Asian, blue suit, no more than eighteen.

Darren pulled up his zip and walked behind the youth as if to wash his hands. Turning fast, he grabbed him by both arms and threw him forward, cracking his head against the wall; brought his knee up fast into the base of his spine and struck his head against the wall a second time. A kick between his legs as he pulled him round; an elbow in the face.

There was a wallet in the inside pocket of his suit; two notes, a twenty and a ten, folded in his top pocket.

"Better call the manager or something," Darren said to the man entering as he left. "Some bloke in there's fainted. Done himself a bit of damage."

"Sorry," he said to the girl with a smile. "Caught short. You know how it is.

"Come on," he said, once they were on the pavement. "Get down to the corner, we can pick up a cab."

Darren's room was an upstairs front: curtains at the window that neither met nor matched, bed, table, wardrobe, chair. He kissed her and asked her name, offered her coffee and she offered him a cigarette.

"Milk's off," he said, coming back with two mugs. "Have to have it black."

"It doesn't matter," she said.

Darren sat beside her on the bed. "I want you to do something for me."

Oh, yes, she thought, though there was something about the way he said it that made her think that might not be exactly what he meant.

"Hang on," he said and disappeared a second time. When he came back from the kitchen there was a pair of scissors in his hand.

10

The black cat sprung onto the stone wall at the sound of Resnick's footsteps, purred and paced and turned as soon as he was in sight, stretched his head towards the passing touch of Resnick's hand. Inside the front door, a second cat trilled and ran towards the kitchen, while Resnick stooped and scooped up the usual unappetising batch of mail. Gas bill, electricity bill, a personal computerised letter from his bank manager offering to make him a loan on the most friendly of terms. The third cat was sitting on the hall chest, opposite the stairs; the fourth . . . There was a metallic clunk as Resnick entered the kitchen, a saucepan lid wobbling across the floor, a bewhiskered face peering from inside the pan.

"One of these days," Resnick said, "you'll wake up in there too late. End up as stew."

The cat jumped out, unimpressed, and rubbed himself against Resnick's legs.

Dizzy, Miles, Bud, Pepper.

A letter with handwriting he recognised but couldn't place. Inside its clear wrapper, this quarter's copy of *Jazz FM*. More reviews of reissues he would love to buy, but the technology was failing him. You could count the vinyl albums in Virgin or HMV on the fingers of both hands. Cassette or CD. Oh, well . . . Perhaps next month he'd take the plunge. Have a word with Graham Millington, he'd have a CD player, bound to; chosen by his wife after a careful perusal of *Which?;* something that would bring Andrew Lloyd Webber's greatest hits into their home with all the sterility they deserved.

Impatient, Dizzy jumped up onto the worktop and Resnick, not unkindly, pushed him down. He opened a tin of kidney and beef heart and forked the contents into the four coloured bowls, sprinkling a little KitEKat supercrunch with liver and game over the top.

OPEN this envelope NOW and read all about your FREE holiday in the Algarve. Resnick tore it in two and tossed it in the bin. The way Dizzy kept pushing Bud out of the way and chomping his food as well as his own, it was no wonder Bud stayed so thin.

The coffee beans were dark and shiny in the palm of his hand and he brought them, momentarily, to his face to savour the smell. Stocks were running low; tomorrow or the next day he must remember to call in at The White House and buy more.

While the water was dripping through the filter, he arranged thin slices of Gruyère cheese, slivers of smoked ham, halved black olives, onion, several pieces of sun-dried tomato and, finally, some crumblings of blue Stilton on top of two thick slices of light rye bread. Careful to keep them level, he set both pieces on the grill pan and slid them beneath the flame, which was already burning.

Taking hold of Dizzy firmly and holding him in one hand, he unlocked the back door and released the black cat into the garden. If he was still hungry, he could forage out there.

When it had become clear that Resnick's marriage was over, his wife of six years setting off for pastures new, his first reaction had been to sell the house, find a flat, make a statement that now he was on his own. But the kind of energy required to go through that process had been lacking. Whatever else the house was—big and rambling for two, absurd for one—it was comfortable. He called Family First and made them a present of the three-piece suite from Hopewell's that had almost cost a second mortgage, took himself down to the auctions at the cattle market and replaced it with something older, broken in, the shape of other lives already impressed into the upholstery.

So he had stayed there and got on with his life and, opening the door one day to say no thank you to a pair of neatly suited young men who wanted to interest him in attending a class in nondenominational readings from the Bible, a skinny young black cat had wandered in, ribs visible through falling fur. Resnick had fed him with chicken scraps and cheese and warmed milk. The cat had bolted the food, all the while glancing round nervously, and as soon as both saucers were licked clean, dashed to the door and demanded to be let out.

Three days later, he was back.

Then the second day.

Then every day.

The first time the cat jumped onto Resnick's lap and allowed himself to be stroked, Resnick was listening to the Prestige album, *In the Beginning.* You know, the blue fold-out cover with the beautiful picture of a handsome Dizzy Gillespie boxed in red. "Oop Bop Sh'Bam" with Sonny Stitt on alto, Milt Jackson on vibes. Dizzy's solo taking them into the final theme, vocal coda, slurred notes at the end.

"Dizzy." Resnick had smiled, feeling the new weight beneath the cat's improving coat, and the animal had looked back at him with wide green eyes.

A few months later, a younger cat had appeared.

Miles: who else?

The following year, Pepper and Bud had strayed and

stayed. Resnick fed them with little fuss and they grew used to his odd hours, demanding as little of him as he did of them.

He drank some more of the black coffee and started on the second open sandwich, olive oil from the sun-dried tomatoes sliding into the cracks of his fingers and making small stains to join those he was already wearing on his tie. Last time he had tried, the assistant in Sketchley's had given him a you-must-be-joking look and handed him his ties back.

The letter lay on the small table alongside the easy chair, beside the telephone, resting on the cover of the Spike Robinson he was now playing. The stamps, the air-mail sticker, he could only think of a couple of people who might be writing to him from the States, but neither of them from—where was it?—Maine? Pete Barnard was a jazz fan he knew, a dermatologist who was now working in Chicago, and Ben, Ben Riley, he hadn't heard from Ben in ages, seemed to have lost touch, but when he had, Ben had been out in Montana somewhere, wearing a deputy's hat and driving a Jeep. Surely that wasn't Ben Riley's writing?

Of course, it was.

Here I am, Charlie, out in Ellsworth, Maine, enjoying the good life and working none-too-hard for the county police department.

The first of the Polaroids Ben had enclosed showed him with his hat and badge and holstered gun and, those aside, it wasn't only the handwriting that the intervening years had changed. Ben was a lot fuller in the face, something akin to jowls hanging down towards a neck that showed a tendency to spread over his shirt collar. Gun belt and trouser belt served to support a sagging stomach that would have been more alarming had it not been for the expression of contentment on Ben Riley's face.

Getting myself across to the east of the country has worked out fine, especially since I met Ali, my second wife.

Resnick wasn't sure that he had known about the first. *Mentally, she's made me face up to a few things, knuckle down, cut back on the drinking and learn to take myself more seriously. Of course, young Max has had a lot to do with that.*

Alison was a broad-faced blonde who stared straight at the camera lens as if daring it to talk back. She looked thirty-four or -five, ten years younger than Ben, arms folded across her chest, wearing a check shirt and blue jeans. Max had her hair, his father's eyes and looked pretty steady on his feet for the two years Ben assigned to him elsewhere in the letter.

Put together some of that holiday time you're never using and get out here and see us, Charlie. There's this little restaurant right by the Grand Cinema, serves the best Thai food outside the Pacific. I guess, whatever else has happened to you, you do still enjoy your food.

The music clicked off and the cat that had wandered onto Resnick's lap jumped down again and ate the fragments of ham that had dropped to the floor. Resnick slid the letter and the photographs back into their envelope and walked across the room, poured himself a drink. In 1981, when Resnick had been standing in that garage, staring into Prior's face, reaching out to take his gun, Ben Riley had been the first officer through the door.

11

"What the hell happened to you?"

"Nothing. What d'you mean?"

"I hardly recognised you."

They were in the café on West End Arcade, opposite the bottom of the escalator, Darren and Keith, the place in the city where they met, mornings, table close against the window. Every now and then there'd be some woman, short skirt, ascending in front of their eyes.

Keith was still staring at Darren, gone out. "How much't cost, get it done?"

Darren ran a hand over his close-cropped hair. "Nothing."

"How d'you mean, nothing?"

"Got someone to do it for me."

"What someone?"

"Some girl."

There was an old boy in the corner, chewing his way through two of toast, careful to break off the ends of brittle crust rather than risk his teeth. A young mum with a tired face was dipping her baby's dummy into sweet tea and pushing it against the child's squalling face. Couple of retro-punks waiting for the record shop back down the arcade to open, rifle through the racks of rare singles they couldn't afford to buy.

"'Nother tea?"

Keith nodded. "Yeh, ta."

"Anything to eat?"

Keith shook his head. "Skint."

"I'm buying."

While they were waiting for the sausage cobs, Keith marvelled at the difference Darren's haircut made to his face. Suddenly it was sharper, harder, his nose seemed larger, jutting out from the centre of his face; and the eyes . . . Keith didn't think he'd ever noticed them before, not really, blue-grey but bright, dead bright, as if for the first time they'd been let out from under a cloud.

"So what d'you think? Suit me?"

"Yeh. Yes. It's good. Really is."

"But you didn't recognise me, right?"

"Well, I . . ."

"When I come in, you said—"

"I knew, but not straight off."

"It's the hair, right?"

"Yeh, of course. . . ."

"Anyone as saw me before, just *saw* me, that's what they'd pick on, what they'd say—hair, he's got all this curly hair."

"Yes."

"That girl yesterday . . ."

"The one you got to cut it off?"

"The one in the building society. Lorna."

"'S'that her name?"

"Lorna Solomon."

"What about her?"

"I was wondering . . ."

"Yeh?"

"If she walked in here now . . ."

"Which she won't."

"But if she did."

"What about it?"

"If she'd know who I was."

Keith watched Darren lift the top off his cob and smear the pieces of sausage with mustard, shook tomato sauce over his own until it lay in it, like a puddle. Darren had been likely to go off at half-cock before, quick fits of temper: dangerous, though he hadn't looked it. Now he did. As Darren bit down into his cob and grinned across at him, Keith saw again that newfound glint in his eyes and felt a chill slide over his skin because he knew then that Darren was capable of anything.

Any thing.

"Shouldn't take that long," the workman said at the door to Resnick's office. "Hour or two at most."

Resnick nodded and picked up a cluster of files from his desk, resigned to losing the use of the room for the rest of the day.

"Just got a call from forensic," Millington called over the noise of furniture being dragged across bare floorboards.

"And?"

"Seems there's some kind of logjam. Lucky to get anything this side of tea time."

"Managed to dig out three more witnesses, boss," said Divine. "Out at Sandiacre. Couple stuck their heads out after they whacked into the road sign, nothing new there, but this . . . Marcus Livingstone . . . had his motor nicked from outside a newsagent's less than quarter of a mile away. Heard this engine revving like crazy, realised it was his own. Got to the door in time to see them driving off down Longmoor Lane."

"And we're certain it's the same pair?"

"Likely."

Resnick nodded. "Which direction, Longmoor Lane?"

"South."

"Double back this side of the rec," said Millington, "Junction Twenty-five. Once they're on the motorway, any place from Chesterfield down to Leicester in a half hour."

"'Less they carry on going," Kevin Naylor said, "swing round Chilwell and Beeston and back into the city."

"This car," Resnick asked, "it's been reported missing?"

"Yes, boss. Vauxhall Cavalier. D reg. Not turned up as yet."

Resnick nodded. "Let's put some pressure on. Have a word with Paddy Fitzgerald, Graham, make sure uniform patrols keep their eyes skinned."

"Right."

Resnick turned back to Naylor. "That witness yesterday . . ."

"Lorna," Naylor said. "Lorna Solomon."

Divine sniggered.

"How good a description could she give of the youth who threatened her?"

"Pretty good, sir. Detailed."

"It agreed," said Lynn Kellogg, "with what I could get from Marjorie Carmichael. Not that I'd like to rely on her in court."

"But from the pair of them—if we needed to—there's enough to bring an artist in, get a composite?"

Naylor and Kellogg glanced at each other before answering. "Yes, sir," said Naylor.

"Yes," said Lynn.

"Kevin, this, er, Lorna . . ."

"Solomon, sir."

"Did you take her through the pictures we've got on file?"

"Not really, sir. Wasn't time. And I thought anyway, you know, by now we'd likely have prints and . . ."

"Bring her in. Sit her down. Can't do any harm."

"'Specially," whispered Mark Divine behind Naylor's head, "if you can get her to sit on your face."

"Something else, Mark?" Resnick said.

"No, boss," Divine said, wiping the smirk from his face.

"Anybody?"

"I thought I'd see if I can talk to the manageress," Lynn Kellogg said. "If she's not turned in at work, I've got her home address."

"Right. And Mark, call the hospital, check the situation with Harry Foreman. Long as he's out of immediate danger, find out when we might be able to have a word. We still don't know conclusively which one it was clobbered him."

Harry Foreman's X rays suggested several hairline fractures of the cranial cavity and damage to the ossicles of the middle ear. He was sedated, mostly sleeping, being fed by means of an IV drip. In one rare moment of apparently clear consciousness he asked a student nurse what had won the three-thirty at Southwell; in another asked why his wife, Florrie, wasn't there to see him. When the ward social worker made enquiries, she discovered that Florence Foreman had died in 1973, having contracted pneumonia after a fall in which she had dislocated her hip.

Rebecca Astley had been prescribed an anxiolytic by her doctor, which she had purchased in the form of Diazepam from her local Boots. Now she was lying on the settee in the living room of the flat she shared with a management trainee from Jessops, a duvet wrapped around her to keep her from getting cold as she alternately watched an old John Garfield film on Channel 4 and reread the Barbara Taylor Bradford she'd bought for the flight to Orlando. She didn't think anyone from head office would be round to see her so soon, but just in case they did, she had put a little makeup on her face and made sure her best dressing gown, the one with the lavender braiding, was close to hand. She only hoped that neither Marjorie nor Lorna had taken the opportunity to make her look bad; Marjorie she could trust, but Lorna . . . She made it a rule never to speak ill of anyone, but Lorna Solomon—it wasn't just that she was common, that wasn't altogether her fault, what she didn't have to be was such a bitch.

"Where d'you get it all?" Keith asked.

"All what?"

"All this money, what d'you think?"

After spending the best part of an hour and more change than Keith could count on video games in the place above Victoria Street, they were sitting in Pizza Hut, waiting for the waitress to bring their order.

Darren winked. "Got it from the girl, didn't I?"

"The one you picked up at Michael Issacs?"

"Which other girl is there?"

"What'd she want to give you money for? She cut your hair, you should have paid her."

Darren reached under the table and cupped his crotch in his hand. "She got paid all right. Couldn't get enough."

The waitress, trying not to notice the way Darren seemed to be fondling himself, put down their Meat Feast Supreme and left them to it.

"Then you wouldn't know a lot about that, eh, Keith?"

Keith made a face and lifted a slice of pizza onto his plate, reached for a tomato from the help-yourself salad Darren had piled high as he could, gluing the ingredients together with blue cheese dressing.

"Day comes, you get your cock out of your hand and up some slag's twat, she'll think she's been stung by a gnat and start to scratch."

"I'd be pleased if you'd moderate your language," said a woman in a red hat, turning round from the booth behind. "There are young children here who don't want to hear that kind of talk."

"Oh, yes," said Darren, on his feet to get a better look at the family scene, mother and grandma and a couple of kids under ten wearing school uniforms. "And where d'you think they came from, then? If it wasn't some bloke slipping a paper bag over his head, getting you bent over the bed and fucking you rotten?"

The trainee manager was keen, only her second week in the job, there in a flash. "Sit down, please, sir. If there's some kind of a problem . . ."

"What it is, Della," Darren said, reading her name off her badge, smiling, "my friend and I, we ordered two portions of garlic bread to go with the pizza, the garlic bread with the cheese topping. Seems to be a long time coming."

12

When Lorna saw Kevin Naylor come through the door of the building society office, something inside her gave a clear and definite lurch. Mind you, something like that had been happening pretty much every time anyone came in, right from when they'd first opened. Her mum had told her last evening when they'd talked on the phone, take a few days off, you shouldn't go straight back, not after what happened; her friend Leslie, when she'd called round, see how Lorna was, she had said more or less the same. Even Mr. Spindler had wondered if she oughtn't to take one of her statutory sick days.

But, no, she'd felt all right, no bad dreams, nothing like that. After all, it wasn't as if anything terrible had actually happened.

Still, there it was, this roll of her insides whenever she heard the door ring open, whenever she saw it begin to swing back. It was just that, well, when she realised it was Kevin, her insides gave it that little extra. Nothing wrong with that: only natural.

"I was wondering," Kevin had said, "if you could spare a little more time."

It had been Lorna's idea to stop off on the way and pick up some lunch.

"We have to eat, don't we? I mean, no law against that."

She suggested the Chinese takeaway just across from the lights on Alfreton Road, more or less opposite the garage. From there it was easy for Kevin to double-back around the block, park on the Forest, the broad swathe of concrete where weekends they did Park and Ride.

This time there were no more than a dozen or so cars there, mostly parked close together. Funny how people tended to do that, as if there was safety in company. Kevin had drawn up away off from the others, facing up towards the trees.

"This is nice," Lorna said. "How's yours?"

Chewing, Kevin mumbled something that might have been "Fine."

Lorna had chosen prawn crackers, sweet and sour pork; Kevin the spare ribs. She leaned a little against the inside of the car door now, watching him lick the sauce from his finger ends.

"We should do this properly sometime."

"What's that?" Kevin asked.

"Eat Chinese. You like it, don't you? Chinese food?"

"I like this."

"That's what I mean. Only one evening, in a restaurant, what do you think?"

"I don't know."

"You mean because of your wife?"

Kevin shook his head. "She doesn't like Chinese. Says it's too salty. Makes her ill."

Lorna was lifting a piece of pork towards her mouth with a plastic fork, grinning.

"What?"

"I wasn't thinking of asking her," Lorna said.

Kevin looked up through the windscreen towards the

cluster of trees; someone in an off-white sheepskin coat was walking a pair of Sealyhams, holding their leads unnaturally high, the way he'd seen owners do on television, Dog of the Year Show from Crufts.

"Where do you go?" Lorna asked.

"You mean to eat?"

"With your wife, yes."

"I don't know as we do, much."

"But, like, something special?"

"Like what?"

"Anniversary."

For their last anniversary, their third, Kevin had sent a card, bought flowers, stood in line at Thornton's for one of those little pink boxes for which you choose your two special chocolates before the assistant ties it up with pink ribbon. The lights had been off at Debbie's mother's house when he'd arrived, all save for the one that was always left on in the porch to put off burglars. After waiting three quarters of an hour, Kevin had left the flowers on the doorstep with the chocolates, gone home and taken a bacon and egg pie from the freezer, sat down in front of "Eastenders" and eaten it out of the foil, not quite warmed through.

"Nothing special," he said.

Inside the car it was getting warm, the windows beginning to take on a film of steam. Lorna offered him the last of the prawn crackers and when he shook his head, she broke it in two with her teeth, biting with a light crunch, slowly. A fragment of cracker, white, stuck to one corner of her mouth, white against the fine, dark down of hair.

She was looking at his hands, resting on his lap. "You ever take it off?" she asked. "You wear it all the time?"

She was staring at the wedding ring on his hand.

"Sometimes," he said.

Lorna nodded. "My sister's husband—they've been married eleven years—she's quite a lot older than me—would you believe it, I'm the youngest?—anyway, he claims, her

77

husband, he's never removed his wedding ring since they got married. Not for one second. D'you believe that?"

"I suppose . . ."

"But you, you said sometimes. Meaning . . . ?"

"It's a little loose. Not quite as tight as it should be. Sometimes, if I'm washing my hands . . . in the shower . . ."

She thought about Kevin taking a shower; standing there, his back towards her, water splashing over him. His backside.

"We ought to get going," Kevin said, looking at his watch.

Lorna raised an eyebrow the way she'd seen Julia Roberts do it once, that movie.

"To the station," Kevin said.

"Look at some photos, that's what you said."

"That's right."

"If it's there, I'll know it. I mean, the way he came over to me first off, not a care in the world. The look on his face when he pushed through the bin bag and told me to fill it. No way I'm going to forget that."

Kevin switched on the engine, but Lorna wasn't through talking.

"You know what gets me?" she said. "What really gets me?"

He looked at her: no.

"When Spindler came in this morning, that's the area manager, oh, he was nice enough to Marjorie and me, good job well done, all the flannel—not that he was going to give us any money for it, no bonus, nothing like that. All the thousands we saved them. But, no, what's he droning on about all the time is Becca, poor Becca and what a terrible shock she had, how it's affected her. Makes me sick. It's not as if anything happened to her. Wasn't her that got a hammer aimed at their head. No, there she is hopping up and down on one leg, practically weeing herself." She stopped, reading the expression on his face. "Sorry, I'm boring you, rattling on."

"No, it's not that. It's just . . ."

"We ought to be going."

"Afraid so."

Kevin released the hand brake and slipped the car into gear.

"What you ought to tell your wife," Lorna said as they were turning right onto Forest Road West, "next time she goes Chinese, ask them to leave out the monosodium gluta-mate. You can do that, you know. Tastes a lot less salty."

13

By midway through that afternoon, they had what looked like a breakthrough. Forensics had finally come up with a couple of prints, forefinger and thumb, plumb on the hand brake of the abandoned car. Whoever had been driving had known enough to wipe around the steering wheel with a cloth—probably the one smeared with engine oil stuffed beneath the front seat—had thought of the gear handle too, but somehow missed the brake. There were a couple of partials on the chrome handle, driver's side, one of which was a near match for those inside, the other from a different hand altogether.

Even better, scene of crime had found a beauty smack in the middle of the side wall of the building society, where the flat of the hand had gone slap against it. The officer, dusting it down, had scarcely been able to believe his luck. Three fingers, close to perfect, almost as clear as if whoever left them had been in custody. "Now roll it lightly, one side to the other, even pressure. Good."

Somewhere short of six o'clock the match came through, faxed back up the line. Keith Rylands: eighteen years of age, five feet five and a half, nine stone six pounds. Six months, youth supervision order, 1988–89, theft from a motor vehicle; 1990, four months on remand, taking and driving away without the owner's consent; six months, Young Offenders' Institution, Glen Parva, two more charges of TDA, one associated charge of stealing from a vehicle dismissed through lack of evidence. Last known address—29 Albert Avenue, Gedling.

Divine showed Rylands's picture to Marjorie Carmichael, who tutted and sweated and finally agreed, yes, it could be him, could be the one. Lorna Solomon wasn't a great deal more definite. "Thing was, you see," she told Kevin Naylor, "I never saw him much more than out the corner of my eye. It's the other one I was looking at, the one with the hammer." Becca Astley was sorry but she had a terrible headache, a migraine really, she couldn't concentrate at all, no way she could be sure.

"What d'you reckon?" Millington asked. They were sitting in an otherwise unoccupied interview room, Resnick's office, as he had suspected, resembling a YTS convention of young plumbers.

"No trace on the other print, the one on the door?"

Millington shook his head. "Not so far."

What they did have was an artist's impression, a narrow-faced young man with a mass of tightly curled hair: it would be in the evening editions of the *Post,* screened on both "Central News" and "East Midlands Today." Not exactly "Crimewatch," but it might yield results.

"Nothing on file about this Rylands's known associates?" Resnick asked.

"Doesn't sound as if he had any. Pathetic little bugger."

"Okay," Resnick said, pushing back his chair, "I'll get Lynn to drive me out there. See what's what. Sooner that than hanging around here without a place to call my own. Mooching about the corridors. Starting to feel like the Ghost of Christmas Past."

"Okay, okay," Darren called. "Stop the car, stop the car. That's it. Here, right here."

Keith had driven the Cavalier into the NCP car park near the Rutland Square Hotel and swopped it for a silver-grey Honda Accord with a rusted rear off-side wing and two pairs of walking boots wrapped in old newspaper down by the backseat.

Keith wriggled himself up to his full height. "Hey, this is—"

"I know where it is."

"You're not going to try knocking it over again?"

Darren gave him a look that warned Keith there was such a thing as having too much to say—what he ought to do, stick to the driving and leave the thinking to him.

"Then why are we—" Keith persisted.

"Shut it!" Darren hissed and pointed at the clock on the car's dashboard. "That working? That right?"

"Far as I know."

Twenty-eight minutes past five.

"Right, then," Darren said, opening the car door. "Wait here."

The office was due to close at five-thirty; ten, fifteen minutes for sorting stuff out, finishing up, they ought to be coming out. Darren remembered the slight hesitation when he'd spoken her name, but nothing more, real cool—"How may I help you?" Looking back at him through those big glasses, blue-framed. He'd liked that. "This gentleman has a query. Perhaps you should deal with it yourself." Took nerve, that. Not a sign of wobble in her voice. Different situation, Darren thought, she and him would get along. Him and Lorna. He'd wondered sometimes what it'd be like, going with a tart as stood up for herself, not just someone to be poked and pushed around.

Resnick was pleased to sit back, let Lynn Kellogg get on with the driving. When he'd been younger, not long joined the force, he'd evinced an interest in cars because it had seemed the thing to do. What you talked about in the canteen when it wasn't how many pints you'd swilled down the night before, how many times you'd got your leg over. As he'd got older, got promoted, he'd gradually felt able to let it drop. It was a while now since he'd talked about all three.

"Called round to see Rebecca Astley this afternoon," Lynn was saying. They were heading down Carlton Hill, about to pass St. Paul's school.

"Bit of a wasted visit, I hear," Resnick said.

Lynn smiled. "Don't know what they think they're doing, giving her branch office to manage. Couldn't even manage to get out to the kitchen, fetch a glass of water to take these pills. Expected me to do it for her."

Resnick laughed, imagining the expression that would have been on Lynn's face when she'd walked back into the room, handed her the water.

"On and on about this migraine. That was the way she said it—*me-graine*. As though it was some rare disease. Instead of a posh name for a headache."

Lynn slowed behind a self-drive van, signalled to turn left into Gedling Road.

"All she was interested in talking about was what a shock it had been. That and the bunch of flowers been sent to her from head office. 'I don't want to brag,' she said, lying there on the sofa, 'but it does show what a lot they think of me.'"

"Didn't tell her what you thought of her?" Resnick asked.

"Tempted." Lynn grinned. "Wouldn't have been worth wasting my breath."

Twenty-nine Albert Avenue had a newly fitted wooden door with a circle of bottle glass at normal head height. The windows were double-glazed with aluminum fittings. A dormer window poked out from the front of the roof; a satellite dish was attached to the wall. STUART BIRD, read the sign to the side of the small front garden, PAINTER & DECORATOR—ESTIMATES GIVEN WITHOUT OBLIGATION.

"You must want my husband," Christine Bird said. "He'll not be back until seven, maybe later. He's got a job on over Newark way."

Resnick assured her she was the one they wanted to see and she showed them into a front room that smelled of furniture polish and Windowlene. A small boy lay on his stomach in front of the TV, watching a cartoon video, pausing it every time the black cat went flying into an old-fashioned kitchen dresser, swallowing plates and bowls and cups before crashing to the ground with them inside him.

"This is Jason," Christine Bird said.

Jason rolled onto his side, stuck out his tongue, then rewound the tape and played the section through again. Christine went over and turned down the sound, turned up the flame behind the fake log fire and took a cigarette from the packet of Players Extra Mild which lay on the marble shelf above the stone surround.

"It's your other son we're interested in," Resnick said.

It took her five attempts to light her cigarette. "He's not here," she said.

"Do you know where Keith is?" Lynn Kellogg asked.

"I haven't seen him, not for a couple of days."

"And you don't know where he might be?"

"I didn't say that." Tapping away ash nervously with her finger.

"We have reason to believe—" Resnick began.

"Don't," Christine Bird interrupted him. "I don't want to know what it is he's done. Not this time. Not anymore."

"You don't happen to know where Keith was yesterday afternoon?" Lynn asked.

Christine Bird got to her feet and crossed the room. Reaching down, she switched off first the television set and then the video and when her five-year-old started to whine and complain, she gave him a look that said, Not this time, and he read it well. "Why don't you go out into the garden?" she said. "Or upstairs to your room?"

"If I do, can I . . . ?"

"One," she pronounced emphatically. "One only. Go on. You know where they are."

"Twix," she explained as Jason left the room.

Neither Resnick nor Lynn Kellogg said a thing.

Christine Bird fidgetted with the blinds, the kind that have scalloped edges. She stubbed out her cigarette and immediately took another from the packet, sliding it back before she could light it.

"My husband . . ." she started.

"Stuart, he's been very good . . ." she tried.

"Keith . . ." she began.

This time she lit the cigarette, pushed a hand up through her hair. There were lines tracking away from the corners of her eyes, slender pouches of skin below them; the eyes themselves were grey, narrowed against the plume of smoke that coiled upwards past her face.

"When we started going together, Stuart and me . . . You see, he'd been married himself, still was, legally. I mean, their divorce, it hadn't come through. One of the things he felt bad about was the thought of leaving his kids. That was the way he saw it, though I don't think it really was like that. Not as if, anyway, she'd have agreed to let him take them with him, and even if she had, well, it's difficult to see how he would have managed. Three of them, you see.

The youngest just eighteen months, much younger than his other two." She drew on the cigarette deeply; stared at her hands. "They had her as a way of trying to sort things out, keep them together."

Rings. Clear polish on her nails.

"When it became clear that we were going to live together, get married, I know—I know, though he never, not in as many words, although he never said it—I know what he wanted was the two of us living together. Starting fresh. Room for his kids to come over, stay weekends or whatever, of course. But nothing more. What he didn't want was, well, what he didn't want, though again he never came right out and said it, was Keith. Living with us. Here."

Three people's breath in the double-glazed room.

"Apart from anything else, he could never understand, you see, why Keith's dad didn't want him there, why Keith didn't want to live with him. To be fair, I think he would have kept him, been happy enough to, but by then they were having these awful rows, Reg was drinking more and more, no real job, and Keith just kept on at him, on and on, prodding away till, of course, Reg—his dad—struck out and, I mean, they just couldn't go on that way, so I said to Stuart, 'Stuart, after we're married and we've moved into the new house, he's got to come and live with us. Keith. Till he's old enough, maybe, to have a place of his own.' "

Ash drifted towards the pleats of her skirt and, absent-mindedly, she brushed it away.

"Keith hadn't been in any really serious trouble by then. Oh, there'd been, you know, silly little incidents, shoplifting, sweets and things, nothing to write home about. Just the way kids do. And truanting. One term he'd skipped off almost as much as he was there. On account of bullying, that's what he said. He's small, you see, Keith, small for his age. Not that he used to be, not when he was little; well, they all were then, little. Around ten or eleven, though, when the other lads started shooting up, Keith, he seemed to stay the same.

"And they teased him for it, beat him up, you know what they're like. Keith, he found the only way to get them on his side was act the fool, make everyone laugh, clown around in class. Which meant, of course, getting in trouble with the teachers instead. Clever, he'd been, back in the juniors. All his reports, lively, that's what they say. Bright. That all changed."

She stubbed out her cigarette in the ashtray on the mantelpiece; stayed there for some moments, staring at the wall.

"When we came here and we asked Keith if he wanted to live with us, he jumped at it like a shot. Stuart was very good with him, took him off to one side and talked to him about how it was important to turn over a new leaf, do well at school."

She glanced at the door before going on.

"When Jason came along, he was lovely with him, Keith, at first; playing with him, parading him up and down. I think it changed when Jason was able to get out of his pram, his cot, move about. Crawl and then walk. Stuart was working more, further and further away, having to, no choice about that, and I was busy with the house, one thing and another. Little Jason, he was really quick, into everything, and before either of us knew it, Keith was up to all sorts, only this time it was serious. Cars and the like. Always mad about cars. First we knew, three o'clock one afternoon, I go to the door, two policemen standing there; in uniform, not like the two of you.

"Course, when Stuart heard about it he went wild, really lost his temper. Hit him. After that it was never the same. I think Keith would have moved back with his dad, but Reg was having troubles enough of his own.

"Last time, when Keith was sentenced, Stuart said if he gets in trouble once more after this, I'm not having him back inside the house. No matter what."

Christine's fingers fumbled out another cigarette.

"Even if it means the end of us, I asked him and he just stands there, you know, looking me flush in the face and says, yes, even if it means that."

Resnick noticed, as if for the first time, the even ticking of the clock.

"He'll be with his dad," Christine Bird said. "Over in the Meadows."

Keith sat hunched forward in the Honda, fidgetting with the tuning of the radio. Five minutes back he'd caught a snatch of M. C. Mell'O', but since then it was GEM-A.M. or static, difficult to decide which was worse. Darren was still leaning against the wall opposite the small parade of shops, shifting his weight every now and then from one foot to the other.

Keith watched him now, stepping away from the wall suddenly, getting ready to move. And there, back across the street, the building society door opened and the girl with blue-framed glasses, the one they'd tried to hold up, stepped out onto the pavement.

14

"I did think that was nice of Mr. Spindler, didn't you?" Marjorie said. "Considerate. Calling round in person, to make sure we were all right."

"About the least he could do," Lorna replied, watching the older woman turn the key in the lock, once, then twice.

"He is a busy man," Marjorie said.

"And we just saved several thousand pounds of his company's money."

"You know, Lorna," Marjorie said, dropping the keys down into her bag, "you really ought to do something about your attitude."

"My att—"

"I sometimes think it's the only thing holding you back."

Lorna half-turned, vaguely aware of someone walking towards them across the street. Where the hell's it got you, Marjorie? she felt herself wanting to say. All those years of back-peddalling and going out of your way to be nice?

"Look at Becca, for instance."

"What," asked Lorna, more than a little steel in her voice, "has Becca got to do with it?"

"Look at the way she's got on as fast as she has. I know she's intelligent, degree and all, but why do you think she's got where she has?"

Lorna stared at Marjorie's doughlike face, waiting to be told.

"It's because she knows how to behave towards people; especially people like Mr. Spindler. She's nicely spoken and she's always well turned out—"

"And if it would help her career, she's not above taking Spindler into the back office and giving him a quick wank."

"Lorna, really!" Marjorie flushed bright red from the nape of her neck to the roots of her hair. "I can't imagine what you . . . I can't believe . . . I'm going to pretend I never heard you say that."

"Fine," Lorna said. "Believe what you like." And, turning fast on her heel, she came close to colliding with Darren, who had slowed his pace on hearing raised voices, but continued, nonetheless, towards them.

"I'm sorry, I . . ."

"'S'okay," Darren said, chirpily. "No harm done, eh?"

For a moment they were stationary, Darren close enough to see his new face reflected in the curved lenses of Lorna's glasses. Lorna looking at him, this tall, skinny youth with the shorn head and the beaklike nose and those protruding grey-blue eyes.

"Closed up?" Darren jerked his head sideways towards the door.

"Half-five."

"Well"—Darren shrugged—"call in another time, eh?"

And he was walking on down the street, hands in his jeans pockets, whistling.

"You don't know him," Marjorie said. "Do you?"

"I don't think so," Lorna said, watching as Darren began to cross back to the other side of the pavement, lower down. But, somewhere inside, she felt that, yes, she did.

Resnick contacted the station, told Graham Millington to get Divine and Naylor down to the Meadows sharpish. If Keith Rylands was there, no sense letting him slip away because nobody was watching the back door. The sky seemed to darken abruptly as Resnick and Lynn Kellogg passed over the railway bridge on London Road, the carriage lights of short sprinter trains standing out clearly—commuters waiting to be shuffled back to Langley Mill, Attenborough, Alfreton and Mansfield Parkway. Ahead of them the traffic slowed almost to a standstill. In the car alongside, a thirtyish executive in a white shirt, sleeves rolled back just above the wrist, added another Benson Kingsize to the pollution levels and listened to the up-to-the-minute traffic report on local radio, confirming where he was and why.

"Heart attack before he's fifty," Lynn said caustically, glancing sideways.

"Maybe he takes long healthy walks," Resnick said. "Off into Derbyshire. Couple of squash games a week and visits to the health club."

"And I'm about to get put up to sergeant," Lynn responded.

"You will. All in good time."

"Meanwhile, I'm still at the bottom of the pecking order, counting through my check stubs each time I go to Safeway."

"You're not doing so bad."

"Aren't I?"

"You're still only twenty-five."

"Twenty-six."

"You'll get there."

Lynn eased the car forward a whole fifteen yards. "How old were you, when you made sergeant?"

Resnick could remember being summoned to the old man's office, stomach bowling googlies all the way along the corridor, not being able to get the grin off his face afterwards, so that four hours later when Elaine opened the door to him she knew. "Nigh on thirty," he said.

"And that was CID?"

Resnick shook his head. "Transferred back into uniform to get the promotion."

"Can't see me doing that. Rather stay where I am."

"It wasn't so bad. Good experience, really. And I was back in CID inside two years. Jack Skelton had just got bumped up as well; he was my D.I."

Lynn laughed. "I can just see him, briefings every morning, checking how you were all turned out." She shot Resnick a quick look. "Smart suit, well-ironed shirt and tie."

Resnick joined in with the laughter. "He tried."

A gap appeared ahead in the traffic and Lynn accelerated smartly into it.

Divine was hard up against the back door, hoping against hope the suspect would try and do a runner; a strained groin had kept him out of the rugby squad for the past three games and he'd dearly love an excuse for landing a couple of good right-handers. Naylor sat behind the wheel of the second car, end of the alley. Resnick pulled on his raincoat and headed for the front, Lynn half a pace behind.

Before Resnick could try the bell, use the knocker, the door opened and a bald man stumbled out, ripe with the smell of ammonia which comes from clothes steeped in stale urine and alcohol.

"Hey up!" Resnick stepped sideways swiftly, halted him with the flat of one hand.

"Wha' . . . ?"

"Reginald Rylands?"

"Na."

"He does live here?"

The man's head moved forward and back as his eyes tried to focus. "Downstairs. Try down . . . stairs."

But, by then, Rylands was in the hallway, the head of the cellar steps, and walking forward. "You looking for me?"

Resnick showed his warrant card, identified himself and Detective Constable Kellogg.

"You'd best come in," Rylands said.

"Be on m'way," slurred the bald man, stepping between Resnick and Lynn Kellogg and onto the street.

"Is he okay?" Resnick asked.

Rylands nodded. "Long as nobody stands too near him with a lighted match."

Inside the kitchen, Resnick turned down the offer of tea, took in the empty quart cider bottles on the floor, several days of unwashed pots and plates. Lynn hung back in the doorway, careful for the sounds of anyone making a dash for the front door.

"Something about the house?" Rylands asked. "One of the lodgers? I'm properly registered, you know, approved. Least till the EEC start in on toilet bowls and sinks."

"It's not that." Resnick shook his head.

"Then it's Keith."

"You tell me."

Rylands eased a finger inside his mouth, scraped away at something stuck between his teeth with a nail. "Got to be, hasn't it?"

"How's that?"

"Always in trouble, isn't he? This thing and the other."

"And recently?"

Rylands shook his head. "No idea. 'Less it's motors, is it? Cars. Can't keep away from them. That what it is?"

From one of the upstairs rooms came the strangulated

tenor of Josef Locke and Resnick grimaced: popular films sometimes had a lot to answer for.

"You do know where your son is?" Lynn asked.

"No."

"We understood that you did."

Someone of similar musical tastes to Resnick opened a door above, shouted loudly and then slammed it shut. Josef Locke faded back into insignificance.

Rylands looked with interest at the white fibre from the heart of last night's chicken tikka, suspended from his finger end. "And who'd that be from?" he asked.

"We've just been speaking to Keith's mother."

"Oh, yes, the former Mrs. Rylands, light of my life."

"She seemed certain that Keith was here, staying with you."

"And I thought he was staying with her and old Stuart, the handy man par excellence. Funny, isn't it?"

"She said she hadn't seen Keith for a couple of days."

"Me neither."

"You haven't seen him?"

"You heard right."

"Since when?"

Rylands shrugged. "Thursday, Friday last week. You sure you wouldn't like a cup of tea?"

Resnick's expression suggested that he was.

"Well, I'll just make one for myself, if you don't mind."

He was on his way towards the sink with the empty kettle, but Resnick was standing in front of him, blocking his way.

"We have reason to believe your son might have been involved in a serious matter."

"I daresay. Now, if you'll . . ."

Resnick took the kettle from his hand and set it down. Lynn stepped to one side in the doorway to let Divine through. "Sorry, boss, getting dead bored out there.

Thought I'd get to where the action was." Reading the question in Resnick's face, he added, "Kev's out back, not to worry."

Rylands had retrieved the kettle.

"Tea up, then, is it?" Divine grinned.

"No," Resnick said. "It's not. Not till we've got a few more answers."

"Well, that's it then, stand-off. Afraid I can't tell you what you want to know."

Resnick could just smell the alcohol on his breath, not insistent, but there. Steady drinker now, he thought, controlled. Likely doesn't start till eleven, eleven-thirty of a morning, no acceleration till late on, eight or nine at night.

"You know it's an offence," Divine was saying, "withholding information."

"How can it be an offence if I don't know anything?"

"You'll not mind," Resnick said, almost casually, "if we search the house."

"Should I?"

"We'll see, shan't we?" Divine smirked.

"If you've a warrant. You did think to bring a warrant?"

"Too cocky by half, boss," Divine said, nodding towards Rylands. "Been here before."

"Have you ever been in trouble with the police?" Resnick asked.

"Who hasn't?"

"Recently?"

Lynn Kellogg responded to footsteps on the stairs and moved out into the hallway; a man wearing stained khaki trousers and a Fair Isle jumper two sizes too tight was carrying a nondescript brown dog towards the door, one hand round the animal's mouth. Before his objective was reached, the dog wriggled out of his arms and barked.

"No animals," Rylands said to Resnick. "It's in the rules. Plain. So daft he thinks I don't know he's smuggling it in and out."

"This trouble . . ." Divine began.

"Let's get back to your son," Resnick said.

Rylands's shoulders slumped and this time Resnick allowed him to fill the kettle, set it on the gas. "You any of your own?" he asked Resnick. "Kids?"

Resnick gave a quick shake of the head.

"If you had, maybe you'd understand. I don't suppose you ever stop caring for them, feeling something, but . . . the rest of it, the day to day, the way they're fucking up their lives." He stood with his eyes closed for as much as twenty seconds. "If I knew where he was, I'd tell you. Time inside, real time, he might learn a lesson. If not, least happens, he'll be out of harm's way. Not able to do anything stupid."

"You think he might?"

"Only every sodding day."

"Then you would tell us where he was?"

"If I knew," Rylands said. "Like a shot."

"You'll not mind, then, if we take a look around?" Divine said. "Warrant or no?"

"Forget it, Mark," said Resnick, beginning to turn away. "He's not here, it's okay." And to Rylands, turning in the kitchen doorway, "If you do see him, what you might do, persuade him to come in. Own accord, go better for him."

Rylands nodded.

"Barring that, give me a call. Resnick. Detective Inspector."

Rylands nodded again. "I'll remember."

Behind him, the kettle was starting to boil.

———

"You get a whiff of him?" Lynn asked. They were outside on the pavement, the opposite side of the narrow street, looking back at the house. "Like he worked in a brewery."

"Starting to feel a bit sorry for him," Divine said, "way he was going on about his lad."

"You and Kevin," said Resnick, "I want you keeping the place under surveillance. All night if necessary. My guess, the youth's been staying here and he'll be back."

15

He hadn't recognised him at first, not for certain; only later, watching Rylands fake his way through sincere parenting, had Resnick been able to slip the younger face over the old. A trick of memory. Tighter, eyes screwed up against the smoke, the lights. Sweat that slid down the channels of Rylands's face, sprayed from nose and forehead as he jerked his head from side to side. Slow smile that would glide into place when, on the stage in front of him, either tenor or guitar would strike a serious groove. The way he would arch back on his stool, sticks a blur as patterns and paradiddles grew from his hands.

Drinking even then, but didn't they all?

Pints of best bitter slopping across the boards: quarter bottles of scotch or vodka passed from hand to hand.

Pills.

Without an effort of imagination, Resnick was there, too many bodies crammed fast, rhythmic thump of dancing feet, sweat that seemed, like raindrops on a windscreen, to rise directly up the walls. Girls you walked back along the Trent, whose interest waned when finally you told them what you did, whose hands eased free from yours, who moved a pace apart.

Walking all over me like that. It's a wonder I didn't go flying back down the stairs.

Elaine.

Resnick had looked for her again, other evenings when the band was playing "In the Midnight Hour," "My Girl," "I've Been Loving You Too Long." Scanning the crowd for that half-serious face, angry, mocking eyes. When next he did encounter Elaine, it would be another place, another circumstance.

The music had changed, too. Instead of soul, rhythm and blues, it was slim young men decked out with purple eyeliner, stars glittering on their cheeks, songs about ancient forests or stars in the skies. Resnick stopped going.

Rylands had beaten him to it: one week Resnick had walked in, together with Ben Riley, and there had been someone else behind the drums.

Rumour was a name band had made Rylands an offer, a group, and he was back on the road, up and down the M1 more times than Peter Withe and Tony Hately combined. There was talk of a record that should have been a hit. To the best of his knowledge, Resnick had never heard it.

He wondered how many years Rylands had been back in the city, if he still played? A pub, maybe, on the outskirts, requests from the customers, keyboard and drums. Draw for the raffle, roll on the snare and a cymbal crash. Blokes pushed up onstage, half-pissed, by their mates, dropping the mike midway through some half-remembered song.

Wondered what Rylands really thought about his son.

Any of your own? Kids?

Without realising what he was doing, Resnick had climbed the stairs to the top of the house.

All those times I'd walk in here and see the expectation rise and fall in your eyes. Fancy a cup of tea, Charlie? Not what you wanted to hear. What you wanted was for me to walk in and say I was pregnant.

Through windows that needed cleaning, Resnick looked down on muted streetlights, the road that curved away in front of the house, the road not taken, not by him.

What Elaine had finally said when she had walked in: *Charlie, we need to talk.* He knew then—the tone of her voice, the look in her eyes—that she was leaving him. Just not when.

Downstairs he checked with the station: Divine and Naylor were still on obs, no sign of Keith. It was a little shy of eleven P.M.

Resnick realised that his instincts could have been wrong. He set aside the idea of going back out there and mooched into the kitchen, began opening and closing cupboard doors. Appetites excited, cats pushed at his ankles, slid their sleek heads across his feet. It wasn't simply finding himself face to face with Rylands for the first time in how many—twenty years? It was more. Other bits and pieces of the past were nudging their way back into his consciousness, rubbing themselves against the back of his mind.

Rylands.

The Boat Club.

Ben Riley.

Elaine.

Prior.

Ruth James.

In the front room he rooted through the shelves of records, albums he'd collected since he was in his teens. On first and second search he couldn't find it, wondered if he could have lent it to someone long ago, if maybe Elaine had taken it, memories of that first time they had met.

He doubted that.

He finally found it inside the sleeve of another record,

Serge Chaloff's *Blue Serge*—not bad, Resnick thought, for an impromptu overcoat. A four-track EP with a laminated cover, soft-focus picture of the singer, head bent, before the microphone. *Ruth James & the Nighthawks.* 1972.

Resnick slid the record onto his hand: a memory of her hand struggling to push back the air. The pallor of her face, auburn of her hair. He dispersed the worst of the dust and set it on the turntable, changed the speed. The stylus stuck near the start and when Resnick eased it gently on, the vocal had already begun.

> *All those dreams and wasted tears,*
> *Every minute, every second,*
> *The worst of all my fears*

He had been called to a burglary, January 'seventy-four, one of those big houses off the Mansfield Road, divided into flats and then divided again. A warren of rooms in which clothes hung drying in front of a two-bar electric fire and every squeak of conversation came through the partition wall. Cooker behind a screen in one corner, the bathroom down the hall—only hot water enough to cover your knees, the plug hole circled round with other people's pubic hair. A rusting fire escape that climbed up from the overgrown garden at the side. Too many windows with a faulty catch. One man, working alone; he had got through four rooms before Elaine came out of hers to go to the toilet and there he was, trying the door across the hall.

"What the hell d'you reckon you're about?" she'd shouted, grabbing at his arm.

The burglar—dark shirt, jeans, wearing gloves—had bolted for the stairs, out through the main door, the lock of which he'd slipped as soon as he'd got inside.

"Sure you're okay?" Resnick had asked, self-conscious inside her room, Elaine sitting on the only chair.

"Um? Oh, yes, I'm fine. Fine."

"You were lucky."

She looked at him then, questioning.

"When you reached for him, that he didn't react."

"He ran."

"I know. What I meant, he might have felt provoked. He might have hurt you."

She smiled: "Like you, you mean?"

Resnick's eyes had smiled back. "I didn't know if you'd remembered?"

"Someone your size? All over me? I had a bruise on my instep that lingered for weeks. Not to mention my big toe."

"Bruised, too?"

"Worse."

He gave her an enquiring look.

"It came off."

"The toe?"

"The nail."

"Oh."

She continued to sit there and he continued to stand where he was, watching. Somewhere above, a cistern was noisily refilling.

"Shouldn't you be looking for clues?" she finally said.

"That fire escape," Resnick said, embarrassed, "it's like an open invitation."

She smiled again; it was a good smile, strong, not ingratiating. "Sooner burgled than burned."

"What I was thinking, window locks—"

"We've been on to the landlord for months."

"Maybe now he'll pay some attention."

She got to her feet. "And maybe not. Anyway, who cares? By then I'll have moved."

"By when?"

"Week after next."

She could read the disappointment in his eyes: just when I've found you again.

"Do you think you'll catch him?" she asked at the door to her room.

"Honestly?"

"Of course."

"If he's a regular, if we pick him up for something else . . . Otherwise, no. Probably not."

He stepped out into the middle of the corridor and she looked at him again. "Are you always that honest?"

"I hope so. I try to be."

"Don't you find that a hindrance in your work?"

He couldn't tell from her expression whether she was teasing him or not. He couldn't think of anything else to say. Before he had reached the head of the stairs, she had gone back inside her room and closed the door. Three weeks later a card arrived, the envelope forwarded from central station. On the front was a photograph of a saxophone, black and white; on the reverse Elaine had written, *Maybe you'd like to call round and check the security arrangements?* along with her new address.

Elaine.

And Ruth James.

This was their story, too.

Empty arms and empty promises
And ten more wasted years

16

"Donner kebabs," Darren said. "Two. Cokes. Cold ones."

The assistant shook his head. "Sorry, closed now. Everything switch off."

"Closed," Darren observed. "What we doin', standing here?"

"Everything switch off. . . ."

"Yeh, you said. So either switch it fucking on again or find us somethin' to eat quick, 'cause we're fuckin' starving."

With a slow shake of his head, the assistant lifted the lid from one of the metal containers. "Meat," he said. "No pita, no bread."

"So stick it in something else," Darren said, being reasonable. At least now they were getting somewhere, talking the same language, almost.

"I don't know if I want . . ." Keith began, watching the slices of grey meat being lifted into two polystyrene trays.

"Course you fucking do," said Darren. And to the man: "Some of the chilli sauce on there, right? Come on, Jesus, shake the bloody thing! And how about the Cokes? Christ! Call this cold?"

Darren emptied the contents of his pocket out onto the counter in a clatter of coins. "Have that. 'S'all I've got. And, hey! You really want to smarten up your act around here, you know? Sweep all this shit up off the floor and do something about that thing you're wearing—more stains than Keith's jockey shorts. And hey, hey! First thing tomorrow, go to one of them places up the market, get a badge cut with your name on, stick it right there, on your lapel. People know what to call you."

"Tony," the assistant said.

"Tony, yeh, right." Darren leant an elbow on the counter and patted him none too lightly on the cheek. "Tony. You remember what I said, huh? Better than having them walking in off the street, Stavros, Stavros, all the time."

"Not a bad bloke," Darren said through a mouthful of meat. "For a Greek."

"I think he's Cypriot," Keith said. They were walking along Lower Parliament Street, strolling really, taking their time.

"Same thing," Darren said.

Keith shook his head. "I think he's Turkish."

"That's what I said. Same fucking thing."

A black and white cab came towards them, signalling to turn right down Edward Street, and Darren stepped out into the road and waved him down; then, as soon as the driver slowed, he waved him on again.

"Forgot," Darren explained. "Skint."

Keith nodded and looked at his watch; new battery just last week and it had stopped again. It had to be well past two. "I ought to be getting back," he said.

"What's the rush?" Darren lifted the last of the meat with fingers and thumb, tipped up the container so that the chilli sauce ran into his mouth, belched, and sent the container skimming across the street into the doorway of the Gas showrooms. "Tell you what, fucking donner tastes like shit."

Keith thought he was going to be sick.

"Stay over at my place," Darren said. "Sleep on the floor."

"Thanks," Keith said. "My old man, he'll be—"

"What? Waiting up to tuck you in?"

Keith thought, chances were, his old man was up at all, a good bollocking was all that was on the cards.

Darren took Keith's silence for assent. "You know what I hate?" he said. "Walking round without money in my pockets. Where's the nearest cash machine?"

They waited until a punter in a loose grey suit, late from one of the clubs, punched in his personal number and withdrew a hundred pounds.

"Got a light?" Keith said, blocking his way.

Darren hit him from behind: twice was enough, the third one just for the fun. Five crisp twenties, never saw the inside of the bloke's wallet. Thank you for your custom, please come again.

A little after four, Keith woke on Darren's floor with a sore back and a stiff neck and the certain sure knowledge that he was going to die. An hour later he was still cuddled up to the toilet bowl, head resting on the chipped enamel. There can't be any more, a small long-suffering voice told him. But there always was.

———

Divine and Naylor were parked along the street from Rylands's house; two or three people had entered, lodgers most likely, none of them any chance of being Keith.

"Know what we ought to do when we're relieved?" Divine said. "Get ourselves out on the old Nuthall Road. See if there's any talent hitching a lift back Heanor way." Divine winked. "Help 'em out, right?"

Naylor looked through the windscreen towards the soft glow of lights that hung over the city centre.

"How long's it been, Kevin?"

"Since when?"

"Since your precious Debbie took herself off to her mum's? Your kid along with her."

Naylor shook his head. "I don't know." Only the months, weeks, days.

"Hardly makes you a married man, then, does it?"

"That gives me the right to go picking up sixteen-year-olds?"

Divine winked. "Gives you the right to a bit of fun."

"Your idea of fun, not mine."

"Jesus, you're a miserable bugger. No wonder she upped sticks and left you."

"Look . . ."—Divine was really getting his rag—"she hasn't left me. That's not the way it is."

"No? How is it then?"

"She's staying at her mum's while we work things out."

Divine laughed in his face. "Never sodding talks to you. How can you be working anything out?"

"That's rubbish."

"Is it? Go on, then, you tell me. When were you last round there? See the kiddie? Talk, the pair of you, without her old lady gobbing and gawking?"

Naylor got out of the car and mooched up the street towards Queen's Walk. As if it wasn't bad enough, his father having a go at him over the telephone, his mother writing those letters—Kevin, she is our granddaughter. . . .

"Tell you what," said Divine when Naylor climbed back into the car. "All the women I've had since joining the force. Names, vital statistics, likes and dislikes. And, hey! Outside the knickers don't count, okay, Kev?"

By the time Millington and Lynn Kellogg took over, it was the coldest part of the night. Lynn had brought a large thermos of tomato soup and Graham Millington had four spinach pasties his wife had bought from Sainsbury's, reheated and handed over wrapped in foil. The car engine they ran intermittently, needing the heater to stop all feeling from leaving them below the knees.

"The wife's talking about Corsica this year," Millington said, "but I'm not so sure."

"You know that bloke I used to go out with?" Lynn said.

"The cyclist?"

"Yes, that's right. Had a card from him the other day. Heard nothing in over a year. Did I have anything fixed for my holidays and, if not, what did I feel about the Tour de France?"

"Too hot, that's what concerns me."

"France?"

"Corsica."

Lynn gave the thermos a shake before pouring out what remained. Her mother had been angling on at her, nothing direct but making it clear all the same, next leave Lynn got she should spend it at home with them. It's your dad, Lynnie, he's not what he was. . . . What he was was a stick of a man, old before his time, wandering between the hen houses instead of sleeping. Likely as not, out there at this moment, checking for foxes, flicking his torch on and off and all the while talking softly, as if his presence not only scared off predators, it kept the birds safe from salmonellosis, aspergillosis and blackhead.

Outside the light was flirting with the sky.

"Come on," Millington said, firing the engine, "he'll not show now. Let's get back to the station. Get a decent cup of tea."

They'd been gone scarcely fifteen minutes when Keith came round the corner, walking slow. Darren had got fed up with the sounds of Keith throwing up, and when the diarrhoea had kicked in, that had been enough. "Here," throwing him some Ajax and a balding lavatory brush. "Clean that mess up and then fuck off. I'll see you tomorrow."

Keith let himself into the house quietly but not quietly enough. His father was on the cellar stairs with a jack handle in his hand. "Figured you for a burglar."

"Figure again."

"Christ, you look awful!"

"Thanks," Keith mumbled and just got to the toilet in time.

"Thought you'd like to know," his dad said through the door, "police were round earlier, looking for you. I don't know what you've been up to, but when you get out of there, I've a good mind to give you the hiding of your miserable life."

What happened later that morning meant that as far as the police were concerned, Keith Rylands was all but forgotten.

17

The time switch on the main safe was activated to open at nine-fifteen. Road works caused by the need to replace thirty metres of sewage piping had brought about a traffic bottleneck, and the security van delivering cash for the start of business was slightly delayed. It finally appeared at nine-thirteen, three minutes late. The bank guard set aside his copy of the *Express* and moved to unlock the outer door. Two men wearing blue-grey uniforms and sky-blue protective helmets climbed down from the cab of the van, called out a remark about the traffic and proceeded to unlock the rear doors.

A bottle-green Granada drew up across from the security van and a woman wearing a high-collared wool coat got out of the passenger seat and began to walk towards the bank.

The first security man was inside the van, passing down sacks of coins to his colleague, who was loading them, side by side, into a low wooden trolley.

The bank guard set the ramp against the stone step and used the side of his shoe to edge it into place.

"I'm sorry, madam," he said, turning towards the

woman in the woollen coat. "I'm afraid we're not open till half-past nine."

The woman, who was a man, pulled a sawn-off shotgun from inside the folds of her coat and jabbed the barrel ends hard against the guard's neck, beneath his jaw.

One of the security men was wheeling his laden trolley across the pavement.

"Move," the armed man said clearly, "and this one's dead."

The Granada was reversing towards the front of the van, two wheels on the pavement, two on the road. A second car, a grey Volvo estate, swerved around the corner and headed towards the rear of the van fast. Before it had come to a standstill, three men, wearing track suits and costume masks, had jumped out.

The security man inside the van had started to leave, one leg over the tail, and now he was back inside, struggling to lock the doors. A blow with an iron bar fractured his wrist; a second, across his shins, fetched him to his knees.

The man in woman's clothing forced the guard to walk backwards into the centre of the bank. Two masked men sprinted past them, heading for the safe. The cashier nearest to them was barged aside.

"If anyone tries to be a hero, they can be the second to die. After this one here."

Shotgun forcing back his head, the guard kept both eyes clenched tight.

Inside the security van, both men, helmets removed, had their mouths and eyes taped shut, back to back.

The contents of the safe were being emptied into double-strength polythene sacks.

By nine-nineteen it was over: a yield, per person, somewhere in excess of three thousand pounds per minute.

———

Resnick was on his way to a meeting with the Home Office pathologist. The remains of a middle-aged man's body had been found in some woods northeast of the city and the possibility was that they might correspond with a missing-person case Resnick had been working on. They were almost there when the news came over the radio. He leaned forward and touched his driver on the shoulder, instructing him to turn round. Parkinson and his corpse would have to wait.

"Boss, you want Kev and me back out at the Meadows or what?" Divine was on the first landing of the police station, eager and open-mouthed.

"Get a couple of uniforms round there," Resnick said, hurrying past. "You'll be needed on this."

In the CID room phones were ringing, some being answered. The furniture had been replaced, the boards—save those in Resnick's office—had been relaid. It was as cold as before, if not colder.

Lynn Kellogg rose from her desk to intercept him. "Just had a call from the hospital. Harry Foreman, seems he's out of danger."

The concern that had leaped to Resnick's eyes faded almost as fast. "Thankful for that, at least. Make a note to get out there and take a statement."

"Today?"

Resnick was already moving on. "I doubt it."

Reg Cossall appeared alongside him in the long corridor, matching Resnick step for step. "What I hear, this is the same team, buggers've changed their MO. Christ knows what we're dealing with now. Bunch of bloody transvestites wearing Mickey Mouse masks. Next we know, sodding students'll be putting their hands up, stunt for charity. Rag week. Awareness of tossing AIDS."

Resnick pushed open the door to the incident room and

let his fellow D.I. enter before him. Most of the chairs were already taken and the air was thickening with smoke. An officer was pinning Polaroids of the two abandoned cars, the Granada and the Volvo, to the board on the side wall, alongside the map showing the route of the gang's escape— that which was certain, that which was conjecture. On a second map the location of the robbery had been newly flagged, joining the four others.

Out front, Malcolm Grafton was shuffling through his deck of six-by-four cards prior to the briefing. Alongside him, Jack Skelton was rehearsing what he would say in front of the TV cameras in an hour's time, wondering if he had made the correct decision in going with the double-breasted blazer instead of the suit.

The door opened again and Detective Inspector Helen Siddons came into the room, acknowledging both Resnick and Cossall with a nod, before moving towards the far end of the rows of chairs.

"Looking for a bloke in drag," Cossall muttered, "there's our man."

Malcolm Grafton coughed a few times and brought the meeting to order. Jack Skelton got to his feet and began to speak.

"Hundred and twenty thousand," Darren said. "More, depending which version you heard."

Keith's face showed no understanding; his skin was the colour of old putty and his eyes were glazed over.

"What's up with you?" Darren said. "Don't you ever listen to the news?"

Keith shook his head: not quickly, not far.

"Over a hundred grand in the time it takes you to wipe your arse."

Across the kitchen, Rylands turned his head but decided to say nothing. He hadn't taken to Darren the first time he set eyes on him, less than five minutes ago when a hammering had brought him to the front door, Darren standing there like a skinhead with a serious personality problem.

"Hey, look," Darren said now. "You got a radio over there. Switch it on, bet there's some bulletin. Something new."

He was staring at Rylands, pointing at the portable Sanyo on top of the fridge.

"It doesn't work," Rylands said. "Needs new batteries."

It had needed batteries for weeks, and he'd bought a fresh set, Ever Readies, last time he'd been to the corner shop, but he'd be buggered if he was going to let Darren know that. Ordering him around in his own house. He wanted to find out the news, let him spend his own money, buy a paper.

"Less than ten minutes," Darren was saying to Keith, "and they were out of there with over a hundred thousand quid. You know how come?"

Keith squinted up at him. "'Cause they planned it?"

"Course they planned it, lamebrain. That's not what I meant."

"Less of the names," Rylands said.

"They got away with it," Darren went on, "because they didn't go in empty-handed. They were tooled up. They had a gun. Shotgun. No one argues with that."

"Who d'you think you are?" Rylands said. "You ever stop to listen to yourself? Something out of *The Untouchables.*"

"What the fuck's that when it's out?"

"See what I mean? Don't even know you're born."

"Come on," Darren said, moving back towards the kitchen door. "We're getting out of here."

"Keith's not well," Rylands said. "He's not going anywhere."

"Bollocks."

"I am feeling rough," Keith said.

Darren took hold of the front of his sweater and hauled him to his feet. "Let's go."

"You," Rylands said. "Let him alone."

Darren's face tightened, eyes suddenly tense and dark—and then he laughed. "C'mon, Keith," he said, still looking at Rylands with the cocky grin the laugh had become. "We're off."

"Keith . . ." Rylands started.

"'S'all right, I'll be fine."

Rylands turned back to where he'd been washing dishes at the sink. The water was already turning cold, the surface swimming in grease. Bits of bacon rind and fragments of egg shell nudged against his fingers. If that was the sort Keith was knocking round with, no wonder he was in trouble.

"Did you hear what happened at that bank?" Marjorie Carmichael said to Lorna as she was unlocking the front door after lunch. "Shotguns and everything. We were lucky that didn't happen to us."

It was only then that Lorna realised who it was had come up to her the previous evening, asking if they were still open, promising that he would be back.

18

"You weren't serious, were you? What you said before?"

"Before what?" Darren was concentrating on getting his score over eleven thousand, his previous best on this machine.

"You know, about . . . well, you know."

"Look, either spit it out or stop going on and on. You're putting me off."

"I meant," Keith said, "about the gun."

"Hey! Why not yell it out a bit louder, might be a couple of blokes over the back never heard what you said." Concentration shot, game over, Darren had been well and truly zapped. "There, see? See what you done?"

Back on the pavement, blinking at the light, Darren ran a hand across the top of his head; his hair had a nice feel to it now, not brittle but soft, a soft fuzz less than half an inch thick.

"Something you got to understand," he said, "I'm not going to spend the rest of my life just hanging round, pulling jobs for a few quid. That's what you want, you better say so now. Me, I'm going to do something with my life. Get some money, real money, get noticed."

With a quick hunch of his shoulders Darren headed off towards Slab Square and, after a few moments' hesitation, Keith hurried after him.

"So what do you think, Marjorie? Do you think I should get in touch with the police and tell them or what?"

It had to be the fourth time Lorna had asked—more or less the same question, more or less the same words—fourth or fifth time in the last hour. Lorna, not wanting to appear too anxious, too nervous either. "Lorna," Marjorie had said, "I don't want to be rude or anything, but you don't think you're being a little paranoid?"

Is that what she was? Or was it the opportunity to spend some more time with Kevin Naylor that had her seeing the would-be robbery merchant in otherwise innocent people?

"It's a shame Becca isn't here," Marjorie said. "She'd know what to do."

Becca knew what to do all right: stay home, send in a sick note and work hard for the sympathy vote. Good riddance, Lorna thought; she and Marjorie could manage the branch fine without her persnickety assistance.

No matter how hard she tried, she couldn't conjure up the youth's face, not exactly—the hair and the nose and the eyes but not a whole face. The walk, though, she could picture that, the slow, cocky strut along the pavement— wasn't that the same walk as the one towards her counter, only the day before?

Here, fill that. Don't keep me waiting.

Well, call in another time, eh?

"I'm going to do it," Lorna said, and reached for the phone. The number was on the card that Kevin Naylor had given to her.

"I'm sorry," Lynn Kellogg said, responding to the call. "He's not here at the moment. Can I take a message?"

"Yes," Lynn said when Lorna had finished, "I'll be sure that he gets it. I can't promise when he'll be able to get back to you, though. It's pretty hectic here today."

Lorna put down the receiver, looked into Marjorie's fleshy, enquiring face and forced a smile. "Well, that's that. Nothing else I can do now."

Naylor had been thinking about his conversation with Divine, Mark sitting there in the car, giving advice for all the world as if, where relationships were concerned, he knew something about it. And then parading his scuzzy list of one-night stands and knee tremblers as some kind of proof that he understood women. What Divine knew about women could be written on the inside of a toilet door and usually was.

"Be hard," Divine had said. "Stand firm, it's the only way. Whatever you do, don't let on you care."

Yes, Naylor thought, and see where that's got you.

The longest relationship Divine had ever had with a woman likely came in short of ten minutes.

It seemed likely that after abandoning the Volvo and the Granada, the gang had doubled back on themselves, possibly using as many as four other vehicles. The only one not wearing a mask was variously described as a slim male, aged between eighteen and twenty-five, and an attractive young woman wearing rather heavy eye shadow and with the faintest suggestion of a moustache. The masks the others had worn had been stolen from a party wear and fancy dress shop the night before and comprised Mickey Mouse, Michael Jackson, the Amazing Spiderman and the Sheriff of Nottingham. The charred remains of what appeared to be several track suits and trainers, together with what could previously have been polystyrene masks, had been found on a patch of waste ground close to the A60, north of Lough-borough. The ashes were on their way to the forensic laboratory without a great deal of hope attached.

The possible identity of the young villain not averse to disguising himself as a woman was currently testing the resources of the Home Office computer.

When Resnick came into the CID room, the remains of a toasted ham and cheese sandwich in the paper bag clutched in his left hand, Graham Millington was slumped back in his chair, overcoat on, hat on, feet on his desk, asleep. Even the first two rings of the telephone failed to wake him.

"Resnick. CID."

Of all the people it might have been, one of the last he would have expected was Rylands.

"No," Resnick said, after listening for several moments. "No, that's okay. I'll come to you. Half hour to an hour. Yes. Good-bye."

When he set the receiver down, Millington was stirring, embarrassed to be discovered asleep.

"Sorry, I don't know what . . ."

"Doesn't matter, Graham, one of those days. Why don't you get off home? Nothing much else any of us can hope for tonight."

Millington, who, one way and another, had been on duty since before four that morning, didn't need to be asked twice. "Reg Cossall said to pass on a message, reckoned you'd know what it was about. Bloke you were talking about the other night, word is, he's likely to get his parole."

Well, so Resnick had been wrong.

"Bad news?"

"Maybe not," Resnick said. "I'm not sure."

Millington resettled his trilby on his head. "Get back now, might be able to watch a bit of snooker before the wife gets back from Russian."

"Taken against it, has she?"

"Not that so much. She'll have me taking off the tiles in the bathroom. Reckons on changing them for that Italian blue."

"G'night, Graham."

Resnick rustled around for what remained of his sandwich, listening to Millington whistling "The Dance of the Sugar Plum Fairy," fading and off-key.

The pub used to be crammed full of medics from the nearby hospital, laughter and large gins and well-honed accents that cut through the ambient sound like scalpels. Now the health authority had shut the place down and sold the site to a consortium of developers whose plans ranged from high-income architect-designed flats to a covered piazza. It not only left the pub quieter, it made it quicker to get in a round of drinks.

Lynn Kellogg's turn, spotting Naylor enter before she'd finished her order and asking for an extra pint.

"Message for you," she said, passing Naylor his Shipstone's. "Lorna Solomon. The building society raid. Will you get back to her. Here, she left her home number as well."

Struggling not to blush, Naylor took the piece of paper and, without looking, pushed it down into his breast pocket. All he would have had to have done, that lunchtime sharing Chinese in the car, was reach over and she would have slid into his arms. Was that what he wanted to do? The way he'd talked about himself and Debbie, as if there was nothing there, nothing left. What was the truth? He sat forward, moving in on the conversation, trying to forget the slip of paper folded inside his pocket, sipping his pint.

19

Rylands had vacuumed the house, the landings and the stairs, from top to bottom. The carpet from the hall he had ripped out and temporarily replaced with some lino offcuts he'd been storing in the cellar. He had borrowed a ladder from a neighbour and cleaned the outside windows, scraping away grime which had gathered for years. For a tenner, another neighbour had lent him a five-hundred-weight van for long enough to cart seventeen bags of rubbish, mostly old bottles and cans, to the household tip. The hall carpet, sodden and stained, had been hauled away, together with a battered suitcase of old clothes and two cardboard boxes of burnt pans, chipped and cracked china and packets of food long past their sell-by date.

The cleanup had begun half an hour after Keith and Darren had left: too early for Rylands to have begun drinking and he hadn't had a drink since. Shaving, he observed it was the first time in months the razor hadn't shaken in his hand and nicked neck or cheek. Before his shave he had taken a bath, long and hot; after it, he dressed himself in clean clothes—a pair of grey trousers that had once belonged to a best suit, a white shirt he ran over with an iron, grey pullover with a V neck in need of a little darning. Black shoes with leather uppers that he had polished and buffed. His hair he trimmed as best as he could before brushing it flat.

Only when all that had been done did he dial the station and ask for Detective Inspector Resnick by name.

Now he and Resnick sat across from each other in Rylands's cellar room, Resnick on the slightly sagging easy chair Rylands had dragged down earlier.

"Nearly got shot of that lot today," Rylands said, pointing at the piles of yellowing music paper on the floor. "Must go back twenty, thirty years. Couldn't in the end—stupid, isn't it, what you cling on to?"

Resnick nodded over his mug of coffee, neither as strong nor as dark as he would have liked. Rylands was drinking the same, smoking a hand-rolled cigarette, thin as a baby's finger.

"I recognised you," Rylands said. "Oh, not exactly who you were, don't suppose I ever knew that, and if I did, well, I'd forgot, but the face—yes—all those nights standing there, close to the band."

Resnick nodded, remembering.

"Most men just went there for the girls. The beer."

"I met my wife there."

Rylands gave a rueful smile. "There you go."

"Stepped all over her feet."

"Dancing?"

Resnick shook his head. "Just being clumsy."

"They say that, don't they? About coppers. The old joke."

Resnick was looking at him.

"Big feet."

Resnick continued to wait, guessing that whatever Rylands had invited him there to hear, it wouldn't be easy to say. There were things itching at the edges of Resnick's mind, too, demanding attention; memories he was unwilling to scratch. Leave it alone, his mother had been forever saying to him, you'll only make it worse. Well, as far as the sundry blemishes of adolescence, that was likely true.

"You still listen to much?" Rylands asked, not ready yet for the conversation to go where it had to go.

"Now and again. When I get the time. Sundays at the Playhouse; the Arboretum, sometimes. Here and there."

"Some of the old band are still playing. . . ."

Resnick nodded.

"Straight-ahead jazz now. R and B, thing of the past where they're concerned."

"And you?"

Rylands was looking at the snare drums gathering dust on the floor. "No," he said, and then: "Last night, when you were here, looking for Keith. All what I said . . . wasn't necessarily true."

"No."

"He had been here, I had seen him. Said he was going to stay. I don't know—daft, really, I know if you wanted him bad enough you're always going to find him—still, I couldn't just, you know, say. Would've been like . . . shopping him, I suppose. Grassing your own."

"Yes," said Resnick. "I understand." The mug of coffee, lukewarm now, he set on the floor.

"What I said . . ."

"Mm."

"About him being better off back inside . . ."

"Yes."

"I didn't mean that. . . ."

"No."

"Not the way it sounded."

"No."

"All the same . . ." The cigarette had gone out and Rylands relit it, wisps of tobacco sizzling to nothing.

"What he's been in up to yet, cars and that, nothing serious . . ."

"Serious enough."

Rylands looked at the floor between his polished shoes. "This bloke he's running with now, mouth on him like a sewer, treats Keith like shit and all the while Keith looking up to him, lapping it up. I hate to see that."

When he should be looking up to you, Resnick thought.

"How much of it's talk, I don't know. Like I say, the mouth on him. But what he was on about, earlier today, here in the kitchen, what he was talking about was getting a gun. A shooter."

A moment's silence wavered between them.

"Did he say what for?" Resnick asked.

"Not right out, but that bank job, today, he was full of that. How they got away with it on account of the gun." Rylands let the nub end of his cigarette fall into his mug of coffee. "Might all just have been chat, showing off . . ."

"The reason we want to talk to Keith," Resnick said, "there was an attempted robbery, branch office of a building society. Two youths, one armed with a hammer. Something happened, all went wrong; ran off without getting a penny. We found Keith's prints—what might be Keith's prints—on the car they used to get away."

"A hammer," Rylands said thoughtfully.

"Like to have broken this old boy's head for getting in the way."

Rylands nodded. "If it was this Darren, I'd believe it. The way he looked at me, just for a second, today. If he'd had a gun in his hands then . . ."

The rest lay between them, unsaid. Resnick thinking about walking in on Prior, shotgun in his hands.

"Keith knows where he lives?" Resnick asked.

"I suppose so."

"And he's coming back here tonight?"

"Keith?"

"Yes."

"Probably. As far as I know."

"We could pick him up, charge him . . ."

But Rylands was shaking his head. "There's got to be another way."

Resnick leaned back, crossed one leg over the other and waited to hear what that was.

At the top of the cellar steps, Resnick said: "Last night, after I'd been here, I found an old record of 'Wasted Years.' "

"Ruthie . . ."

"Yes."

"Great voice."

"Not still in touch I suppose?"

Rylands shook his head. "Haven't seen Ruth in years. Scarcely since that bloke of hers got sent down. What was it? Twelve years?"

"Fifteen."

"Jesus," Rylands said softly.

"Rumour has it," Resnick said, "he's on his way back out."

"Prior?"

"Yes."

"Jesus," Rylands breathed again.

"I'd best be off," Resnick said, moving away.

"What I heard, you know, back then, be a few scores to settle when he's back on the street."

Resnick nodded. "Possible." He stopped close to the front door. "Ever hear anything, where Ruth is now, give us a ring, okay?"

"Yes, right. Though, like I say, don't suppose . . ."

"This other business, your Keith, let me have a think

about it. One way or another, I'll be back in touch." Resnick held out his hand. "Be good if we could work something out, between us, old time's sake."

His eyes held Rylands's for a long moment, not wanting him to escape his meaning.

"Yes," Rylands said. "Sure. I'll do what I can."

"Good."

Rylands stepped back and watched the inspector out onto the street; when he had closed the door, he leaned his head against the hardness of the wood, eyes clenched shut. He would stay there, exactly as he was, until the urgency to find a drink had passed.

The night was clear and the moon three-quarters full. Resnick needed to walk. Ten, fifteen minutes he would be in Slab Square and could pick up a cab if he wished. Hands in pockets, coat collar pulled up, Resnick walked away.

20

In the square, a fifty-year-old man, trousers rolled past his knees, was paddling in one of the fountains, splashing handfuls of water up under the arms of his fraying coat. A young woman with a tattooed face was singing an old English melody to a scattering of grimy pigeons. Resnick stood by one of the benches, listening: a girl in denim shorts and overlapping T-shirts, razored hair, leather waistcoat with a death's head on the back, standing there, oblivious of everything else, singing, in a voice strangely thin and pure, "She Moved Through the Fair."

When she had finished and Resnick, wishing to say thanks, tell her how it had sounded, give her, perhaps, money, walked purposefully towards her, she turned her back on him and moved away.

On the steps, in the shadow of the lions, couples were kissing. Young men in shirtsleeves, leaning from the windows of their cars, slowly circled the square. Across from where Resnick was standing was the bland brick and glass of the store that twenty years before had been the Black Boy, the pub where he and Ben Riley would meet for an early-evening pint. The glass that ten years ago was smashed and smashed again as rioters swaggered and roared through the city's streets.

No way to hold it all back now.

Inside the house, he showered, turning the water as hot as he dared and lifting his face towards it, eyes closed; soaping his body over and over, the way he did after being called out to examine some poor victim, murdered often as not for small change or jealousy, being in the wrong place at the wrong time. Steam clouded the bathroom, clogged the air, and still Resnick stood there, back bent now beneath the spray, content to let it wash over him.

In the kitchen, he felt the smoothness of coffee beans in the small of his hand. He knew already which album he would pull from the shelves, slide onto the turntable from its sleeve.

The purple postage stamp on the cover, Monk's face in profile at its centre, trilby hat sloping forward, angled away, the thrust of his goatee beard rhyming the curve of the hat's brim. Riverside 12–209: *The Unique Thelonious Monk.* "If only they'd take away the blindfold and the handcuffs," Elaine had used to say of Monk's playing, "it might make all the difference." Resnick would smile. Why play the right notes when the wrong ones will do?

Resnick set his coffee on the table by the chair and cued in the second track.

Monk picks the notes from the piano tentatively, as if it were a tune he once heard long ago and then, indistinctly, through the open window of an apartment down the street. There is more than uncertainty in the way his fingers falter, sliding between half-remembered chords, surprising themselves with fragments of melody, with things he would have preferred to have remained forgotten. "Memories of You."

Moments when it is easy to imagine he might get up from the piano and walk away—except that you know he cannot, any more than when the solo is finally through he can let it go. When you're sure it's over, probing with another pair of notes, a jinking run, a fading chord.

At the track's end, he seems to hear Elaine's feet walk across the floor above: door to dressing table to wardrobe, wardrobe to dressing table to bed. If he went now and pushed open the door into the hallway, would he hear her voice?

"Charlie, aren't you coming up?"

The final weeks when they lay beneath the same sheets, not speaking, not touching, catching at their breath, fearful that in sleep they might be turned inward by some old habit or need.

"Christ, Charlie!" Ben Riley had exclaimed. "What the heck's the matter with you? You got a face like bloody death!"

And in truth he had—because in truth that's what it had been like: dying.

A long death and slow, eked out, a little each day.

Fragments.

"Don't you see, Charlie?"

Once the blindfold had been taken away, it made all the difference.

1981

21

"That the post, Charlie?"

"Mm?"

"I said, is that . . . ? Oh, never mind. I'll get it."

Resnick slurped down more coffee, half an ear on the local news report, mother and her two children narrowly escaping a house fire out in Bilborough, half on what Elaine was shouting from the hall.

"That lad," Elaine said accusingly, coming down the steps into the kitchen.

"Which one?"

"The boy who delivers the paper."

"I thought it was the postman?"

Elaine shook her head. "The paper."

"What about it?"

"Him. It's him. Rides that bike of his right up to the door, hardly time to stuff the paper through the flap and he's off again. Four times out of five, see what happens."

She dropped the *Mail* onto the table where Resnick was sitting. On a torn and buckled front page he glimpsed something more about the new princess.

"Why not have a word?" Resnick said. "At the shop."

"I have."

"And?"

She pointed at the newspaper. "You can see for yourself how much good that did."

"What d'you reckon, then?" Resnick grinned. "Lurk in the shrubbery, flash my warrant card at him? Performing wheelies in a confined space?"

"Go on, make a joke out of it."

"I don't see what else I can do."

"You don't pay for it, that's why."

"I don't read it."

"You don't read anything. Aside from the back pages."

"Better than page three."

"The *Mail* doesn't have page three."

"Shouldn't mind missing bits of page one as well, then."

"God! Something has got into you this morning."

Resnick reached for her hand. "Part of my new image."

"Oh, yes?" Allowing herself to be pulled gently towards him. "What's that, then?"

"Ooh, you know. Light-hearted, silver-tongued."

"Yes?" A smile brightening Elaine's face. "Well, I don't want to disappoint you, but you've still a way to go. And, no. I am not going to spend the next few minutes dallying on your lap."

"Why not?"

"Because it's way past time I finished getting ready for work."

"You look ready to me."

"I said for work."

Resnick's kiss missed her mouth and landed between neck and cheek.

"Do you know how long I spent putting on that makeup?"

"To the second."

"Then you know I haven't got time to do it over again."

Resnick grinned.

"Charlie!" She wriggled to her feet and stood over him, trying hard to look annoyed. "If that's what you're interested in, you should have said so an hour ago."

"I did."

For a moment Elaine's expression changed. "Why didn't I hear you?"

Resnick shook his head and looked away. "I don't know," he said.

The news had finished and Neil Diamond was sounding beefily cheerful in its place. Elaine walked across the room and switched off the radio. Resnick bit into cold toast. There were times when this house they had bought could feel strangely barren and still.

"Can you drop me off?" Elaine asked.

"Sure. I'm in court first thing. Shirehall."

"How long've I got?"

Resnick looked at his watch. "Ten minutes."

"Fine."

Toast in hand, he turned to watch her go and in the doorway she swung back towards him, a smile slipping back to her face.

"Be careful, Charlie."

"What?"

But before he could follow the direction of her gaze, the marmalade had slid from the edge of the crust down onto the welcoming width of his tie.

A little under six months ago, Elaine had taken a new job with an advertising agency which had opened new offices in one of the Victorian factories in the old Lace Market. Open-plan premises, green plants, partners with turned-back cuffs who encouraged everyone to call them by their first names. "It's a good opportunity, Charlie. They've got big plans for expansion and they're really keen to promote from inside."

Her desk was close to one of the beautifully proportioned arched windows and, aside from her keyboard and printer and VDU, held a pair of trailing ivies, a scarlet geranium, a photograph of herself and Resnick at the party celebrating his promotion to detective sergeant, a small furry animal she had had since a baby, a pocket calculator and a large glass ashtray—not that she smoked herself, but her boss did and since quite often he stopped by her desk rather than calling her over to his, it was only sensible to be accommodating.

"Not that there's anything wrong with the way you dress," her boss, the sales director, had said, tapping ash from the end of his cigarette, "but if we saw our way to giving you an advance on your first bonus, d'you think you might see your way clear to spending it on something a little more, well, something with a little more flair?"

She hadn't said anything about the conversation to Resnick. She'd taken the money, spent it, lied about the cost, cutting it by more than fifty percent, and still had to live with the look of incredulity on his face. "What? You spent how much? On that? To sit around at work in?"

Clothes, Resnick thought, were what you put on so as not to appear naked. They were what you covered with paper suits before stepping into a scene of crime.

For that much money they could have hired someone to repaint the outside of the house, replaced the carpet on the stairs, booked that holiday in New Orleans instead of spending a week in a self-catering cottage in Northumbria or risking coming face-to-face with half the rest of the local force on Majorca.

"This do you?" Resnick asked, drawing into the kerb on the corner of High Pavement and Stoney Street.

"Fine." She leaned across the front seat to kiss him deftly on the cheek. "You're not going into the witness box in that?" she asked, looking askance at the stain on his tie.

"Don't worry. I'll hold my notebook in front of it."

Elaine kissed him again and slid from the car. Resnick watched her in the wing mirror, a crisp-looking woman with good legs and brown hair, small leather bag swinging from one shoulder. When it was clear she wasn't going to turn and wave, Resnick pulled away from the kerb and continued along High Pavement towards the Shirehall.

An hour and a half later he was giving evidence against a nineteen-year-old who had walked into a secondhand jeweller's on Castle Gate and tried to negotiate a price for a dozen items which were on the list regularly circulated by the police. The jeweller requested time to give an accurate estimate, asked the youth to come back within the hour. When he did so, Resnick and D.C. Rains had been waiting in the back.

"Good stuff," Rains had said, examining a diamond clip through the jeweller's glass. "Shame to let it go to waste. Owner's likely claimed on the insurance already."

Resnick had chosen not to hear.

"And at any time, Sergeant, when you and Detective Constable Rains were taking my client into custody, were you aware of the detective constable threatening my client?"

"No, I was not."

"You neither saw nor heard the officer propositioning my client at all?"

"I'm not sure what you . . ."

"You were not in the police vehicle when Detective Constable Rains said to my client, 'There's half a dozen more down to you and you're going to cough for them or I'll see how your balls fit inside a pair of garden shears'?"

"Those exact words?"

"Did you hear your colleague utter those words, Sergeant?"

"No, I did not."

"Nor anything like them?"

"Not to the best of my knowledge."

"But Detective Constable Rains and yourself did question my client about other alleged offences?"

"In the course of our interview with him, yes."

"This interview, Sergeant, would this have been held in the police station?"

"Yes."

"Not in the car?"

"I'm sorry?"

"The police car taking my client back to the station, the interview did not take place there?"

"I told you, the—"

"What was said to my client in the car?"

"I'm not sure, I mean, not exactly. But very little of consequence. As far as I remember."

"Perhaps you would like time to refer to your notes?"

"Thank you, but there's nothing in my notebook about any such conversation."

"It was silent, then, the journey?"

"For the most part, as I recall, yes."

"You were driving?"

"Yes."

"And D.C. Rains?"

"Was in the passenger seat alongside me."

"Leaning over that seat to talk to my client, who was handcuffed in the back?"

"He may have, I don't . . ."

"You don't recall, yes, Sergeant, we're getting used to your convenient lapses of memory . . ."

"I . . ."

"I put it to you, however, that you must have been aware that your colleague was leaning over towards the rear seat in which my client was travelling, both his wrists handcuffed behind his back, leaning over and telling him in no uncertain terms that if he refused to own up to at least six other cases of burglary, he would personally emasculate him?"

"I have no recollection of any such conversation."

"Nor of the detective constable reaching into the rear of the vehicle and grasping my client's testicles in his hand and twisting them so viciously that my client cried out and kicked the back of the seat and, finally, almost lost consciousness."

"No."

"You were not aware of any of these things I have described taking place?"

"No."

"In which case, Sergeant, my client must be lying?"

"It seems possible . . ."

"And the doctor who examined my client at the police station and found signs of severe bruising on and around the area of his testicles, he was lying, too?"

"That's not for me to say."

"You are not saying very much at all, are you, Sergeant?"

"I am giving evidence as to what happened as best I remember . . ."

"So you keep saying. And, as the court is becoming distressingly aware, your memory, Sergeant, is not of the best. Neither, apparently, are your powers of observation."

Smarting, standing there in the witness box in his slightly shabby suit and his freshly stained tie, looking neither directly at the barrister questioning him nor at the judge, but directly in front of him, Resnick made no reply.

"You were *in* the vehicle?" the barrister asked.

"Yes."

"Sleeping."

"Driving," Resnick said. "I was driving. My attention was on the road, the other traffic. I was concentrating on what was going on outside the car, rather than inside."

"How convenient!" The barrister made no attempt to contain his sarcasm.

"Well," Resnick said, "it meant that we reached the station without accident."

"In which case, Sergeant, I suppose we should congratulate you on a job well done. I'm sure that after this, your superiors will look favourably on any request you might make to continue your career in traffic control."

Resnick's eyes narrowed and, behind his back, his hands clenched and unclenched several times.

"Thank you, Sergeant. I have no further questions. You may step down."

Half an hour later, Resnick was across the road in the County Tavern, washing down a cheese and onion cob with a pint of draught Guinness. He'd already had two whiskies at the bar to catch his nerves and his head was still throbbing. Rains was the last man he wanted to see coming through the door and there he was, bouncing up the steps to where Resnick was sitting, flashing a smile to match the watch strapped to his wrist.

"Owe you one, Charlie. Several, in fact." His open hand pounded Resnick on the back. "Word is you stonewalled in there like the best. Place in the next Test if you don't watch out."

He held out his hand and Resnick ignored it, bit down into what was left of his cob.

"So, then, Charlie, I'm buying. What's it to be?"

"Nothing."

"Charlie, come on. I—"

"Nothing."

Rains pressed both hands together flat, as if praying, raised them till they were resting against his mouth: a familiar gesture. "Okay, have it your own way." He took a step back. "That supermarket blag—we've got a meet tonight, half-seven."

Resnick watched him go, a tall man, an inch under six foot, slim-hipped, expensive suit, dark hair professionally styled and cut, handsome, twenty-nine years old.

What Rains had actually said to the terrified youth in the car was: "There's half a dozen more down to you, you pathetic little arsewipe, and if you don't cough for the lot of them, I'll whip your grungy little bollocks off with a pair of secateurs."

22

The gang had robbed a Securicor van of eight thousand pounds, give or take the small change. They had driven a Transit into its path in the loading area outside the new Sainsbury's superstore and three men with stocking masks had jumped out of a BMW which had skewed to a halt hard behind it. Shoppers had scattered towards safety, leaving laden trolleys abandoned. If the youngest of the security guards had not taken it into his head to be a hero, it would all have gone as smoothly as the two similar raids the gang had carried out in the preceding months.

But, for whatever reason, misguided or noble, the twenty-five-year-old part-time archaeology student had hurled himself at the legs of the nearest robber, bringing him down, the money sack that he'd been carrying tumbling clear.

In the confusion and clamour that followed, only these things are certain: the robber, who was rugby tackled, suffered a damaged kneecap, which, when the atmosphere was damp, bothered him to this day; the money sack somersaulted into the path of a small girl, little more than a toddler, who was running from her mother, stopping her in her tracks, causing her, in fact, to topple against it, her young body keeping it secure and reducing the gang's haul by approximately one-fifth; the nearest of the other masked men to the incident, immediately and without hesitation, brought the sawn-off shotgun he was carrying to his shoulder and fired both barrels into the guard's face and body. Several hours of surgery succeeded in removing almost all of the 0-0 pellets from his neck and cheek, shoulder and chest, and he was deemed fortunate to be left alive.

Fourteen detectives and numerous uniformed officers had been devoting most of their waking hours ever since to tracking the gang down. A lot of overtime and a lot of shoe leather and, for those of them with wives or lovers, a lot of broken promises and recriminations.

"Elaine, look, I'm sorry . . ." Resnick said into the phone.

"What?"

"I'm going to be back late."

"Why are you telling me, Charlie? Late's what you always are."

"This might be later."

She made no attempt to suppress the sigh. "If you're any later than quarter to eight in the morning, I'll have left for work."

Resnick saw Reg Cossall watching him as he set down the receiver. "Bastard, in't it, eh, Charlie?"

Resnick slowly shook his head.

"After my third time," Cossall said, lighting another Silk Cut, "I thought as how I'd got it sussed. Never give 'em reason to expect 'owt, they won't be disappointed." He blew smoke at the ceiling and laughed low in the back of his throat. "Cow shoved off anyhow. Took every one of my suits, that good Crombie coat I had, shirts, socks, trousers, piled 'em all up in the back garden, chucked a can of paraffin over and burned the bloody lot. Women! Different bloody race, Charlie, and it don't pay to forget it."

"All right, gentlemen. Settle down now. Let's see what we've got." Jack Skelton, two years an inspector, transferred up from Stevenage and still pretty much an outsider, was on his feet and looking round the room expectantly. A nice result here was what he needed to get his feet under the table and he was going to push everyone as hard as it took until it was over.

What they had, Reg Cossall reckoned afterwards, was about as much use as a eunuch in a brothel. They were in an after-hours drinking club on Bottle Lane, crowded round a table in the last of a succession of small rooms, Cossall and Resnick and Rains and four or five others. Any pretence at moderation, just a pint before hitting the road, had long since flown out the window. Now it was spirits, doubles, Resnick dodging the occasional round, wanting to pace himself, knowing all he had to do was get up and leave, knowing that once you'd passed a certain point it's the hardest thing in the world.

Skelton had been with them in the pub earlier, his shout, a few pleasantries and then the suburbs awaited. But Jack Skelton had rank for reason, had a young kiddie, a girl named Kate, waiting for him to kiss her good night; he had a wife, something in hospital administration, professional woman. Expectations he had to fulfill.

When Resnick made inspector, things would change; like Skelton he could make his excuses and leave, knowing full well the men were glad to be shot of him, free to talk, to call him names behind his absent back.

When he and Elaine had a child . . .

"What d'you reckon then, Charlie?"

"How's that?"

"What Rainsey here was saying, these blaggings down to Prior."

"I thought we'd been through all that?"

"We have."

"Checked him out."

Rains leaned forward, jabbing his finger at the air. "Pulled him in twice, brief right alongside him, all through interrogation, every step of the sodding way."

"The way it's meant to be," Resnick said.

"Bollocks!"

"Alibied to the armpits, wasn't he?" Cossall said.

"In bed with his old lady, middle of the afternoon . . ."

"I should fancy!"

"Not if you'd seen her you wouldn't. Face sour as last week's milk. Real scrubber."

"What's his form again?" Resnick asked, interested almost despite himself.

Rains eased back in his chair. "Couple of stretches, aggravated burglary. Fancied him for a post office job, eighteen months back, his face all over it but nothing we could prove. That time, reckoned he and the wife had driven her mother up to Harrogate, bit of shopping, afternoon tea."

"Family man," said Cossall quietly. "That's nice."

"Villain, that's what he is," Rains said. "Nothing else." He leaned forward again, looking into their faces. "What d'you think he's been up to this last eighteen month? Filling in his Spot the Ball coupons?"

Cossall shrugged and Resnick checked his watch and Rains downed his scotch and got to his feet. "Another of these and then I reckon we go round and knock him up, see what he's got to say."

"What grounds?" Resnick asked.

Rains winked. "Information received. Reasonable suspicion. Probable cause. Who gives a toss? Scotch, Reg? Charlie? Vodka?"

Resnick shook his head.

"Suit yourself."

"Jesus, Charlie," Cossall said, watching Rains disappear in the direction of the bar, "most of us get tireder as the night gets longer—each hour he's awake he gets bloody brighter."

"Think there's anything to what he says?" Resnick asked.

"Prior? He'll be into something right enough. His sort always are. That's not counting shagging his missus the wrong side of *Blue Peter.* Maybe it wouldn't hurt to give him a tumble at that."

Resnick shook his head. "Not like this. Not now."

"Be off his guard."

"For how long? No warrant, we're not going to find anything. Get him down the station and he'll be back on the street before breakfast. Besides, state Rains is in, no telling what he might get up to."

"What, Charlie?" Cossall laughed. "With you there to hold his hand?"

"You'd go along with it then?"

"Like hell as like! Way Rains's getting himself pumped up, time he gets there, be near enough out of his skull."

Rains arrived back with doubles all round, setting one down in front of Resnick as if he'd never said a word; from the gleam in Rains's eye he'd slipped in an extra one while being served.

"Here's to us, then." Rains raised his glass in front of his face. "And here's to a life of crime." He downed the whisky in a single swallow. "What d'you say, then, skip?" He rested a hand on Resnick's shoulder. "Time to see if Prior's all tucked up?"

Resnick got to his feet, leaving his drink untouched. "Time we all went home. Got some sleep."

"Bollocks!"

"Come on," Resnick said.

"Keep your hands off me," Rains said. "Leave me a-fucking-lone."

"Quietly," Resnick said. "I'll walk with you down the square, cab it home."

"I don't need a cab, I've got my sodding car."

"Leave it where it is. You don't want to drive."

"Who says?"

"You're drunk."

"Who's fucking drunk?"

Reg Cossall stood up heavily, taking hold of both their arms. "This isn't so good. People are starting to pay attention. What say we hold it down?"

Rains swung himself clear of Cossall's grasp. "The rest of you can do as you like. Just don't try and fucking interfere."

Resnick caught up with him near the foot of Bottle Lane. Rains was leaning forward against the wall, urinating onto the uneven cobbles and his own feet. The car keys were in Rains's right-side coat pocket and Resnick had found them and fished them out before Rains could react.

"You can have these back in the morning. Now get home and sober up. And don't go within a mile of Prior. Clear?"

Rains's eyes were glazed and he shook his head from side to side, bringing Resnick into focus.

"You've got no—"

The index finger of Resnick's right hand stopped no more than two inches from the centre of Rains's face. "Don't tell me what I can or can't do. Not you. I spent one of the worst mornings of my life in court today, bending over backwards to keep the shit off your shoes. I'm in no mood to do the same thing twice. Now get home and get yourself sorted out."

Resnick let the keys fall into his own pocket as he turned away; glancing back from the corner of Bridlesmith Gate, he saw Rains had not moved. Resnick hailed a cab rounding the square and gave his address.

"Good night?" the driver asked pleasantly.

"Yes," Resnick said. "Terrific!"

―――――

Only the front hall light was on and Resnick switched it off as he went through to the kitchen. There was a piece of Stilton in the fridge and the remains of some pasta Elaine had made in a covered bowl. He shook some Worcester sauce onto the pasta, cut slices from the cheese and sat at the kitchen table with the local paper. Fifteen minutes later, shoes in hand, he climbed the stairs to bed.

Elaine was tucked in on herself, most of the covers dragged over to her side. Resnick undressed quickly, sliding in alongside her, finding some space beneath the sheet.

"Charlie," she said softly. "Is that you?"

"Yes."

"Charlie," Elaine said, turning towards him, "you smell of drink."

23

Resnick had his feet behind his desk before eight and by eight-fifteen Rains was standing in front of him with an apologetic grin.

"Way out of line last night, sorry."

Resnick drew breath.

"Try not to let it happen again, eh?"

"Right," Resnick said.

"No hard feelings?"

Resnick shook his head. "No."

Rains held out a cupped hand and Resnick dropped his car keys down into it. Rains smiled. "Tell you something interesting," he said. "Bloke got picked up this morning, Rossi. Early hours. Shinning down a drain pipe out near the castle. Neighbour got up to let out the cat, spotted him, phoned in. Your mate Ben Riley got out there in time to help him to the ground. Once he got him talking, hardly get him to stop. Put his hand up for twenty break-ins going back two years. Says there's more but he wants to cut a deal."

"Go on."

Rains shrugged. "Usual kind. Not so keen on going back inside. Something about four walls, not good for his nerves. He wants to trade."

"Information?"

"What else has he got?"

"You know what we stand to lose? Lies and half-truths, God knows how many hours chasing after things we can't make stick."

"All the same"—Rains was nodding—"one little tidbit —reckons he knows something about the Sainsbury's job. Reckons he knows the driver, friend of a friend."

"Name?"

Rains shook his head. "Not yet. Not so easy."

"Okay," Resnick said, "get him in an interview room. I'll have a word on high."

Rains went off smiling.

On his way back from talking to Jack Skelton, Resnick ran into Ben Riley on the stairs; Ben, still in uniform, sergeant's stripes in place. When Resnick had applied to return to CID, his friend had opted to stay put. "Not me, Charlie, all that hanging about in pubs, rubbing shoulders with the scum of the earth. Rather keep them at a distance—close as the end of this truncheon, that's about as close as I want to get. And besides, I like the uniform. Smart. Lord alone knows what you'll look like when you're back in civvies. Without you get Elaine to sort you out every day and I can't see her being much in the way of that."

"Just off to have words with the chap you arrested," Resnick said.

"Tried to kid me he was from Visionhire." Ben Riley laughed. "People had complained about trouble with their picture; he'd gone out to sort out the aerial."

"Four in the morning without a ladder?"

"All part of the service, he reckoned. That was before I

got him to turn out his pockets. Three picklocks, a chisel and a six-inch metal rule."

Resnick grinned and continued up the stairs.

"Pint later?" Ben Riley called after him.

"Doubt it."

"You'll be at the match Saturday?"

"I'll try."

"Don't bloody try. Be there."

Melvyn Rossi was a shortish man with a weepy left eye and skin like chalk. Son of an Italian father and a Scottish mother, he had fetched up in the Midlands by default. Seven years of hard graft in his father's ice cream business in Dawlish had ended when his father discovered he was unsystematically skimming off the top. His mother, who had returned to her native Inverness long since, had never had much time for him anyway. Melvyn had met a man on a long-distance coach who had told him you could pick up women in the city like fruit from the trees. True, Melvyn discovered, though his fellow traveller had neglected to point out that you were expected to pay for them.

Rossi would break into the back of a house in St. Anne's or by the Arboretum, steal what cash he could find, fifteen minutes later hand it over for the dubious pleasure of taking his clothes off in an upstairs room with a single-bar electric fire, a narrow bed and a red light bulb.

It was the crabs that cured him of that particular habit.

Now he spent his money on horses and beer and an ever-growing pornographic video collection. There were times he wished he'd never turned his back on the world of 99s and orange zooms and water ices in five identical flavours, and this was one of them.

When Resnick entered the interview room, Melvyn Rossi was sitting at the plain wooden table, Rains standing close behind him, patting Melvyn benevolently on top of the head.

"Melvyn's decided to be a good boy," Rains said. "Melvyn's going to tell us everything we want to know."

Which wasn't exactly true. As Resnick had suspected, what he told them in the space of almost four hours didn't amount to a great deal. Aside from the burglaries that Rossi had carried out single-handed, the rest was a mixture of insinuation and evasion. Rumour and counter-rumour, most of which could not be substantiated, none of which would have stood up in court. Always assuming Rossi would have agreed to repeat his allegations under oath, which was almost certainly not the case.

And if he had, what judge, which jury would believe him?

Melvyn Rossi leaned first on that elbow, then on this, dabbed at his weeping eye with the corner of a handkerchief, smelled his own sweat.

"The Sainsbury's robbery," Rains prodded again, "where the guard got shot. You know the driver."

"I told you."

"Tell us again."

Melvyn had been in a pub on the Alfreton Road when the landlord locked the doors from the inside and proceeded to throw a party. Melvyn had almost certainly got himself invited by accident. Some time later he was squashed up in a corner with a redheaded woman he knew was on the game, feeding her gin and thinking she was better-looking by the minute. He had one hand on her leg, the other fingering her fleshy shoulder like it was Plasticine, when she started telling him about the time she'd been paid for a foursome by two real villains, hard nuts the pair of them, fivers all over the bed, the one of them bragging about how he'd taken close to ten thousand from a security van outside a supermarket.

"Name?" Resnick asked.

"That's what I can't remember."

"Name!" Rains shouted, leaning hard into Melvyn's face.

"Honest, I can't remember. Maybe she never said."

"And the woman?"

"Mary, Margaret, I don't know."

"Perhaps," Rains said slowly, looking across at Resnick, "you could let Melvyn and me have a few words in private. See if that wouldn't help his memory to come back."

Resnick stared back at him. "Not such a good idea."

"In that case, why don't we push him back in the cells and let him stew? All right, Melvyn, you decide you've got something more to say to us, something serious, you let us know. Otherwise . . ."

Rains made a gesture of wiping his hands clean down the lapels of his jacket and moved towards the door.

"Look," Rossi said, "I'm doing my best."

Resnick nodded. "The trouble is, Melvyn, it isn't good enough."

An hour later Rains had a quick word in the custody sergeant's ear and let himself into Rossi's cell. Less than a quarter of an hour after that, he was back in the CID room, hovering close to Resnick's desk, waiting for the sergeant to get off the phone.

"Frank Churchill, otherwise known as Chambers, also Frank Church. Address in Basford."

Resnick looked at the smile toying at the corners of Rains's mouth. "Funny thing, isn't it," Rains said, "memory? Way it comes and goes."

Frank Churchill had gone, too. "Manchester," the woman who came to the door said, "hope the bastard gets washed down the drains where he belongs."

"You'll not mind if we come in, love?" Rains said. "Take a look around."

"Help your bloody selves."

They found several pairs of underpants, odd socks, a striped tie that looked as if it had been used as a belt, a plastic tube of hair gel and an empty deodorant spray, a ticket stub from the Odeon, several dog-eared western paperbacks written by an ex-postman from Melton Mowbray.

"If you find him," the woman called out onto the street after them, "tell him not to bother coming back bloody here!"

"We could phone Manchester CID," Resnick said. "Ask them to keep an eye out. Chances are he might be known up there, too."

Rains nodded, checking the rearview mirror as he backed the car away from the kerb. "Vice squad, I'll see what they know about a redheaded tom called Mary."

"Or Margaret."

"Whatever. See who else was taking part in this little foursome, who else had reason to celebrate. Working it back, I'd say it couldn't have been more than a couple of days after the Sainsbury's job went down."

24

Mary MacDonald had been out since eight o'clock that evening. Short black skirt, black tights, high heels that pinched, a once-white blouse that hung open over the tops of her breasts. The fake fur, hip length, she wore unfastened. By ten, Mary had been approached seven times, the car slowing as it neared the kerb, window wound down, face—always white, usually middle-aged—leaning towards her.

"Looking for business, duck?"

It was as far as the transaction had progressed. Head withdrawn, window up, the car pulling sharply away, looking for what? Someone younger, slimmer, sexier, closer to their damp and furtive little dreams?

Mary watched the same cars driving round and round the circuit, some of them never going beyond the first exchange, discussion of terms—"Any place to go? Strip? How about the night? Have you got a friend?" Mary lit a cigarette although she was supposed to be giving it up, leaned back against the stones of the high wall, paced slowly up and down.

From the corner of Gedling Grove along Waverley Street, hang about on the edge of Raleigh Street then back again, heels clicking on the pavement as she climbed back up the hill. Across Waverley Street, the trees of the park were dark and losing shape and through them she could just see the lights of the Arboretum Hotel. Some nights the landlord would let her sit at a table near the bar, sipping at a rum and black, slipping off her shoes, now and again reaching down to rub her feet. Other times, the look on his face would be enough and if she were thirsty enough, fed up enough, she would walk the other direction, up onto the Alfreton Road, where the publicans were less fussy about their trade.

The car came round again, maroon, she'd noticed it before, gliding slowly past the railings, slowing down, smoothly accelerating away.

This time it stopped.

No movement.

Then the window winding down.

Whiteness of a face.

Mary MacDonald walked across the street.

"Charlie, have you seen this?"

"What?"

"On the box. Right now. The news."

Resnick wriggled awkwardly backwards and withdrew his head from beneath the sink: if anything was guaranteed to make him feel incompetent, it was being bent over double with a full set of washers and an adjustable spanner.

"Charlie!"

"All right." Resnick rinsed his hands beneath the tap, looked for the towel, couldn't find it; he was wiping his hands down his trousers as he stepped into the living room. On the screen an overturned bus had been set ablaze and was blocking a city street; the lights of other, similar, fires burned in the background. A youth, scarf half-masking his face, ran towards the camera and hurled a bottle. The microphone picked up the crash of glass, the whoosh of flame.

"Belfast?" Resnick asked.

Elaine shook her head. "Brixton."

Resnick moved closer to the set and sat down.

Mary MacDonald rented a room on Tennyson Street: three-quarter bed and wardrobe, melamine table, chair, fixed unsteadily to the wall a gas fire that made a small explosion whenever she bent towards it with a match. On the tiled shelf above it were a couple of buckled postcards sent by an aunt in Derry, a plastic flower in a slender china vase, a photograph of herself and her friend Marie at Yarmouth, holding up ice creams and wearing funny hats, laughing so much they were forced to cling on to each other so as not to fall down.

"Mary, is it?" the man said.

"I never said . . ."

He was younger than the average punter, not fat either, tall, not bad-looking. What did he want with her?

"Mary, then?"

"I never . . ."

"I know, you never said."

"Then how . . ."

"Do I know? Well . . ." Smiling. "You look like a Mary to me. Good Catholic girl. Perhaps we met at Mass."

"I never go."

"Nor me."

Mary's throat was strangely dry. "I don't understand."

"No need. Now, why don't you take off those clothes?"

She held out a hand. "Pay me first. You've got to pay me first."

"Oh, yes, don't you worry. I know the rules. Rituals. Better than most." Reaching into his coat pocket for his wallet. "Now, what did we agree? Fifteen?"

"Twenty."

The pink of his tongue showed at his mouth as he smiled. "All right, then, Mary. Twenty it is."

Police in uniform, some still wearing their blue jackets, others down to shirtsleeves, stood in the otherwise deserted street, amazed. A young officer, twenty-one or -two, looked up into the camera's lens and one side of his face was dark with blood. Stones, half-bricks and bottles continued to land. Sirens and fire engines could be heard, overlapping, continuous. Smoke filled the edges of the screen.

"I can't believe it's happening here," Elaine said.

"Here?"

"This country."

Resnick nodded. London seemed far more than a hundred and twenty miles away.

The telephone rang and Elaine picked it up, listened for a moment and held the receiver out. "For you."

"Are you watching?" Ben Riley asked at the other end of the line.

"Unbelievable, isn't it?"

"Is it?"

"How d'you mean?"

"How long," Ben Riley said, "before it spreads up here?"

On the screen, police were holding shields over their faces, slowly advancing down a tree-lined street under a hail of missiles. "Hold your line!" a hoarse voice shouted. "Hold your line!" A man Resnick's age, who had already lost his helmet, staggered back, struck on the side of the head, and the line broke. Youths, black and white, surged through.

The newsreader's voice tolled over the scene. "Our community relations are as good as can be expected," said the Metropolitan Police Commissioner, Sir David McKnee.

Backed away by the fire, Mary held her tights bunched up in one hand. Aside from the shoes he had told her to put back on her feet, she was naked. The man had removed his jacket, hung it over the back of the chair, loosened his tie.

"Don't want to get over-personal, Mary, but that body of yours, bit of a bloody disaster area if you ask me. What I mean, must've seen better days."

She was beginning to wonder whether any of the other girls had seen her get into the car, if any of them knew the man and might have had good reason to have noted his number. Wondering whether, naked or not, she could get past him and out of the door, down the stairs and into the street. Wondering how much she would get hurt.

"What I think, Mary, way I look at it, what we're here for, looks don't so much matter. If they did, well, they wouldn't come trolling out here, would they? They'd be back in the middle of town in some hotel, waiting for the discreet knock on the door. None of your cheapskate twenty-pound job there." He pinched the loose flesh of her arm between finger and thumb. "No, bloke comes out here, all he wants, something to slop around in."

"Bastard!" she spat at him, automatically flinching from his reply.

What he did was smile. "Frank," he said. "Frank Churchill, that how it was with him?"

She blinked and stuttered her feet. The fire was starting to burn the backs of her legs. A piece of her skin was still tight between forefinger and thumb.

"You remember Frank? The night of the party. Just the four of you. Pissed on cheap champagne."

She remembered her and Marie giggling so hard they liked to have wet themselves. The blokes hollering and grabbing and finally one of them fishing out some cocaine and insisting on sniffing it off Marie's backside, sniffing it up through a fifty-pound note. Her and Frank and Marie and . . .

"Who was he, Mary?"

"Who?"

Finger and thumb twisted just a little, not too much, enough. Tears came to her eyes and the backs of her legs were red and tender and the insides of those bloody shoes biting into her ankles.

"Who, Mary?"

"I don't know."

"Don't make me—"

"Swear to God, I don't know."

"Mary!"

"Ow!"

"Mary."

"He never said, I—"

"All that time, you must've heard his name. Must've called him something. Frank. He must've—"

"John."

"What?"

"John. I think that's what he called him."

"John."

"Yes."

"You're sure?"

"Yes, I think . . ."

"You're sure?"

"Yes. Yes. John."

"John Prior."

"I don't know."

"That's who it was."

"If you say so. I said, I don't know. He never said his other name. I don't know."

"John Prior, that's who it was."

"You know already."

"I know."

"Then why all this . . . ?"

"Confirmation, nothing more."

"Oh, shit!"

"What?"

"Shit!"

"What now?"

"You're police, aren't you?"

"Am I?"

"Police, you rotten bastard!"

"Steady."

"Pig!"

She thought he was going to punch her in the breast, but the fist opened up and he stroked his fingers around the deep brown of her nipple. "Maybe later, we can have some fun, eh? For now, why don't you get over on the bed, take the weight off your feet, take a look at these pictures, see who you recognise? Okay, Mary? Okay?"

Resnick was in the front room, transfixed by the ten o'clock news. A half-cup of coffee sat close by him, cold. A virtual no-go area had been hewn out of that part of South London, roads blocked off by vehicles overturned and set on fire. Rubble and glass were strewn across the streets. All along Brixton High Road, shop windows had been smashed through, allowing youths to loot at will. Discarded as too heavy, the settee from a three-piece suite lay on its back across the kerb.

The sky at the upper edge of Resnick's TV set burned with an orange glow.

Elaine stood behind him, hand resting on his shoulder. "Poor Ben," she said.

Resnick turned to look at her.

"If it happened here, you'd be all right. Now. He'd be out there, in the front line."

Resnick nodded.

"I could never understand," Elaine said, "why he didn't move into CID, same time as you."

"Fondness for regular hours. That and being out on the street."

Elaine looked past him towards the television. "These days, I should have thought, last place anyone'd want to be. Any of you."

Resnick got up and switched off the set. "Bed?" he said. "Early night?"

"All right."

Within fifteen minutes, the rhythm of Elaine's breathing had changed and she was asleep, leaving Resnick to replay the images of the evening. How long before it spreads up here?

On the corners of Hyson Green and Radford groups of men were congregating, hands in pockets, heads down. By the early hours, well before light broke in the sky, the first crates of empty milk bottles had been taken.

Mary MacDonald sat alone in her room, squatting down before the gas fire in her pink candlewick dressing gown, praying that her friend Marie would never have to go through what she had that night; praying that what he had forced out of her would not end up in the papers, be read out in court. Simply praying.

And Rains?

Fast off the moment his head touched the pillow, sleeping the untroubled sleep of the just.

25

"Time to get out, Charlie," Ben Riley said. "That's what it is."

Resnick laughed. "Just see you behind the counter of some pub, running a little newsagent's somewhere. You'd be in your grave inside a twelvemonth."

"Better like that than hit over the head by some yob with shit for brains."

"I don't know." Resnick shook his head.

"Christ, Charlie, you saw them. All that talk about police harassment, racism, that was just an excuse. Smashing things for the sake of it, looting. Don't tell me that's political. That's theft. That's greed."

Resnick sighed and bit into his bacon sandwich. When Ben's shift matched, they would meet there at Parker's, eat breakfast, talk. More often than not about the way Chedozie had run the opposition ragged the week before. But not today.

"I'm serious, Charlie. I'm leaving. Not the force. The sodding country."

Resnick looked at him. "You've never said."

"Not mean I haven't thought."

"But you'd have said. Something anyway."

"Would I? Don't you have any pipe dreams nestling away in that head of yours? Things you wouldn't even tell Elaine?"

Resnick shook his head: his problem, where Elaine was concerned, was that he made his dreams all too clear. The day he'd spotted alphabet wallpaper in Texas Homecare and told her it would look just right in the small bedroom; the way he glanced at her expectantly when she came in from the bathroom, those times of the month when he knew her period was due.

Ben Riley folded the slice of thin buttered bread in half, then half again and began, slowly, to wipe it round his plate. "You don't think there are things she doesn't tell you?"

"I don't know."

Riley looked at him quizzically, not quite believing.

"Well, she's ambitious at work," Resnick said, "I know that. Wants things for the house . . ."

"And that's all?"

Resnick finished his coffee, too weak as usual, nodded over at Ben Riley's empty cup. "Another tea?"

"Best not. Time, almost, we weren't here."

Outside the café, the traffic entering the city from the south and west was thickening. Pretty soon the island would be jammed tight. A fireman, wearing a red and white Forest shirt above his uniform trousers, walked past them towards the fire station alongside. The two policemen watched him till he had disappeared through the broad entrance, neither one wanting to be the first to walk away, each sensing there were still things left unsaid without recognising what they were.

When Resnick finally arrived, the police station was humming with the previous night's events in London. He had scarcely shown his face in the CID room before being summoned to the inspector's office. Rains was already sitting there, relaxed in a chair beside Skelton's desk, one long leg crossed casually over the other.

"Looks as if we've a break in the Sainsbury's job," Skelton said, pressing the tips of his fingers together in front of his irreproachably ironed shirt. "Witness prepared to swear she heard Prior and another man—"

"Churchill," Rains interrupted, "Frank Churchill."

"Heard Prior and this bloke talking about carrying out the robbery, bragging about it."

"More than that," Rains prompted.

"Using the gun."

Resnick looked away from the inspector, staring at Rains hard. Rains recrossed his legs and smiled disarmingly back. "Who was this?" Resnick asked.

Rains shrugged. "Some tom."

"They spoke about the shooting in front of her?"

"Sure."

"It seems they were clear which of them had fired the gun," Skelton said.

Resnick still hadn't moved his eyes from Rains's face.

"Prior," Rains said quietly, leaning forward slightly as he mouthed the word. "John Prior, what happened to that poor bastard of a guard, it was down to him."

"And she'll swear to that, in court if needs be, the woman?"

"She'll swear to it all right." Rains smiled. "On her life."

Prior lived in a nondescript suburban-looking house overlooking Colwick Wood Park. Some mornings it was quiet enough to hear the kids singing to the teacher's piano in the nearby Jesse Boot Junior and Infant School. Step across from the house and there were the bowling green, the recreation ground, the reservoir. At the far side of the park lay the greyhound stadium and the race course. There were roses here and people quietly walking their dogs; men and women wearing white sitting on the steps of the bowls pavilion comparing notes about the bias of the green.

One car swung round into Ashworth Close and parked, three men to watch the rear of the house. The other cars, two of them, came from opposite directions, slowing to a halt at either side of a milk float making late deliveries.

Skelton waited until the milkman had cleared before giving the order to move in. Prior's wife was in her dressing gown at the door, bending down to pick up the two pints, when the detectives raced up the path, Rains at their head, Resnick not far behind.

"Just right," Rains said, pushing past. "Tea all round."

"John!" Ruth Prior screamed. "John, it's the police!"

Heavy men shouldered her aside and one of the bottles slipped from her hand, glass shattering to a hundred tiny pieces on the step.

Prior was half out of the bedroom, pulling on a pair of jeans, when Rains charged up the stairs.

"What the fuck's going on?"

Like the card in a magician's trick, Rains's warrant card was in the palm of his hand. "John Edward Prior, I am arresting you in connection with the theft of . . ."

Already, other officers were starting to search the premises.

"Get out of my house!" Ruth Prior shouted at the man pulling clothing from the hall cupboard. "You bastards, you've got no right."

"I'm afraid that's not the case," Jack Skelton said, holding the magistrate's warrant in front of her eyes.

"Fuck you!" she said, anger contorting her face.

"Why don't you get yourself in the kitchen, love?" said one of the detectives. "Mash tea."

"And fuck you, too!"

Aside from the fact that she was older, her hair had darkened into chestnut brown, there'd been some thickening around the waist and legs, she wasn't so very different from when, as Ruth James, she had flailed her arms in front of the band at the Boat, moaned and sung the blues.

They hurried Prior up the steps and into the station, laces of his brown shoes still undone. "I'm not opening my fucking mouth till I've seen my solicitor."

"Course not," the custody sergeant said agreeably. "As it should be. Now, if you'll just empty your pockets out onto there."

Ruth walked into the bedroom without expecting anyone to be there and found Rains feeling through the contents of the chest of drawers that had been tipped across the double bed.

"I thought you bastards had all gone."

"Clearly not." Straightening, smile curling from one corner of his mouth. "Some of us bastards are still here."

She watched his hands smooth across the pale shades of her underwear, almost delicate.

"Does something for you, does it?"

Rains's smile became a question.

"Women's knickers?"

"Depends who's inside them."

"Go round pinching them from washing lines?"

"I said—"

"I heard what you said."

He lifted a pair of her pants, white, lace at the front, plain and shiny at the back; all the while he was fingering them he was looking at her.

"Still appreciates you, does he? Touches you? Like this? After all these years?"

She grabbed a bottle of moisturiser from the dressing table and threw it at his head; tore the garment from his grasp and hurled it back across the room; aimed a blow at his leering face and he caught her wrist as her fingers were only inches from his cheek.

"Got to be compensations, though, married to a villain. Secondhand excitement. Holidays in Malta, Costa del Sol. Never knowing where he is at nights. Who he's with. Jumping every time the doorbell rings."

She pulled hard and he let her go and she stood there close to him, her breathing loud in the quiet room. Car doors slammed in the street outside. A voice calling Rains's name.

"You know," Rains said softly, "I did you a misservice. Took you for a slag. But I was wrong. You're not that at all. Here."

And before she knew what he was doing, he had seized her hand and pressed it between his legs, laughing when the surprise jumped in her eyes.

"Not many women," Rains said, stepping round her, around the end of the bed towards the door, "can make me feel that way. Not without even trying."

Ruth was still standing there, staring across at her reflection in the dressing table mirror, when she heard the front door slam shut, the last car drive away.

"What I'd like to do," Skelton said, "is ask you to take us through it once again."

"No way."

"To be certain we have the details . . ."

"No."

"No room for any doubt . . ."

"No!"

"I think, Inspector, my client has answered your every question as fully as you could wish. I'm afraid I can really see no further purpose being served here, other, of course, than an attempt at intimidation."

"Investigation," Skelton corrected him mildly.

"Investigate my arse!" Prior said.

Just perceptibly, Jack Skelton flinched. Sitting beside him, Resnick leaned forward, drawing Prior's attention. "What can you tell us about Frank Churchill?" he asked.

Prior shrugged and shook his head.

"Does that signify a no?" Resnick asked.

"It means I've got a dose of Parkinson's—what d'you think?"

In his notes, the young D.C. wrote: Prior gestured no, nothing.

"How about Frank Chambers?" Resnick asked.

Prior turned aside in disgust and a look from his solicitor told him to respond. "No," Prior said.

"Frank Church?"

"Never heard of him."

"What about," asked Skelton, apparently studying the marks on the tabletop with interest, "Mary MacDonald?"

"Was she there?"

"Where?"

"Up that supermarket, wherever? That's what you've got me here for, isn't it? So I want to know, what's she got to do with it, this . . . Mary whatever-her-name-is?"

"Miss MacDonald," Skelton said, "was present on an occasion when you and Frank Churchill—"

"I told you, I don't know any—"

"Shh!" Prior's solicitor said, raising a hand in warning. He knew from experience it was when they lost their temper that his clients gave it all away.

"When you and Frank Churchill," Skelton was saying, "talked about the raid on the security van, openly admitted taking part—"

"Don't waste your breath!" Prior said with scorn, leaning his chair back onto its rear legs.

"And when you admitted being the one in possession of the gun which seriously injured one of the guards . . ."

Prior's chair rocked back forwards fast and he was on his feet, arms braced against the table's edge, glaring into Skelton's face.

"Mr. Prior," his solicitor said, alarmed, half out of his seat. "John."

Resnick and the D.C. had moved near enough simultaneously, closing on Prior from either side, the constable's notebook spilling onto the floor. Skelton blinked and little more, his hair still brushed back and perfectly in place, tie knotted with deft correctness at the neck of his cream shirt.

By whatever mechanism Prior brought himself under control, it took forty, possibly fifty seconds to work. Time-a-plenty, Resnick thought, to have squeezed back on the trigger of a gun.

"My client would like a break," the solicitor said. "A drink."

No one seemed to hear him.

"If you're going to talk about firearms," Prior said once he had sat back down, "people getting shot, I've got nothing further to say."

But when neither Skelton nor Resnick responded, he said, "This woman, fetch her down here. Let her say that to my face. Stick me up in an identity parade. Anything. 'Cause I tell you this, either one of you's made her up or she's lying."

When Rains and two other officers arrived at the furnished room in Tennyson Street, all the signs were that Mary MacDonald had gone. The clothes, the personal knickknacks, even the sheets from the bed, had all disappeared, leaving a thin stained mattress and a box of kitchen matches close by the gas fire.

One of the postcards of Mary and her friend Marie had slithered almost from sight, wedged against the cracked lino by the door.

For the best part of two hours they knocked on doors, rang bells, came no nearer to knowing where Mary MacDonald might have gone. All they could do now was show the picture of Marie to the vice squad in the probability that Marie was also on the game, hoping against hope that she hadn't done a bunk at the same time.

The CID room was oddly quiet, the click and hiss of cigarette lighters, irregular sounds of men breathing. Jack Skelton sat on one of the desks, shirtsleeves rolled evenly back upon his wrists. "House, garage, garden—we turned up nothing. The only witness we might have had has disappeared. We don't seem to be any further along with Prior in this business than we were a week ago."

Rains lifted his head as though to intervene, but, under the inspector's eyes, ducked it back down and continued examining his shoes.

"We're going to have to kick him loose."

"Any point hanging on to him till morning, sir?" one of the detectives asked.

"If you can give me one," Skelton responded.

He could not. Nobody could.

"Right," said Skelton, levering himself to the floor. "Release him. Now."

26

Resnick had returned home around seven that evening to find Elaine engrossed in the spreadsheets she had over the dining-room table, the radio defiantly tuned to Radio Two. Computerised figures and Barry Manilow: for Resnick an eminently resistible combination.

"Anything to eat?" Resnick said over her shoulder.

She didn't look round. "Cold chicken in the fridge."

"You?"

"I had lunch."

"It's supper."

"I'm not hungry."

Resnick opened a pot of Dijon mustard and dipped pieces of three-day-old chicken into it, eating absentmindedly as he scanned the local paper, the urban ghetto scare stories in the *Mail*. In the front room he put a record on the stereo, realised he wasn't listening and switched off.

"How about the Club? I wouldn't mind a drink."

Elaine turned slowly. "The Polish Club?"

"Where else?"

"I thought you'd allowed your membership to lapse?"

Resnick shrugged. "A chance to rejoin."

"You go. I ought to finish this."

For some moments Resnick struggled to summon up the interest to ask what *this* was. "Maybe meet me there later?" he said.

"Maybe."

"I shan't be late," he called from the hall.

If Elaine responded, he failed to hear.

Somewhere in his teens, for reasons he would have found difficult now to clearly remember or define, Resnick had turned against his parents' Polish culture. Perhaps it was no more than what teenagers did. The young Resnick as James Dean. He recalled seeing the film *Rebel Without a Cause,* most of his sympathies flowing to Dean's father, poor Jim Backus, wearing an apron and embarrassed, standing mortified upon the stairs, flinching from the anger of his son's tirade.

For Resnick it had been less dramatic, more gradual; little by little he had stopped answering his parents in their native tongue, speaking in his own instead. The boys at school had rechristened him Charlie long since and Charlie he had been happy to become.

Sitting now with an iced glass of lemon vodka, he felt he was visiting a strange country, stranded in the past. Photographs on the walls of men in uniform, decorations for lost wars. The bartender in his neat white jacket looked along at him and smiled. At round tables heads were lowered in desperate conversation. Suddenly standing, he swallowed down the remainder of his vodka and pushed through the doors into the street.

The city was soft red brick, broken by green trees. For more than an hour he walked it aimlessly, nodding to people whenever they passed.

———

The phone rang a little shy of four A.M. and Resnick reached mistakenly for the alarm. By the time he had propped himself on one elbow and lifted the receiver, Elaine was awake as well, looking at him reproachfully from her side of the bed. Resnick listened, grunted a few times in agreement and broke the connection.

"What is it?" she asked as he swung his feet towards the floor. "This time of night."

"Morning," Resnick said, beginning to assemble his clothes. "It's morning, more or less. They found a woman, Mapperley Plains, out on the golf course."

Resnick read the question in her eyes.

"No," he said. "She's alive. Pretty badly beaten, apparently. They've taken her to Queens."

"Why phone you?"

Without looking in the mirror, Resnick was fastening his tie. "Case I'm involved in. Some chance there's a connection."

"Charlie," she said when he was at the door.

"Yes?"

"Nothing. It doesn't matter. You'd better go."

Car headlights cut soft channels through the slight mist; the surface of the grass was bright with dew. Unseen, birds stirred up the day. There was still an indentation where the body had been found, midway to the seventh hole, nestling the edge of the rough. Yellow tape marked off the spot.

The uniformed officer who had found her was still there, peaked cap circling round and round between his fingers, Panda car parked close with the others, static and occasional voices from its radio spilling out across the green.

"Caretaker rang in," he told Resnick, "reckoned how he'd heard this car. Couple of break-ins past month or so. Worried this might be another. Drove out and checked around like. Just on my way when I heard this sound." His gaze flickered away to the markings on the ground. "It were the girl."

Resnick nodded, understanding the startled expression that survived at the back of the young officer's eyes. He and Ben Riley had been that young once, stumbling upon their first assault victims, pretending that it didn't affect them, needing to show they didn't care.

"No doubt who she is?"

The constable shook his head. "Bag was off in the bushes. Must've got thrown, no telling who by."

Versions of the scene were already playing themselves out in Resnick's mind.

The handbag was plastic, creased shiny black. Inside were several tissues, crumpled and used, a lipstick labelled Evening Rose, three Lillets, a packet of condoms with two remaining, a small tan diary in which little had been written —entries Resnick recognised as the names of pubs, a handful of names—at the front; on the page headed Personal Details, she had written Marie Jacob, five foot three, brown eyes, brown hair, no birth date, an address in Arnold.

Resnick remembered the photograph Rains had brought in from Mary MacDonald's empty room, two women on the front at Great Yarmouth, smiling, squinting their eyes against the sun. Mary and Marie.

"She'd been cut," the constable said. "Across the face. Here."

With the tip of his index finger he drew a line diagonally down from below the lobe of his ear, almost to the cleft of his chin.

"And beaten. Knocked around pretty bad. Time I found her, this eye, it were good as closed."

Resnick nodded, picturing it clearly. "No sign of any weapon?"

The young P.C. shook his head.

"Give the light half an hour, maybe a little more. Then get a search organised. Thorough. Every blade of grass. If the weapon's here, we want it found."

They could wash away the caked blood and the dirt, replace the blood, lessen the pain; what they could not do was remove the fear.

"I don't know," Marie said in an accent so soft that Resnick had to lean over her face to hear. "I don't know who he was."

Her lips were swollen and cracked.

"I met him, earlier, you know. We were on the golf course for a bit of business when he started in hitting me, no reason at all."

She motioned that her mouth was dry and Resnick lifted the glass from the bedside table, was gentle as he could be, one hand raising her head so that she could drink through a bendy straw.

"No," she said, voice fading near to nothing, "I never knew him. Never saw him before."

When Resnick held photographs before her, she blinked her eyes and barely shook her head. She cried. Resnick sat there till the staff nurse tapped him on the shoulder and then he left.

"Believe her, Charlie?"

"No, sir. Not really. Could be telling the truth, of course, but no, I don't think she's giving us all she knows."

"Just a feeling, or have you got something more?"

"Just a feeling."

Skelton stood by the window, looking out. Below, a line of lock-up garages, factories with raised roofs and a few neat streets of council houses beyond. In the middle distance the floodlight towers of both soccer grounds pushed up against the sky. Further still, the green of a solitary hill. "Prior," he said, turning back into the room. "You think Rains could have been right."

Right as Rains: it didn't even raise a smile.

"Don't want to, do you, Charlie?"

"Maybe not."

"No more your methods than mine."

"No."

"But within hours of us lifting him, both women Rains says might have dropped him in it . . ." Skelton shook his head. "One's in hospital, terrified half out of her wits, and the other . . . Well, we don't know where she is at all, do we?"

"Manchester," Resnick said. "They're still checking."

"Let's hope with some success."

Resnick thought about Marie Jacob's face and prayed the inspector was right.

"Couple of uniforms checked her address," Skelton said. "Nothing useful there at all. But then, they wouldn't look with your eyes."

"I'll get out there," Resnick said. "Poke around."

Skelton nodded, giving each of his shirt cuffs a little tug before turning back to the window. When he had applied for the transfer, accepted the promotion, he had failed to realise how different it would be, less than a hundred miles north and close to the Trent. How hard to slot in. He hoped that, as his wife was in the habit of suggesting, he had not perpetrated one of the major miscalculations of his life.

27

Resnick spent forty minutes with a sixty-eight-year-old man who was convinced he had come about his stolen bike. "Locked the bugger up in the entry an' everything. Right t' the bloody fence. Side entry, along of the house. Safe enough you'd say, aye, so did I. But it weren't, you see. Some clever sod's snuck round there with bolt clippers, right through bloody lock, less time than it takes to crack an egg. Wouldn't mind so much, but I've had that bike—Raleigh, good 'un, made good 'uns in those days—had that bike, must be—what?—well, dozen year at least. Maybe more. Who'd want to steal a bike like that? Spite, that's what I put it down to. Spite or cussedness, 'cause they'll not get much for it. All them fancy coloured jobs with half-assed handlebars and great thick frames, that's what they want nowadays. Not solid and dependable, like mine."

He looked across his back kitchen at Resnick, a wiry man with a shiny bullet head and a neat greying moustache, braces hanging down either side of his trousers.

"Got so," he said, "you can't leave anything out your sight more'n a minute or it's gone. Thieving bastards'd have the shirt off your back if they thought as they'd get away with it." He shook his head. "That bike, my lifeline were that. Now it's bloody gone."

Resnick phoned through and checked the crime number, established that no progress had been made. Truth was, though they might catch the thief, the bike would already have been sold intact or stripped down for parts.

He accepted several cups of tea, each stronger than the last, sipping from a thick china cup, the inside of which was stained with overlapping rings of orangey brown. Trying hard not to look at his watch, he listened while the man talked about his son in Australia, the grandchildren he had never seen, the stroke that had taken his wife—God rest her —early from the world. Agreed that Tommy Lawton was the best centre forward this country had ever had—bits of kids nowadays with these flash cars, won't as much as kick a ball without there's someone there fanning 'em with a cheque.

Resnick had seen players on the County side the past few seasons, would have found it difficult to kick anything without the aid of an on-the-pitch injection.

"I don't want you to think," the man said, showing Resnick to the door, "as I'm one of those who can't keep up with the times, forever rattling on about how much better everything was when they were young, 'cause I'm not. Not by a long chalk. But I'll say one thing and I know you'll bear me out, folk were a lot more honest in them days, folk round here, ordinary folk I'm talking of now, like you and me. Why, twenty year back, I'd gone off down the shops, I'd not so much've bothered to've locked this front door, never mind bike. Now—well, you know about now well as I do."

Resnick thanked him for the tea and walked past the bushes of roses that needed pruning, out of the gate and onto the street. The house was three doors down from Marie Jacob's address and the old man thought he might have seen her once or twice, but couldn't be sure. "Time I might have looked at a bit of skirt," he'd said, "now you are going back a fair while. Not that I wasn't above a thing or two when wind were in right direction." And he'd winked and grinned and Resnick had grinned back, men together, talking the way men did, in the old days and now.

Marie Jacob had lived with her aunt, a short, plumpish woman who was struggling to move an easy chair down the stairs and into the middle room when Resnick rang the bell. He took off his jacket and helped, finally forcing the legs past the frame of the final door with a shove that stripped away several layers of paint and the skin from his own fore-finger.

"Here," Clarise Jacob said, "let me put a plaster on that. You'll not want it turning all gangrenous on you, sure you won't."

Despite his protestations, Resnick found himself sat firmly down while the woman fussed and cleaned and smeared his finger with Germolene before wrapping it in Elastoplast with a technique which leant heavily on the early Egyptians.

"I never asked her a great deal, you know, about her life. I mean, she's a grown woman." Clarise smiled. "More so than me. I'm only four foot eleven, did you know that? Can't even see over the counter at the bank without I've got my high heels."

"Marie," Resnick prompted. "You don't know who she might have been meeting last night?"

Clarise Jacob pursed her lips. "Like I say, I was never one to interfere. As long as, you know, she came across at the end of the month with her little bit of rent." She looked at Resnick directly. "Family or no, bills've got to be paid. Either that or we'd all be out on the street."

Exactly, Resnick thought, where Marie was earning her money in the first place.

"You'd know, though, what time she left?"

"I would. I would. You're right. It couldn't have been before ten, on account of I was still watching the box. I make a habit of turning it off, you know, right at the start of the news." She studied Resnick's face seriously again. "It's not good for you, that's the thing, too much of it, you see."

Whether she meant television or news, Resnick wasn't clear. "I wonder," he began, getting to his feet.

"If you can see her room. Oh, sure. Though those two boys earlier, they did the same." She escorted him up the stairs. "I'll not speak ill of her behind her back, specially after what happened, but, you'll see, the tidiest soul on this planet she was not."

The walls were covered with posters of rock stars and the previous Pope; almost every available surface was covered with a riot of clothing, garments of all designs and colours.

"The officers who searched earlier," Resnick asked, "they weren't responsible for this?"

"Oh, no. They did a bit of tidying up."

"Did you ever hear her," Resnick asked, "mention a man by the name of Prior? John Prior?" He was back downstairs now, towering over Clarise Jacob in her tiny hall.

"I'm sorry," she said. "I'm not being a lot of help at all."

Resnick slipped the lock on the front door. "Anything you think of later that might be relevant, give me a call. I've left my name and number."

"All right. And, ooh, when you're making out your report, it's Clarise with an S, R-I-S-E. Everyone always gets it wrong. Bye-bye."

Eleven minutes past two: if I were a social worker, Resnick thought, I might consider I'd had a pretty good morning. The Fiesta in front of him swerved outwards to avoid an aging pigeon and Resnick braked hard, then swore as the engine stalled. He had vaguely intended to call in at home, but that was enough to change his mind; if he took one of these turnings to the right, that would bring him down onto the Mansfield Road. He was humming one of those Parker tunes with an unpronounceable name, beating his fingers against the wheel, when he saw a woman walking out of a house a little off to the right. The house was quite substantial, thirties probably, set back from the road; the woman, wearing a blue suit, smart, turned her head to look back at the man who was now locking the front door and she was smiling. It was Elaine.

Resnick accelerated clear, took the next road to the left, a narrow street curving back up the hill, swung in between two parked cars, switched off the engine and applied the brake. Suddenly, in the sealed space of the car, he could hear his own breathing, smell his own sweat. He was starting to shake.

Elaine, leaving the house, low heels clipping the flagged path beside the gravel drive. A suit that had cost a month's wages and more. Graceful turn of the head and slow. A smile he had seen before. Beside the front garden shrubs, the low stone wall, a sign which read FOR SALE. The man at the front door, pocketing the keys. Volvo parked at the kerb, dark blue. It had been a long time now since Resnick had seen that smile.

When his breathing was back to normal and his hands steady, he continued up the sloping road, circling an irregular block.

The Volvo had gone.

Slowly, Resnick slid into its place.

VIEWING STRICTLY BY APPOINTMENT ONLY across the bottom of the sign.

The garden was orderly, just the grass perhaps in need of a trim. The curtains at the upstairs windows had been drawn a uniform third across. Below, the rouched blinds had been set to deny any nosy passerby an easy glance. Resnick sat there for a quarter of an hour and nobody walked past in either direction; there was no sign of movement from inside the house, no sound.

He got out of the car, locked it, and walked up to the front door. Two locks, a Chubb and a Yale. The gate beside the garage was bolted, but a tall man could reach the bolt end on tiptoe. It took seconds, not minutes, to slip the back-door lock with an Access card he rarely, if ever, used. Two glasses had been rinsed and left on the drainer to dry; they were not dry yet. Nothing else in the kitchen suggested recent occupation. The air was flat and smelled faintly of lavender; the central heating had been switched off.

Faint, he could see the marks their feet had made upon the stairs.

The toilet had recently been flushed, a fragment of paper flat against the inside of the bowl, a single curl of hair floating dark upon the water. The taps of the hand basin were slightly damp to the touch, bubbles of lather on the purple soap.

In the second bedroom, at the back of the house, the pillows bulked unevenly against the quilted headboard. Resnick lifted up the floral duvet and eased it down towards the foot of the bed, lowered his face towards the imagined indentations at the centre of the sheet. Careful, they had left no marks. What remained, unmistakable, was the sour-sweet smell of sex: another scent, the natural odour of Elaine's body, clinging to it lovingly.

28

Rains had half of a chicken rogon josh in a plastic container and he was offering it round the CID room when Resnick came in. "How 'bout you, Charlie? Never known you to say no to some free grub."

Resnick said no.

He went over to his desk and sat shuffling through meaningless pieces of paper, applications for courses, arrest forms, incident reports. Back across the room someone got the most from the punchline to an old joke and someone else laughed. Phones rang and were answered. Business as usual.

Rains dumped the container in the metal bin, wiped his fingers on a pocket handkerchief, lit a cigarette. "That woman, Charlie, Prior's wife. Knew her, didn't you? Some time back." He perched on a corner of Resnick's desk, leg swinging. "Know her well?"

Resnick opened one of the drawers and took out a notebook, spiral bound.

"Anything I say may be taken down?" Rains grinned.

Not for the first time, Resnick caught himself wondering how it was that Rains managed to dress the way he did on a

D.C.'s salary. According to gossip from officers who claimed they'd been there, the interior of Rains's flat looked like something out of an ad for expense-account living. The car he had parked downstairs was a two-year-old Golf GTI.

"You do know her?" Rains said. "Ruth Prior?"

"Not really. Not personally. Who she is, that's all. Who she used to be."

"Some singer, right?"

The last time Resnick had heard her, or maybe the next to last, she had done a version of "I'd Rather Go Blind," so slow he thought, listening, time must have stopped.

"Yes," he said. "She was a singer. Local, mostly. Blues, soul, stuff like that."

"Sort of Tina Turner?"

"If you like."

"Without the tan."

Resnick said nothing.

"And she gave it up to marry him, Prior?"

"I suppose so."

"No kids, though, eh?"

"Not as far as I know."

Rains let himself down from the desk. "How long d'you reckon it is, then? Since she jacked it all in for a life of domestic bliss?"

"Must be five years at least. Six?"

Rains grinned. "No wonder."

Resnick's expression: what?

Still grinning, Rains cupped his crotch in one hand. "Ready for a taste of something fresh."

"Is she?"

"Yeh. See it in her eyes. Just might not know it yet herself, that's all." Midway between Resnick's desk and the door, Rains looked over his shoulder and winked. "Married women, they're a cinch."

———

When Elaine got home a shade after six-thirty, she assumed Resnick had not yet returned. It was only after making herself a pot of tea and opening the tin of lemon creams that, wandering between rooms, she noticed his jacket on the bannister rail.

"Charlie! Charlie, are you here?"

It was quite likely that he could have been in and gone out again; certainly, his car hadn't been outside.

"Charlie?"

She sat in the comfort of their new settee—the arguments there had been before she'd felt able to go into Hopewells and put a down payment on *that*—drank her tea and leafed through a magazine. Unable to concentrate, she knew that something was troubling her: she didn't feel that she was alone.

"Charlie? You're not in bed, are you?"

The bedroom was empty, her dressing gown diagonally across the foot of the bed where she had left it. A pair of discarded tights were on the floor near the wardrobe and she scooped them up, dropping them in the laundry basket as she walked out of the room towards the last flight of stairs.

"Charlie, whatever are you doing here?"

He was sitting in an old easy chair that had come from his parents' home, the fabric along the arms worn smooth until the original pattern had all but disappeared.

"What are you doing up here?"

There was new wallpaper on the walls, an old carpet on the floor, a whitewood chest pushed into one corner of the room. Cartons and boxes that had never been emptied since they had moved. Some of them—God!—Elaine knew were stuffed full of rubbish she had kept since leaving school: reports, magazines, pocket-sized diaries crammed with spidery writing, fevered accounts of first kisses and half-conjured dreams. In there somewhere was a scratched

Parlophone single: the Beatles' "I Want to Hold Your Hand."

"What on earth are you doing?"

"Thinking."

"What about?"

It was too dark in the room for her to be able to clearly see his face. Only the light from the stairs lengthening Elaine's faint shadow.

"You don't normally come up here."

"Sometimes I do."

It occurred to her that were she not able to see him, she might have had difficulty in recognising his voice.

"What are you thinking about?" she asked.

"Work."

"That girl, the one on the golf course?"

"Yes, that."

Elaine took a pace back towards the door. "I've not long made some tea."

Resnick nodded. "I'll be down."

She hesitated a few moments longer before going back downstairs. When Resnick eventually followed, the tea had grown stewed and cold and Elaine was washing salad to go with the grilled chicken breasts they were having for their meal. As Resnick crossed in front of her, taking a beer from the fridge, she didn't say anything more about the incident and neither did he.

"Ready in about half an hour, that okay?"

"Yes," Resnick said, pouring the beer over near the sink, "that'll be fine."

Prior was channel-hopping, switching between the highlights of the Eurovision Song Contest, a studio discussion about law and order in our cities and an interview with Spurs' Argentinian midfield player, Osvaldo Ardiles. "If they win the Cup, it'll be down to that little bastard," Prior said over his shoulder. "Lawyer, too, back home." Prior laughed. "Ever end up in court, reckon I'll ask for him. Ossie for the defence. Good, eh?"

"Wonderful."

He reached out and caught her by the wrist. "Christ, Ruth! What is it with you lately?"

"Lately?"

"Every time I open my mouth, all I get's this great put-down."

Ruth pulled away, rubbing at her arm. Sometimes he didn't know his own strength; sometimes, she thought ruefully, he did, and knew enough to hit her where the bruises didn't show.

"Jokes," she said. "The same old jokes. Maybe I'm fed up with them."

"Yeh? What else you fed up with?"

"Oh, you know. Life. Think I'll go and stick my head in the oven, end it all."

"North Sea gas." Prior smiled. "Don't work no more. Better off locking yourself in the garage, leave the car engine on."

"You'd like that, wouldn't you?"

"Don't be stupid."

"I'm not stupid."

"I know, I know."

"Stuck round here all the time, I might as well be."

"Get out then?"

"Oh, yes? And do what?"

"Get a job."

Ruth laughed. "Only place you'd let me do that'd be a convent."

"Not likely. Let them nuns get a look at you."

"Stop it! Just stop it!"

"What? Ruthie, what?"

"Going on. This joke, this fantasy. As if I was some kind of sex queen."

"You still get blokes turning their heads after you in the pub, in the street."

"Yes?" She moved close against him, her hip brushing his arm as he sat in the chair. "If I'm so sexy, how come I'd need to be on 'Mastermind' to remember the last time we made love."

From the sudden change of expression on his face, she thought he was going to take a swing at her, but the phone rang and she jumped to her feet. "I'll get it," she said.

She recognised his voice straight off and it was like him grabbing her hand again and pulling it against him, although she pretended that she didn't.

"Come on," he said. "You know who it is?"

"You want to speak to John?" she asked.

Rains laughed. "I wondered if you fancied meeting for a drink?"

For some time after she had broken the connection, Ruth stood in the still quiet of the hall, staring at the way her fingers curved around the sharp red of the receiver, the tarnished gleam of the ring biting tight below the knuckle. From the living room came the sound of Prior's mocking laughter, the oompah bass and fractured vocal of the Icelandic entry.

Resnick had watched the discussion, the Police Commissioner's assertions that he would never countenance No-Go areas in the capital; the search for an appropriate police response, which veered between a return to community policing, ordinary coppers on the beat, to the advanced technology of CS gas and the riot shield.

"What do you think?" Elaine asked as the programme came to an end.

"I don't know," Resnick said, "but Ben reckons we'll soon get the chance to find out firsthand."

"Want anything before bed?" Elaine asked. "Tea or anything?"

Resnick shook his head. "Think I'll sit up for a while. Listen to some music."

Elaine thought about offering to sit with him, till she saw which record he was pulling from the shelf. That bloke who played piano like a man with no arms.

"Don't sit too late then."

"I'll be all right. You get some sleep."

Resnick poured a vodka and took it over to his chair; found the track he'd been hearing, off and on all day, inside his head. Ten, eleven single notes, seemingly unconnected, fingers jabbed down against the keys, till suddenly, the steady rhythm of the bass, swish of brushes against the snare and the vibraphone takes over, finding a line, a melody where none had existed before. July 2, 1948, New York. "Evidence."

29

The main office of Hilton, Lockett was on Trinity Square, where the fumes from the waiting buses and the cars waiting for spaces in the National Car Park were enough to lessen life expectancy a good five years. Resnick walked into the square past the *Post* building, pausing to look at the special offers on art paper in the stationer's window and buy a packet of mints from the newsagent's. He hoped he wasn't developing a sweet tooth.

There was no mistaking the man he'd seen leaving the house with Elaine. Leaning now over one of the young women at her desk, smiling as he made some remark. He was several inches shorter than Resnick himself, slim; the suit, dark blue with a narrow stripe, was the same as he'd been wearing then. The same or similar. The young woman laughed and the man moved across the office to his own desk near the rear.

There were several people inside, couples, browsing the property details: houses under £40,000, houses under £65,000, houses under £85,000; £85,000 and above. There was a photograph of the detached house on Richmond Drive in the window; save for the two figures who had been outside, it was exactly as Resnick remembered. And well above the eighty-five-thousand mark. Good: he was pleased Elaine wasn't selling herself cheap.

Resnick pushed open the door and stepped inside. Three faces looked up at him expectantly. Ignoring them, Resnick went to the appropriate section and lifted a sheet detailing the Richmond Drive property from the rack.

"A very fine house, sir." He was blocking Resnick's path, professional smile in place, scent of violets faint on his breath. "Excellent value."

Resnick nodded and took a step to the side.

"Was it that particular property you were interested in, that particular area? We have a number of others. . . ."

Resnick knew if he stayed there another minute he would hit him, full in the face. "No," he said, pushing past, "this is fine for now."

Out on the street he screwed the paper down into his jacket pocket and hurried between heavy green buses towards the lower edge of the square. One hand against the railings outside Jessops, he caught his breath: not since he had been in uniform, confronted by a gang of youths shouting abuse and spitting in his face, had he felt such a need to lash out, strike back. Although he hadn't admitted it at the time, almost certainly hadn't been aware that it was so, this had been one of the reasons that had nudged him into CID and out of the front line. The urge to strike back, more than that, to hurt, actually hurt. It frightened him.

Inside the Victoria Centre, he skirted round the mothers and toddlers, mothers with prams, climbed the central stairs to the upper floor. Passing between the stalls laden with vegetables and fruit, the rows of hanging plants and cut flowers, he took his stool at the Italian coffee stall. One espresso, full. He had scarcely received his change before ordering a second. And a third. He withdrew the property details from his pocket and smoothed them out upon the counter. *This substantial property provides an excellent opportunity for purchasing a large and established residence in this exclusive and much sought-after area of the city.*

"Thinking of moving?" Maria asked, setting his third espresso in front of him.

"Something like that."

She moved away to serve another customer as Resnick turned over the sheet of paper. *Viewing earnestly recommended,* it said in thick letters across the bottom of the page.

The police car was parked across the street from the station and Ben Riley slid from the passenger side when Resnick approached, Ben not in uniform, wearing the same sports coat and flannels he stood in on the terraces deploring another County attack gone wrong.

"Where the hell've you been?"

"Why?"

"Nobody seemed to know where you were."

Hands in his pockets, Resnick shrugged his heavy shoulders.

"You all right?" Ben Riley was craning back his neck, looking at Resnick keenly. "Okay?"

Under his friend's gaze, Resnick looked away. "Fine. Why?"

"You look dreadful."

"Thanks."

"All the more reason for lunch," Ben urged him.

Resnick shook his head, glanced towards the station. "I can't."

"I'm paying."

"I've got things to do."

"And you have to eat lunch."

"I'll get a sandwich."

"And indigestion."

"Sorry, Ben." Resnick stepped into the street. "Some other time."

Ben Riley's hand reached for his shoulder, holding him back. "Work, Charlie. This is work. Believe me. This is stuff you'll want to hear."

"Excuse me, sweetheart. Love. Miss. Another couple of pints, please." Ben Riley beamed and offered the waitress his glass.

Resnick flattened his palm over his and shook his head.

"Half?" the waitress asked.

"Thanks."

They were in Ben Bowers at the top of Derby Road; if you angled your head round sharply enough, it was possible to see Canning Circus police station through the window. Ben Riley was eating his way through a steak, T-bone, medium rare, french fries, broccoli, new season's peas. Resnick had ordered the lemon sole, sautéed potatoes, salad. The only other diners were on expense-account lunches from the insurance company offices along the road.

"So picture this," Ben Riley was saying between mouthfuls, "there we are, eleven-fifteen, eleven-thirty, whatever, on our way out of the pub, taxi waiting, all of a sudden there's this commotion across the street. Two couples, blokes in their Friday-night suits, women wearing dresses so thin you can see the goose pimples on their arms from where we're standing—"

He broke off as the waitress set the glasses on the table; used the blade of his knife to dab English mustard onto the reddish end of his steak.

"Where are we?" Resnick asked. "This pub?"

"Woodborough. You know, the country and western nights."

Resnick didn't like to think about it. He had never understood how a grown man, otherwise fully in control of his faculties, could break down and cry at the sound of Hank Snow singing "Old Shep."

"Anyroad, there I am, few more sheets to the wind than rightly I care for, looking over there, hoping it'll all calm itself down, storm in a biryani, when one of these blokes knees the other one right in the groin. Woman I'm with, instead of hauling me off, she's all for a bit of action. 'Go on, then. You can't turn your back. Go over and get them sorted.'" He cut off a wedge of meat and chewed at it thoughtfully. "I get halfway across the road, bloke who's been hit unlocks the boot of this car parked at the kerb and comes up with a gun."

If he didn't have all of Resnick's attention before, he had it now.

"Bloody shotgun!"

Resnick set knife and fork quietly down and pushed away his plate.

Ben Riley grinned. Two insurance executives across the aisle were hanging on his every word. "Where there'd been a lot of shouting and commotion, everyone was suddenly quiet. Three of them staring at this shotgun and the chap with it looking ready to take the other bloke off at the knees."

By now the entire restaurant was silent, wanting to know how it had worked out.

"He was so engrossed in what he was doing, didn't seem to hear me at all. Got right up behind him, tapped him on the shoulder. Jumped half a foot in the air, dropped the gun." Ben Riley was smiling broadly, enjoying the audience. "Got a foot on it, showed him my warrant card, that was about that."

You could hear breath being released around them on all sides, click of utensils on china, conversations resumed.

"Seemed the car he was driving wasn't taxed, his driving licence had been withdrawn six months previous and, of course, he didn't have a licence for the gun. I get the names and addresses of the others, make sure my woman gets a taxi, me and him go back inside the restaurant—pretty fair tandoori, by the way, specially when it's on the house—anyway, we get to talking, he's worried about this motor thing, needs it to get around, can't believe he was so stupid as to threaten this bloke with the gun. Been mates—what? —four years, but that's not what's really putting the shits up him, what is, he had that gun earmarked for somebody else. One of the things he's into, a little buying and selling on the side. It's in police custody, how can he sell the gun?"

Resnick could feel the small vein vibrating at the side of his skull. "Did he say who he was going to sell the shotgun to?" Hoping against hope, not really believing what Ben's reply was going to be, but knowing all the same.

Ben Riley leaned forward across the table and lowered his voice. "Prior. John Prior."

Resnick picked up his knife and fork and cut across the fleshy section of lemon sole. His appetite had come back.

The man's name was Finch, Martin Finch, and they didn't talk to him in one of the interview rooms at the station; they talked to him in Ben Riley's Vauxhall, parked in a lay-by on the Kimberley-Eastwood bypass, east of Junction 26. The temperature was such that the windows were steaming over, three men in that confined space the best part of an hour, Finch's sweat holding his shirt flat and wet to his back, running into his groin. Finch wanted to reach down and scratch, wriggle and set himself to rights. Except for small movements with his hands, he sat quite still, leaning back into the rear corner of the car, grey tongue dabbing at his drying lips. Softly, the four-speaker stereo was playing one of Ben Riley's compilations of country hits.

"The gun that was used in the Sainsbury's job," Resnick asked, "did that come from you?"

Finch mumbled something that could have been yes or no.

"Again," Resnick said.

Audible this time, Finch staring at the condensation on the window as traffic, like blurred ghosts, swished by outside. "Yes."

"You knew what it was for?"

"No."

"You must have had an idea?"

"No. Never."

"The person you sold it to, that was Prior?"

"Not direct."

"Explain."

Over the whine of a steel guitar, George Jones was preparing to get hurt all over again.

"I met up with Frank—"

"Frank Churchill?"

"Yes. Through him I met Prior. After the deal'd gone through."

"They talked about the robbery?"

"Course not."

"But you knew?"

"No."

Resnick wiped his hands along his thighs. "You thought they were going out to shoot rabbits?"

"Maybe." A flick of the tongue. "Why not?"

"You know now," Ben Riley said from behind the wheel. "After last time, no way you can't know."

Finch lowered his face into his hands. Count to five hundred in tens and when you look they'll all have gone away.

Resnick leaned closer along the backseat. "This time Prior contacted you himself?"

"Yes."

"Why not Churchill?"

Finch shrugged. "Maybe he's not around. Who knows?"

"When," Resnick said, "were you supposed to make delivery of the gun?"

"I don't know."

"Don't lie."

"Honest to God . . ."

"Yes?"

Finch's eyes left Resnick and found Ben Riley instead. His temples were beginning to throb; it was increasingly difficult to breathe. "Tomorrow, day after. He's supposed to get in touch."

"How?"

"Phone."

Resnick glanced towards Ben Riley, who gave a quick, almost imperceptible nod. "Go through with it. Go through with the deal. Soon as Prior's in touch, arrangements are in place, you call us."

An articulated lorry went past so fast along the bypass it made the car vibrate. Sweat dropped from Finch's nose onto his mouth and chest. Tanya Tucker asked to be laid down in a field of stone; Billy Joe McAllister jumped off the Tallahatchie Bridge. "All right," Finch breathed eventually. "Okay. Yes. Yes."

30

"Whatever's the matter with you, Charlie?" Elaine was leaning against the living-room door, a glass of white wine in her hand.

What's the matter with you? Resnick felt like asking. Since when did you start drinking at home, this side of seven o'clock especially? Resnick was listening to Charlie Mariano, thumbing through back issues of *Jazz Monthly,* the omelette he'd made earlier balanced cold on its plate at the edge of his chair, largely untouched.

"I don't know," he said, looking at her steadily. "Is something the matter?"

Elaine held his gaze for several moments, clicking forefinger against thumb as she turned away. When Resnick appeared in the kitchen fifteen minutes later, he was wearing his grey raincoat, unbuttoned and unbelted. "I'm going to the match."

"What match?"

"Reserves."

Without humour, she arched back her head and laughed. "Christ! Is staying in the same house with me suddenly that bad?"

He stood on the County Road side, near the halfway line. Rain began to fall in swathes, darkening his coat, seeping through to his shoulders. On the pitch a bunch of youngsters and the odd gnarled professional hoofed the ball out of defence in the hopeful direction of their opponents' goal. Tackles slid fast across the greasy turf and, with so few people in the ground, you could hear, all too clearly, the crack of bone meeting bone.

"Here! Here! Here!" a player called, arms like semaphore. "Get the bastard thing upfield!"

Gripping the metal rail before him, Resnick failed to notice that his fingers had whitened, his knuckles were purple. So many times since the previous afternoon the words had lain on the back of his tongue, waiting to be spoken, and each time he had swallowed them whole and unsaid. *Whatever's the matter with you, Charlie? Is staying in the same house with me suddenly so bad?* He could smell something strange and sweet and it was the scent of violets, filling nostrils and mouth, making him retch. *Married women,* Rains had said, smug and handsome and knowing, *a cinch.*

When, less than five minutes from the end of the match, County's reserve striker latched on to a weak back pass and toe-poked the ball past the keeper for the game's only goal, Resnick could scarcely raise a cheer.

It was a drinking club near the Forest, as unlike the one where he'd been with Resnick and Cossall as it was possible to be. The DJ at the far end of the main room was playing reggae and Rains's was the only other white face at the bar. "Scotch," he said, "large. And a large gin."

He slid a note across the bar and pocketed the change, picked up the glasses and carried them to the far end where Ruth was sitting.

"I told you . . ." Ruth began.

"It's a free country."

Ruth laughed bitterly. "Is it?"

Rains sat himself on the stool beside her, tasting his scotch. Ruth lit another cigarette and poured the gin into her own glass.

"We can't talk here."

"Why not?"

"I'm known. Besides, he might come waltzing in any minute."

"Okay, my car's outside. We could go for a drive." He drained his glass and began to get to his feet. Ruth scowled and looked straight ahead but otherwise she didn't move. Rains settled back down and gestured to the barman for a refill. He thought if there were any real danger of Prior arriving, she would have left the moment she'd recognised him at the door.

Ruth held the glass by the stem, tight, wondering if some kind member was in the entrance hall already, letting Prior know his wife was sitting there, taking drinks from a sodding copper. She could see Rains's reflection mirrored above the bottles, so fucking good-looking it made you want to throw up.

"Another?"

She didn't answer and he took her silence for agreement and bought a large gin. Ruth waiting for him to start in on Prior's activities, how did it feel being married to a villain? He surprised her by asking her how it felt, not being able to sing anymore.

"Not able? How d'you mean?"

"Don't suppose he takes to the idea much, does he? Wife up onstage, on show? Bit old-fashioned about things like that, I should imagine."

Before they were married, Prior had gone everywhere to see her. Step out onto the stage and there he was, somewhere at the back of the room, leaning, smiling. Later, it was, "Jesus, Ruthie! You have to start that caterwauling, every minute of the bloody day?" At first, career going nowhere, bands breaking up around her, record contracts not materialising, she had found it difficult to mind. The joy had gone out and all that was left were torn vocal chords and hard work.

"Don't you wish," Rains said, "you could do it again, now and then, just for the hell of it?"

Ruth stubbed out her cigarette, automatically reaching for another. "It's been too long. Any voice I might've once had's gone."

He put his hand over the one that was bringing the cigarette to her lips. "Maybe then you shouldn't smoke so much?"

She shook him free. "My father, that's what you want to be? My agent? You're short of an act for the police smoker? What?"

Rains waited until she was looking full into his face. "I like you. Talking to you, it's good. I like that. Paying you a bit of attention, I reckon it's too long since anyone's done that. You deserve better. That's all."

Ruth sat there, you cocky young bastard, you're so full of shit; but listening all the same, knowing he was lying, enjoying every word.

When he arrived back at the house, all the lights were out and Resnick assumed that Elaine had got tired of her own company, caught a cab to someone welcoming. But she had gone to bed early, her face blinking back at him from the pillow when he switched on the light. She covered her eyes and he snapped it back off.

"Coffee? Tea?"

"No, thanks."

The usual courtesies.

Resnick spread the coffee beans across the palms of

both hands, lowering his face towards them. Even so, it lingered: sweet sour smell of the sheet, oil of violet on the breath. In the living room he thought of playing Parker's "Lover Man," one of those bruised ballads Billie Holiday sang with Lester Young. Either, he realised, would reduce him further into self-pity. He fetched a notebook from the desk by the window and wrote up that day's conversation with Martin Finch. If anything went wrong, he was going to need all the accurate documentation he could muster.

Almost an hour later he called Ben Riley on the phone.

Ben's voice was quiet and Resnick wondered if there was someone there with him, the woman who had witnessed the incident with the shotgun or someone else. "What's the matter, Charlie? Can't sleep?"

"Sorry, I didn't realise it was so late."

"Not to fret. What can I do for you?"

"That deal today, with Finch? You think it was all right?"

"Will he follow through, you mean?"

"Yes," Resnick said.

"Depends who he's more frightened of, us or Prior."

They talked some more, Resnick reluctant to put down the phone.

"You know what I was on about the other day," Ben Riley said eventually. "About getting out."

"Leaving the force?"

"Quitting the whole bloody lot, lock, stock and barrel. Well, I'm serious. Maybe didn't think I was at the time, but I am. I'm getting out, Charlie. Started looking into it, serious. Got an appointment to talk to the union rep later this week."

Resnick's stomach was hollow and chilled. "Where the hell'd you go?"

A pause and then, "The States, perhaps."

"Don't be daft. Whatever it is you're running from here, ten times as bad over there. New York. L.A. You'd be—"

"Big country, Charlie. Not all cities, you know."

"If it's a quiet life you want, what's wrong with Devon? Cornwall?"

At the other end of the phone Ben Riley sighed. "It's not a quiet life I'm after, Charlie. It's a new one."

Not knowing what to say, Resnick said nothing. "Get to bed, Charlie," Ben Riley said. "Maybe see you first thing? Breakfast, eh?"

"Maybe," Resnick said and rung off.

There was a half-inch of coffee cold in the bottom of the cup and he tipped enough Bell's into it to make it half full. Drank it standing at the foot of the stairs. At the bedroom door he listened to the sound of Elaine's breathing and knew that she was deep in sleep. In the bathroom, he switched on the shower and stood under it for a long time, head bowed. Then went to bed.

31

"Chancy business, Charlie. Can't say it's the way I'd have played it."

"No, sir."

Skelton was in the midst of compiling the duty roster, coloured pins and stickers strategically placed at the four corners of his desk, each ready to be slotted into place. He reminded Resnick of those elderly men at the B.R. Travel Centre, just aching to be asked the quickest way to get from Melton Mowbray to Mevagissey on a Sunday, calling at Wolverhampton and Weston-super-Mare on the way.

"Conspiring to provide a known villain with an illegal weapon, that's the way the courts might see it."

"Yes, sir."

"Still, now it's set in motion, best let it play itself out. But I want a close eye kept, Charlie, understood? A close eye."

Resnick turned towards the door.

"Can't remember, Charlie—squash, that your game or not?"

"Not exactly," Resnick said.

Skelton nodded. "Bit of difficulty finding partners." His

gaze drifted down in the direction of Resnick's gently spreading stomach. "Could do a lot worse than give it a thought. Getting to the age when it pays to look out for these things—health, fitness. Doesn't pay to let them slide."

Resnick gave it some thought while he was enjoying a smoked ham and brie sandwich, light on the mustard, heavy on the mayonnaise. That and other things. Brushing his fingers free of crumbs, he crumpled up the empty bag and dropped it in one of the black and gold litter bins around the square. Time to do a little more house hunting, he thought, crossing towards the old post office building dividing King and Queen streets.

The young woman at the first desk had a complexion like sour milk. "Oh, that would be our Mr. Gallagher," she said in response to Resnick's enquiry. "He's just stepped out of the office for a moment. Is there anything I can do to help?"

Resnick was in the middle of declining when the bell above the door sounded and Gallagher returned, different suit today, a charcoal grey. He had the early edition of the local paper under one arm, a bar of Cadbury's fruit and nut and a packet of twenty Benson king-size in his hand. He handed the chocolate to the young woman and slipped the cigarettes into his own pocket. He seemed to recognise Resnick, but not the exact connection.

"Richmond Drive," Resnick prompted him.

"Ah, yes, of course. You're interested, then?"

Resnick nodded.

"Good, good. Not been on the market for long and already we've had a lot of interest."

"It is empty, though? Vacant possession?"

"Oh, yes. People that lived there moved abroad. France, I seem to remember." He gave Resnick a professional smile. "Do you have somewhere to sell?"

"Yes."

"Perhaps we can help you there. Handle both ends. But first things first . . ." He reached for a leather-bound appointment book. "You'll want to view the property."

"No, that's not necessary."

"But surely you can't . . ."

"My wife's already been round the house."

"Oh, I see. I'm sorry, you didn't say. I . . ."

"Yes. Matter of fact, you showed her round yourself."

Gallagher was thumbing back in his book. "I don't remember . . ."

"Well," Resnick said, a pace closer, "I'm sure you do a lot of that kind of thing."

Gallagher glanced up with a quick, uncertain smile; he was still turning, back and forth, from page to page. "I'm afraid I still don't . . ."

"Probably no reason you should. My wife, come to think of it, she didn't have a lot to say about it either."

"If I could have the name?" Gallagher said.

"Oh, Resnick. Mrs. Resnick. Elaine."

The appointment book slipped from his hand and he caught it, steadying it against his body at the second attempt. Much of the colour seemed to have left his face. He made a guttural, stuttering sound that never threatened to become real words.

"If there's anything else," Resnick said, "you can get in touch at the station. I expect Elaine mentioned I'm a policeman. Detective sergeant. CID."

"What the hell were you doing, Charlie?"

Elaine had been waiting for Resnick the moment he turned the key in the front door; not waylaying him exactly, but there at the centre of the hall, close to the foot of the stairs. He wasn't sure, but he thought she might have had a drink or two to steady her resolve.

"What the hell did you think you were doing?"

He gave her a "What do you think?" look and made to go past her into the kitchen.

"No, Charlie. No, you don't. We're having this out, here and now."

He tried again and physically she blocked him, pushing her hands against his arms. "Talk to me, Charlie. Talk."

He looked into her face. "I don't think I've anything to say."

"Really?" Head to one side, sarcastic. "You surprise me."

"I'd like to think you'd surprised me."

She hit him, fast and unthinking, her open hand smack across his cheek, the edge of her ring catching his lip. When he moved his tongue, Resnick could taste blood.

He walked around her and this time she made no attempt to stop him. Resnick got as far as the back door and realised he didn't know what he was doing there.

"Running out again, Charlie? Another football match to go and see?"

He turned to face her. The anger had scarcely diminished in her eyes.

"You went into where he worked and threatened him."

"He?"

"Philip."

So: Philip Gallagher. Phil. "I didn't threaten him."

"No? Well, that was certainly the way it felt to him. I'm a police officer. Sergeant in the CID. Christ, it's like a bad film."

"I wouldn't know."

"No, you wouldn't. Not on your social calendar too much these days. Films. Nor a lot else, for that matter. Forgetting the football, of course. Late-night drinking, no danger of forgetting that." She laughed, shrill and short and bitter. "We used to go to the pictures, Charlie, I don't know if you remember. Cinema. Dancing. Even the theatre once or twice, although you did have a tendency to fall asleep after the interval. Still—used to do a lot once upon a time, you and me."

"Why do I think this is turning into some kind of an attack on me?"

"Is it? Maybe because that's the way you feel. Catholic guilt, Charlie. All that stuff you thought you'd disowned."

Resnick leaned away from the door. "I should've thought if there was any guilt around . . ."

"I should have the monopoly?"

"You were the one sneaking off in her lunch hour."

"Sneaking off?"

"Making love to another man."

The bottle that she'd opened was close to where she was standing and she poured herself another glass of wine. The bottle was nearly empty. "We weren't making love, Charlie, Philip and I. What we were doing was fucking. There's a big difference." Slowly, she carried her glass of wine towards him. "What you and I do—used to do—that was making love. Tender, Charlie. Careful. Solicitous. What we do, myself and Philip, other people's beds, we fuck!"

He swung his arm and she saw it coming, trying to block him and not quite succeeding, the heel of his hand catching her at the front of the left temple, alongside the eye. The glass she had been holding shattered against the floor. Elaine stumbled backwards, the worktop saving her from falling.

Resnick moved towards her, arms outstretched, apologising; instead of flinching, she lifted her face towards him, daring him to strike her again. Resnick wrenched the back door open and slammed it behind him, unable to see where he was running, half-blinded by the tears of shame and anger in his eyes.

32

"If you were going to hit anyone," Ben Riley said, "you should have had a crack at him."

"Wouldn't do any good," Resnick said.

Ben Riley shook his head. "I'm not so sure about that. And, by my reckoning, nine out of ten people'd think the same."

"That doesn't mean they're right."

"Come on, Charlie. It's a bit late to be bloody reasonable. And he was, if you'll pardon the expression, screwing your wife."

"Not a crime."

"Isn't it?"

Resnick got up from the table and started to pace haphazardly about.

"For God's sake, Charlie, have a drink."

"Better not."

"Some coffee, then."

"All right."

"I've only instant."

"Never mind. Forget it."

Ben had been ironing shirts when his friend had arrived,

bending over the board with a bottle of Jamesons close to hand and a celebration of George Jones's ten years of hits in the cassette deck. He'd switched it off when the doorbell had rung and hadn't felt moved to turn it back on. He doubted if Resnick was ready for "Nothing Ever Hurt Me (Half as Bad as Losing You)," never mind "If Drinkin' Don't Kill Me (Her Memory Will)."

"What are you going to do?" he asked.

"I don't know."

"You want me to go round, talk to her?"

Resnick shook his head.

"You're sure? 'Cause I will."

"Thanks, no. It's hard to see how it would help. It's something we've got to sort out for ourselves."

"Yes, I suppose you're right." He pointed at the bottle and Resnick shook his head. "Just give it a little time, eh?"

"Yes." Resnick sat back down, shaking his head. "I suppose that's the thing to do."

"D'you want to stay here tonight? You know there's plenty of room."

Resnick accepted gratefully, realising that it was no more than temporary respite: a night on the couch away from what still had, painfully, to be faced.

They ate breakfast at Parker's, Resnick sure he would have no appetite, but something—the smell of bacon?—making him ravenous the moment he walked to the counter. Ben Riley settled for tea and a sausage cob, looking on amused as Resnick tackled black pudding, back bacon, tinned tomatoes, double egg, chips and beans.

"Jesus, Charlie. Good job you don't get cuckolded often. You'd be over eighteen stone."

"It's not funny, Ben."

"I know that. What d'you think I'm cracking jokes for?"

Resnick sawed off a slice of black pudding, wiping it

round in the tomato juice before transferring it to his mouth; one of those things, if you didn't think what it was made from, it could taste wonderful.

"Happen we'll hear from Finch today," Ben Riley said without much conviction.

Four firemen, just off night watch, came in talking about a fire on the industrial estate they were all persuaded was arson.

"What worries me," Resnick said, "drifts on too long, Skelton might get cold feet, have him pulled in before Prior's in contact. That happens we're back to square one."

"He'll allow forty-eight hours, got to."

Resnick shook his head, forked up the last of his beans. "No 'got to' about it."

"Should have played squash with him." Ben Riley grinned. "Sweat your way into his good books."

"Yes." Resnick eyed his empty plate. "Can just see me chasing a little green ball after that lot."

"If you want to stay over again . . ." Ben said when they were on the pavement.

"Thanks. Best not. Sooner or later it's got to be faced. Sooner's the better."

"Who you trying to convince, Charlie? Me or you?"

One question Resnick did know the answer to.

Resnick had to take a statement from a thirty-year-old curate who'd witnessed a mugging on his way back from a parochial visit. Another case he was working on. They sat the best part of an hour in a draughty church hall decorated with Sunday-school paintings and posters advertising a fund-raising dance for the end of Lent. As he sat listening, taking notes, asking questions, Resnick tried to imagine Elaine and himself visiting someone like this to discuss their problems. That or a marriage guidance counsellor. Was that what you did when you could no longer speak to each other? Talk through a third party? He was only now beginning to realise they hadn't been communicating: what they'd been doing, opening their mouths, pronouncing words.

"I'm sorry," he said to the curate. "Could you just say that again?"

When he got back to the CID office, there was a sheaf of messages on his desk, the last of them, written hastily in blue Biro, *Finch* and a six-figure number. At the bottom, the initials, barely legible, R.C.

Reg Cossall was out interviewing a remand prisoner at Lincoln Prison. Resnick dialled the number on the paper and after thirty rings no one had answered. He tried again on the quarter hour for an hour and when somebody eventually picked up, it was a girl of around nine or ten who told him he was calling a public call box on Valley Road.

Resnick thought about driving out there and decided against it. Chances were Finch might ring in again, and if he did it was better if he were there to take the call. So he did paperwork, tried not to look at his watch, kept an ear open for Cossall's voice on the stairs.

When Cossall finally returned, he was unusually subdued. The young man he'd been out to see, two days short of his twentieth birthday, had tried to kill himself that morning by puncturing his wrist with the broken end of a fork he'd stolen from the dining hall. When that hadn't worked, he'd broken it again and pushed the pieces down his throat. "All the bastard'd've got was six months suspended. Likely probation." But something about it had got even to Cossall—that degree of self-inflicted pain.

"Reg," Resnick said, approaching. "You took this message. Finch."

"Yeh, wants you to ring him. Regular cat on hot bricks, sound of it."

"I tried. Call box. No one there."

"That's 'cause you tried at the wrong time then, isn't it?"

Resnick showed him the note. "How was I supposed to know the right one?"

Cossall took the slip of paper from his hand. "Sorry, Charlie. Must've forgot to write it down."

"You haven't forgotten what it is?"

"No way. Three o'clock. Four o'clock. On the hour."

It was seven minutes past four. Resnick dialled the number from his desk, held his breath willing the receiver to be picked up.

"Yeh?"

He thought he recognised the voice as Finch's, but he wasn't sure. "Martin Finch?" he said.

"Who's that?"

"D.S. Resnick."

"Why the hell didn't you phone before?"

"Never mind that, I am now. What have you got?"

"He's been in touch. I'm meeting him tonight."

"He still wants to buy?"

"There's something coming up. Pretty soon. Wants it bad. Tried putting him off, tomorrow, but no, got to be tonight or he'll go someplace else."

"Tonight's fine. Where's the meet?"

Finch's voice was like a leaf. "I'm going to be all right here, aren't I? You're not going to get me mixed up in this? If Prior ever susses . . ."

"Listen, I've told you. You won't even be involved."

"Involved to the sodding eyeballs, that's all!"

"Relax. We won't go near him when he's with you. Anywhere near you. Nobody ever has to know. . . ."

"He'll know."

"Just tell me," Resnick said, letting the firmness back into his voice, "where the meet's arranged for, place and time." Nodding into the telephone then, "Uh-huh, uh-huh," writing the details carefully down.

———

Skelton was not long off the squash court; his hair, prematurely starting to grey a little, was brushed back flat upon his head and his face was flushed. He was wearing a navy-blue track suit and white Adidas shoes with green piping. "One thing I'm not prepared to countenance, letting him take delivery of a weapon and then using it to commit a robbery. It's not on."

"Our information suggests whatever's going down, it'll be pretty soon. That time, we can keep him under observation, twenty-four hours. As soon as he moves, we move too."

"And all that needs to happen is we put one foot wrong, someone gets shot, maybe this time they get killed, where does that leave us? I'm sorry, Charlie, the risks are too high. Walk into the super's office with that and I'm as like to walk out again with a flea in my ear as anything. No, we'll do the simple thing and we'll do it right." Skelton looked at his watch. "Incident room, eight o'clock. Make sure everyone knows."

Back in the CID office, Resnick phoned Elaine.

"Look," he said, "tonight, something's come up. I'm sorry. I've no idea what time I'll be back."

"How convenient," Elaine said and hung up.

33

Ruth climbed out of the bath, water streaming down her thighs. She'd lain in there too long, idling with her thoughts, the skin on her fingers ridged and puckered. Reaching for a towel, she rubbed a circle on the steam-covered mirror with her fist. Jesus! Like waking up and discovering you'd turned overnight into your mother. She wound a white towel about her head, began to pat her legs dry with another. *How's it feel, then, after all that time, not being able to sing?* Cocksure bastard with his hands round the glass, nails even and smooth like they'd been manicured, long fingers. *How's it feel?*

"Ruthie, you going to be all night?"

The look in his eyes when he took her hand and pressed it against him. Bastard! Excited, she hated him for that.

"Ruthie!"

Every night I'm kept waiting, she started singing to herself, face blurred in the mirror, gaunt and unfocused. *All those dreams and wasted tears . . .*

Prior knocked loudly on the door. "There's other people in this house, you know."

"Couple of minutes."

"You better be."

There'd been other people, right enough, same old faces along with a few new ones; conversations that petered out the minute she walked into the room. Phone calls that would be terminated at the least chance of being overheard. Something new was in the offing, something big, and he wouldn't say anything about it till it was over. Then there'd be the bragging—"Ought to've seen their faces" or "Like a bleeding dream, Ruthie, clockwork wasn't bloody in it"—the celebrations with champagne swilled down like water and holidays to exotic places. The lies. "Papers, Ruthie, you know what they're like, blow it all up out of proportion. Hardly laid a finger on them." And last time: "All an accident, never should've happened. Wouldn't've done if he hadn't took it into his head to be a sodding hero. Me? Ruthie, come on! When did you ever know me as much as touch a gun?" God! The lies. How she hated the same old, senseless lies.

"Ruth!"

"All right!" She wrenched the door open and moved quickly past, into the bedroom, Prior's voice trailing behind her.

"Jesus! What you been up to in here? Like a bloody sauna!"

Ruth closed the door and unwound the towel from her body, draping it over the end of the bed. In the full-length mirror she saw that her breasts were getting smaller, the flesh over her hips and around her thighs was thickening. Sighing, she closed her eyes. *All those lonely wasted years.* Rains's face, wide-eyed with honesty even as he lied. *I like you. Talking to you.* The beginnings of a well-trained smile edging his face. *You deserve better, that's all.*

Resnick was to be in the lead car with three others, Hallett and Sangster and a new lad called Millington. Skelton

would be in car two with Maddoc and McFarlane and Terry
Docker. "Your show this, Charlie, I'm just along for the
ride." The third car contained Rains and Cossall and Derek
Fenby. Uniforms were providing extra backup, sealing off
the area of the Prior house once the time was ripe. Resnick
had asked for Ben Riley and got him. One officer in each
car was armed.

The first car alone would stand close watch on the pub,
where two plainclothes officers were already stationed, borrowed from outside the city so there was less chance of their
being recognised. As soon as the deal had gone down, the
other cars would close in.

"All right," Skelton said, "nobody loses their head. We
want a result here, not gunfight at the O.K. Corral."

A couple of officers politely laughed.

"Charlie? Last thoughts?"

Resnick was on his feet. "Thanks, sir. I don't think so.
We all know what we've got to do."

"Yes," said Reg Cossall, "make sure that bastard Prior
goes down for a long time."

There were cheers for that.

"Ruth?" He'd changed into light blue slacks, dark crewneck
sweater under a brown leather coat. Tan shoes with tassels.
Where's the gold chain? Ruth thought. "I'm off out. Shan't
be long."

She swung her legs down from the settee. On the TV an
off-duty surgeon was performing an emergency operation
with the assistance of one of the night cleaners and a hastily
sterilised Swiss army knife.

"Going to the club?"

"No," Prior said and winked. "See the well-known man
about the well-known dog."

Ruth looked back at the screen. "Is this the dog that

takes a thirty-eight-calibre bullet or the one that prefers shotgun shells?"

Prior laughed as he closed the door, and over the sound of the TV she could hear him doing a really bad Presley impression down the hall. Now or never, Ruth thought, might be just about right.

The pool tables in the side room were crowded round with onlookers, the occasional shout at a lucky shot or a bad miss rising above the general noise. At the back of the main bar a woman in a floral dress was plying coins into the electronic fruit machine as if feeding a long-lost child. The jukebox cut in with a sudden burst of eighties techno-pop, fighting it out with the landlord's tape of western theme tunes, which was playing through the speakers above the bar.

"What the hell's the matter with you?" Prior asked as Finch made his second return from the gents in fifteen minutes. "Got the runs or what?"

"This ale," Finch said, holding up the glass. "Goes through me like nobody's business."

"So stop bloody drinking it," said Prior, who was sticking to scotch and water, nibbling his way through a packet of nuts, shells overflowing the metal ashtray. "Anyway," he said, pulling back his jacket sleeve to see his watch, "almost time we weren't here. Got the wife to get back to, know how they are."

"Give her one." Finch laughed nervously.

Prior scowled and pushed back his chair. Coins spilled from the fruit machine so liberally that the woman couldn't hope to catch them in her hands. "Parked round the back?"

"Yes," Finch said. "Hang about while I finish this."

Prior took the glass from his hand and set it down. "In your own time. Let's do this now."

They walked out past the pool players, half of them

sixteen at best. There'd been something in the *Mirror* that morning about underage alcoholics, Esther Rantzen or Annika Rice or one of them setting up a telephone help line. "Any kid of mine . . ." Prior had started over his scrambled eggs, but the look on Ruth's face had shut him up. Far as the pair of them knew, any kid of his hadn't been born yet.

"Just left the pub," the detective said into his two-way radio. "Rear car park, the pair of them."

The shotgun was wrapped in a length of wool blanket, sheathed inside thick plastic; the notes were in fifties, rolled tight and held in place with a rubber band. The exchange took less than forty seconds. "Okay," Resnick said into the handset. "We're on."

Fed up with TV, Ruth had climbed onto a dining chair, scrabbled about in a box on the top shelf in the alcove, above Prior's Brian Ferry albums, his Rod Stewart and his Elvis Presley. Paperback books by Wilbur Smith and Jeffrey Archer. The corners of the cover had got bent, one of the edges torn. Nineteen seventy-two. She could remember going into the recording studio still. Manchester. Driving up there with Rylands, through the Peak and along the Buxton Road. Four tracks and it had taken them the best part of a day. Cold in the studio and she'd found it difficult to pitch in key, sent Rylands scurrying out from behind his drum kit to buy a quarter-bottle of brandy.

Ruth wiped away dust with the side of her hand and set the record down. Play it now before he came home. The rawness of the sound took her by surprise, the echo, her voice. Well before the first song was over, she lifted up the stylus, slotted the record back in its sleeve. That moody, soft-focused picture, head down by the mike like she was Janis Joplin. Well, lighting a cigarette, she wasn't Janis; she was alive. Just. Without bothering to get back onto the chair, she tossed the record back up into the box.

Ruth James and the Nighthawks R.I.P.

Hallett drove, enjoying this part of the job, good at it. Followed a stolen Sirocco once, all the way from Exeter to Chesterfield, five different motorways, never spotted once. Now he ghosted eighty yards behind Prior's car as it swung down Southdale Road, turning south through Bakers Fields towards Colwick Park. In the back Graham Millington began to whistle, tuneless and unrecognisable, until the others stared at him and he shut up.

The other cars were slowly closing, east and west.

The palms of Resnick's hands were dry and beginning to itch. Since making his call several hours before, he had not thought of Elaine once.

Ruth had intended to be in bed before Prior arrived back, but she had switched the set back on and a programme about prisoners' wives had caught her attention. Talking to camera, some of their faces had been electronically distorted to avoid recognition. Story after story of impossible journeys by bus and train, often with kids in tow. Month after month, year after year. Stand by your man. If mine gets nicked, Ruth thought, he can sod that for a lark!

Above the television sound she heard the car draw up outside, switched off and went quickly up the stairs.

"Ruth? Ruthie?"

No reply. Prior switched on the TV and flicked through the channels. Highlights from tonight's top-of-the-table promotion battle. He broke off a piece of mature Cheddar with his fingers, popped open a can of beer. If this is the top of the table, he thought after a few minutes, God help the rest of them.

He was lolling back against one corner of the settee, feet resting on the coffee table, when Sangster swung a sledge-hammer at the door, the second time enough to splinter the hinges clean away.

Resnick was first inside, calling, "Police!" Hallett and Millington on his heels. Prior raced from the front room, shouting Ruth's name as he passed the stairs. "Charlie!" Hallett yelled. "Go! Go!" Prior wrenched open the kitchen door and slammed it shut behind him. Ruth, pulling on a robe over her nightclothes, stepped out of the bedroom into a chaos of chasing feet and harsh voices. Prior leaned his weight against the kitchen table and rammed it against the door; through the window he could see the shadowy figures of men at close intervals between the roses.

"Bastards!"

Rains looked up at Ruth from the well of the stairs and winked.

Hallett shoulder-charged the kitchen door and his ankle turned under him, but the door budged back far enough for Resnick to squeeze through. A quick look towards the rear windows, which were still closed. He guessed the side door led into the garage and he was right.

The offside door to the car was open and so was the boot, Prior partly screened behind it, bending low. The only light was that which came through from the kitchen, but it fell across Prior's back and face.

"CID," Resnick said breathlessly. "D.S. Resnick. I . . ."

Prior moved to his right as he straightened and when he did he had the double-barrelled shotgun in his hands. Something banged against the garage door outside, but the hands didn't falter; they were holding the gun quite steady, angled towards the upper part of Resnick's chest.

Peripherally aware of other voices, outside and behind, Resnick could only concentrate on Prior's eyes as they narrowed down, the slight tightening of the finger behind the trigger guard.

The breathing of both men was ragged.

Resnick took a pace forward and cautiously, very slowly, began to open the fingers of his empty right hand.

Something inside Prior changed, like a switch being thrown; his eyes widened and blinked and he began to reverse the shotgun, the barrels towards his own head. Christ, Resnick thought, he's going to kill himself. But the swivelling movement didn't stop until the stock was pointing towards Resnick and he went quickly forward, hand reaching across the roof of the car, to take the weapon from Prior's loosening grasp.

The garage doors slid quickly up into the roof and Ben Riley stepped out of car headlights, concern on his face. Hallett and Millington moved either side of Resnick, turning Prior around, reading rights and warnings as they fastened cuffs about his wrists.

"Did well, Charlie. Star performance."

Resnick turned at the sound of Rains's voice, and there he was grinning from the kitchen doorway, Ruth at his side. Rains had a police issue pistol in his right hand.

"Thought for a minute there I was going to have to use this."

Resnick pushed past them, back inside the house, Ben Riley following him through.

34

Summer in the cities.

Prior was refused bail on the grounds that he might skip the country or attempt to interfere with potential witnesses and jailed on remand. Martin Finch was persuaded to testify that in addition to the shotgun Prior had surrendered to Resnick, he had supplied the weapon that had seriously wounded the Securicor guard and that Frank Churchill had told him it was to be used in a robbery Prior was organising.

When Churchill stepped off the Manchester train, officers were waiting to arrest him.

Resnick was officially commended for bravery and the object of several late-night celebrations in the local force. He found himself celebrating again when the soccer season ended and County were promoted to the First Division of the Football League for the first time in fifty-five years.

He sat in front of a television set with Ben Riley, watching Spurs' other Argentinian, Ricky Villa, plough his way through a maze of players in the Manchester City penalty area and score the winning goal in the F. A. Cup Final replay. When it was over, Ben told him that he'd written an exploratory letter to the Montana State Police.

One of Prior's fellow prisoners came up to him in the exercise yard and told him his wife was getting her leg over with a copper. It took four men to prise Prior away, and by the time they succeeded, the other prisoner had a broken nose and a ruptured spleen.

Resnick and Elaine were talking again, being civil at least; she said she had stopped seeing Gallagher, needing to think things through. There was still a great deal that went unspoken, neither of them willing to prise open what each, in their different ways, was apprehensive to examine.

In June there was more rioting in London and in July the attempt by police to arrest a black youth for stealing his own motor bike resulted in violent confrontations which lasted for three days. Petrol bombs were hurled at a besieged police station in Manchester and riots threatened to tear apart the decaying hearts of many other inner cities: Birmingham, Blackpool, Bradford, Cirencester, Halifax, Huddersfield, Hull, Leeds, Nottingham, Preston, Reading, Sheffield and Wolverhampton. The Prime Minister, Margaret Thatcher, refused to accept either swingeing unemployment or bad housing as causes, putting the violence and looting down to criminal greed.

Police used water cannon, CS gas and plastic bullets to quell the disturbances. And Ben Riley applied to the American Embassy for his visa.

The fag end of July, Resnick, with four days' leave and time hanging wide on his hands, bought white gloss paint and set to work on the skirting boards in the unoccupied top bedroom.

The first time Elaine came up the stairs she brought biscuits and a mug of tea; the second she stood, arms folded, and said, "Charlie, we need to talk. Charlie, I want a divorce."

1992

35

"Pam Van Allen?" people would say. "What kind of a name is that?"

"My husband's."

"Your husband's called Pam?" Same old jokes.

Either that or it was assumed she'd got herself married to a Dutchman, like, you know, that detective on television.

Truth to tell, his name had been one of the most attractive things about him, just the right amount of seriousness and mystery; so much more interesting than her own name, the one she'd been born with, born into, which was Gold. Pam Gold: it didn't exactly have a ring to it. It made her sound, Pam thought, like the wife of a dentist or a lawyer or a psychotherapist, spending her days listlessly shopping for things she already had.

All right, she knew that was a stereotype.

But that was the way people thought. If she weren't careful, she caught herself falling into the same trap—despite the fact that her dentist was called Adams and the lawyer she'd consulted about the divorce had been Mitchell of Haywood, Turner and Mitchell. She had never, knowingly, met a psychotherapist. Though her husband had suggested it on numerous occasions towards the end of their five-year marriage. Five years, two months, thirteen days. After the usual healthy mudslinging, she'd walked away with fifty percent of the resale value of the house and its contents and her husband's name.

"It doesn't make sense," her friends at work said, disappointed. "All that's over. You should go back to who you really are."

But Pamela Van Allen was who she felt she was; it didn't make her think of him at all. Little did. Dandruff and "Mastermind" and pee stains round the toilet bowl. And Pam Gold was a stranger who had once bopped around to Paul McCartney and 10cc., believed in silly love songs and the things we do for love.

Pam Van Allen was a probation officer in the city, thirty-five years old, six years' experience, responsible single woman with a responsible job, showing her identification as she slowed to a stop at the prison gates.

She had worked out a strategy for visits like these. Next to no makeup, just a touch around the eyes, loose cotton jumper under a check wool jacket, plain skirt, three-quarter length. Female, but not flaunting it, no kind of a come-on; clearly feminine, not a dyke. Careful about gesturing with the hands, crossing legs, being overgenerous with the smiles. Know what you wanted to say, questions you had to ask. Firm, not overfriendly, but all the same—what you wanted was their trust.

The first doors rang shut behind her and an internal clock automatically switched on, counting the minutes till she would walk back out again. The man she was going to see had been imprisoned for a decade of his life.

Since that night he'd last called on Rylands and they had talked about the prospect of Prior being released, Resnick had tried to push it to the back of his mind. With the burglary rate taking a steep hike and a spate of quick and savage underpass muggings, that wasn't so difficult. And, of course, the investigation into the highly organised series of armed robberies was, as the phrase went, ongoing. In this connection, Divine had taken to flexing his muscles at a health club in the Lace Market, swopping confidences afterwards with a pair of likely lads who seemed to have more disposable cash than four nights a week as club bouncers would account for. Graham Millington was doing his drinking in Sneinton, hobnobbing with a snout who'd put some good tips his way in the past and just might be about to do so again if the price was right.

The atmosphere in the CID room was tense, simmering, waiting, if not to explode, at least to let off a head of steam. The workmen had finally got the central heating system working again, floorboards had been replaced, furniture dragged from corridors and odd corners; Resnick had his office back to himself. Space to think, plan, enjoy a deli sandwich without being looked at askance. He was polishing off a salami and Gorgonzola on light rye when the phone rang.

"Resnick. CID."

"Neil Park."

Neil was a senior probation officer, a fair-weather County fan, a man whom Resnick trusted and might have liked had not the ambivalent relationship between the police and the probation service stood between them.

"You were interested in who's been assigned to Prior."

Resnick waited.

"Pam Van Allen. D'you know her?"

Resnick had an unclear picture of a woman in her mid-thirties, not tall, darkish hair—not worn long, he remembered, cut quite close to her head. "I think so," Resnick said. "Who she is, anyway. I don't recall speaking to her."

"She's good," Neil Park said. "Reliable. Doesn't take any pushing around."

"Will she talk to me?"

A hesitation at the end of the line, longer than Resnick liked.

"She might."

"But you'll not suggest that she does?"

"That's right."

Thanks a lot, Resnick thought. "Didn't see much of you this season," he said.

Neil Park laughed. "Work's bad enough without suffering on my day off and paying for the pleasure."

Resnick thanked him and rang off. Twenty minutes later, shuffling through the past few days of incident reports, he remembered that Pam Van Allen's hair wasn't really dark at all: it was that shade of grey that in some lights looks almost silver.

What must he have been thinking of?

Prior hadn't reacted to her name. Sat there and answered her questions, briefly, not impolitely, never avoiding her eye. His face was sallow, lines curved from his mouth, his cheeks were lightly sunken in. The accent wasn't local, Pam thought. Oh, there was an overlay, words and phrases; but below all of that it was harsh, southern, London or close.

"You appreciate it'll be difficult," she said. "Readjusting."

He glanced up at her quickly, keeping his head angled down. It was almost mischievous, that look wrinkling his eyes.

Pam hurried on. "Being in here, it's hard not to get . . ."

"Institutionalised."

"Yes."

He spread one hand upon the table, the other resting, loosely clenched, upon his knee. "You'll help me."

She nodded. "Yes. As far as I can." The room was suddenly small and short of air. Sweat ran in a single line along Prior's face, running from his short hair to his close-shaven chin. "Certainly, we'll find you somewhere to live. At first. While you get sorted."

"Somewhere?"

"A hostel. A place in a hostel, that's the most likely."

Prior looked round at the walls. "I thought I was getting out? Released."

"On parole."

"Course."

"The hostel," Pam said, "it probably won't be as bad as you think. Not too many rules. Only common sense. Anyway . . ." Was that her perspiration she could smell or his? "It's only temporary."

"You said."

"While you find your feet."

"Yes."

"Find work."

Almost lazily, Prior shifted position, leaning one shoulder towards her. "You'll help with that, too."

"Of course. Yes. As far as we can. There are contacts we've built up and if they don't pan out, there are workshop places. Retraining. Learning new skills."

Prior fixed her with his gaze. "Sounds great. Can't wait."

Pam began to push her papers together, putting them back in her case. "Well," she said, rising to her feet, "I shall come and see you again. With any luck I'll have more definite news about the hostel place. And we'll have a chance to talk in more detail about your plans."

"Good," Prior said flatly. "I'd like that."

As she made a move to leave, he stood quickly and offered her his hand.

36

Keith had to hand it to his dad—ever since the day he'd decided to stop drinking, stop was what he'd done. If Ladbroke's had been offering odds, Keith would have been down there with every penny he could muster, happy to put it all on his old man to be back on the bottle before the week was out. After all, hadn't he grown up hearing his parents lob promises like hand grenades between them? Listen, you've got my word . . . That's the last time, I swear . . . I'll never ever . . . Cross my heart and hope to die. "Promises," his gran had said once, her sour commentary on the whole affair, "are like pie crusts—meant to be broken."

But here it was, not yet ten in the morning, his father had already stripped the paper from three of the walls in the bathroom and was moving in on the fourth. Consistently, the house was being transformed. The last of his dodgy lodgers had found his belongings, such as they were, stacked against the front wall. Instead of stale beer and puke, it smelled of disinfectant and fresh paint.

"Set the tea to mash," Rylands called from the bathroom door. "I'll be down in a minute."

In the kitchen, Keith delved his hand into a packet of Honey Cheerios and started eating them dry.

"Why don't you sit down, have a proper breakfast?" Rylands said, rinsing his hands beneath the tap.

"Not hungry."

"There's plenty of bread. You could make yourself some toast."

"I said—"

"Okay, okay." The kettle coming to the boil, Rylands made the tea himself, swilling hot water round the inside of the brown earthenware pot and emptying it out before dropping in two tea bags, thinking about it, adding a third. "What you going to do today?" he asked.

Keith pushed the cereal packet back in the cupboard and shrugged.

"I could use a hand in the bathroom. Those tiles . . ."

"No, thanks."

None of the cups and saucers seemed to match and all of the mugs were chipped or cracked: he would have to chuck them out, get himself to the market and get them replaced.

"How about work?" he asked, pouring the milk.

"Huh?"

"I thought you said this week you were going to look for a job?"

"There are no bloody jobs."

"Pork Farms, they need people on the night shift."

"Don't think I'm working in some factory, coming home stinking of meat."

Rylands poured the tea. "Suit yourself."

"If you don't like it, I'll move back out."

"That wasn't what I said."

"Well . . ."

Rylands passed Keith his tea, sat at the kitchen table and started to leaf through the *Mirror.* "Sure you don't want any toast?"

"Sure. Have some yourself, I'm not stopping you."

"Had mine a couple of hours ago."

"What d'you want, a medal?"

Rylands looked at his son, sipped his tea; all that belligerence in the boy's face, clenched fists, his stance. A young lifetime on the defensive, warding off those who were bigger, older, stronger. From the first day Keith had stepped into the secondary-school playground, he had been bullied, made fun of, an easy mark. The few friends he had were usually lower on the pecking order than he was himself: a timid boy, part-Indian, part-Chinese, with silky skin and long dark eyelashes that curved; an asthmatic lad with glasses thick as the bottoms of half-pint mugs. Either that or they were using him for their own ends.

"Seeing that Darren today?"

"Maybe."

Rylands nodded and turned to the sports pages.

"Why d'you want to know?"

"No reason."

Keith was standing close against his father's elbow. "Don't like him, do you?"

"Do you?"

"What sort of a stupid question is that?"

Rylands took hold, not roughly, of his arm. "One it wouldn't hurt for you to think of an honest answer to."

Keith shook him free and stood away. "I'm off out."

"All right," Rylands said. "I'll be here."

Darren had been watching her, Lorna. Nothing regular or consistent, not methodical, just whenever it came into his head, if he was at a loose end, didn't have anything better to do. So he knew the route she took to work, the corner shop where she would stop off to buy a paper and occasionally a packet of cigarettes, more often than not some magazine; he knew the way she walked back, sidetracking sometimes to call at the mini-market and pick up something for her supper—frozen calorie-counter meals and Slimma soups, she went in for a lot of that. Not that Darren could see why.

He'd sneaked up close to the house once, the one where she had her flat; shinned over the wall and stood in the back garden, not really a garden, more of a yard. Leaned against the flimsy shed and watched her undress. Not all the way, not before she'd crossed the room to switch out the light, but far enough to see the last thing she had to worry about was being overweight.

Maybe he should tell her, casual-like, in the newsagent's when she was picking up her copy of *Today*. Helpful words from a friend. No. Let it wait until he was ready to put right what went wrong before. Drift in off the street and saunter over to the counter. Lorna Solomon? You've got a really good body, you know that? Oh, and while you're doing nothing, just empty all of that cash you've got there into this sack.

Real cool: he liked that.

Standing in front of the boarded-up shop down the arcade from the building society, he looked at his reflection in the darkened glass and grinned at himself as he repeated the words. Practice makes perfect.

Taking his time, Darren wandered towards the building society office and looked through the glass door. Fat woman who worked there—now, if anyone needed her calories counting, she did—explaining something to this old couple, expression on her face suggesting that she was going through it for at least the third time. And Lorna alongside her, laughing suddenly at something the man in front of her had said; counting the bank notes out carefully before passing them under the glass. For an instant she looked towards the door and in that instant Darren instinctively dodged back so that neither of them were ever sure—Darren whether he had been spotted, Lorna if she had seen who she had thought she'd seen.

The square was riddled with bikers and hippies and punks with swastikas tattooed onto their faces with blue Biros or shaved into the top of their close-cropped hair. The same old woman stood amidst the same grubby pigeons and scattered them with birdseed and stale crumbs.

Keith and Darren sat on the low stone wall, sharing a piece of flabby pizza, Darren taking drags from a bummed cigarette. What Keith wanted to do was walk into the Park Estate and nick a car, one of those Ferraris or Mercs with personalised number plates that were always so invitingly there. Get onto the motorway going north and see what it really could do.

But Darren wasn't having any. Stupid, he reckoned, to take the risk. Get caught over a bit of fun when they had serious plans. Keith kicked his heels, unable to extract from Darren precisely what these plans were.

"You don't worry. You'll know what you need to know soon enough."

He would never have dared say so, but there were times when Keith doubted Darren had any real plans at all. Except for the gun. That was the one thing it always came back to, almost the only thing he ever talked about now, aside from that woman who worked in the building society and how he wouldn't mind giving her one, how any day now he was going to get hold of a gun. The look on Darren's face when he said it, as though somehow that was going to change everything, change the world.

"Got any cash?" Darren asked. "I fancy a Coke."

Keith shook his head.

"Jesus!" Darren said, flicking away the butt of his cigarette as he stood clear of the wall. "I hate that. Not even enough between us for a drink when you want one." He jerked his head in the direction of the nearest underpass. "Come on," he said.

37

Millington was peering at the screen of the VDU, chewing at the bottom of his moustache and pondering the wonders of modern technology, the overlap between what he'd gleaned from his informant and the facts as known. He still couldn't decide if he were being taken for a ride.

"Anything to go on, Graham?" Resnick said, pausing at the sergeant's desk.

Millington scowled. "Sometimes reckon we'd be as well off with crystal balls."

Across the room a phone rang and Kevin Naylor picked it up. "CID. D.C. Naylor speaking."

Resnick remembered there was a call of his own he wanted to make; he went into his office and closed the door. Down through the window, he could see the track-suited figure of Jack Skelton jogging past the lock-up garages below the main road.

"Yes, of course I know who it is," Naylor was saying. With a half-guilty glance across the room, he angled his chair towards the wall.

"I called before," Lorna Solomon said. "Left messages. You never phoned back."

"I know. I'm sorry. Things have been busy."

"I thought . . ." She hesitated.

"What?"

"You were avoiding me."

"Like I said, it's been busy."

There was an uneasy silence between them and Kevin sensed rather than heard her breathing at the other end of the phone. He wondered where she was calling from, work or home? Behind him, one of the other officers swore lightly and slammed shut a drawer. Graham Millington was whistling something vaguely classical, the music from some advert or other.

"Kevin?"

"Yes?"

"I wasn't sure if you were still there."

He was thinking of sitting close alongside her in the front of the car, the warmth of her arm whenever she moved it accidentally against his, Chinese food and perfume.

"That youth, I've seen him again."

"The one from the robbery?"

"Yes."

"Where?"

"Right outside. Just today."

Naylor swivelled the chair back round towards his desk. "You're sure?"

"Yes. At least I think so."

"It couldn't have been someone else? I mean, a bit like him? After what happened . . ."

"He was outside the door, staring in. When I saw him he jumped away."

"He didn't come in?"

"No."

There was a pause and then Lorna said, "Kevin, it's not the first time. I'm sure I've seen him before."

"He spoke to you, on the pavement outside."

"No, other times. And not just at work, here at the flat. Kevin, I think he's watching me."

Naylor reached for a ballpoint and flicked open the pad on his desk. "You at home now?"

"Yes."

"Best let me have the address."

It wasn't a place that Resnick knew, not the inside of anyway, a wine bar–cum-restaurant on Barker Gate, across the street from the snooker club. The entrance was down a flight of steps off the pavement; the room that you stepped into had a bar away to the left, a few small tables pressed against the right-hand wall, plenty of space to stand in between. Through an archway there appeared to be a second room for more serious eating.

Most of the people near the bar seemed to have strayed in for a drink after work and stayed. Grey suits and cigarette smoke and braying conversation. Pam Van Allen was sitting at the first table, a white wine spritzer in front of her, reading a paperback book. In that light her hair was a metallic grey.

Her eyes lifted from the book as Resnick came towards her.

"Hello. Charlie Resnick."

"Pam Van Allen."

She held out her hand and her grip was brief but firm.

"Can I get you another drink?"

"Thanks, I'm fine."

He went to the bar for a glass of house red and she read another page of her book, a novel about college friends who spend a summer together in middle age, the first time some of them have seen one another in ten or more years. Pam could only think of two people she still knew from university, none from school. All those friendships you're sure will be so important the rest of your lives.

"It's good of you to meet me."

She gave a slight shrug and waited for him to settle down. He was a big man, bulky, the kind who could do with all the exercise he didn't get. A roundish face with serious eyes. Dressed like that, he'd be less conspicuous in the side bar of a pub.

"If you're hungry," Pam said, making conversation, "the food's pretty good. Snacks. Hummus. Things like that."

"Maybe later."

She glanced at her watch, then folded down the corner of the page and closed her book.

Resnick drank some wine. "John Prior. You've been to see him."

Pam said nothing, waited.

"You're happy about the fact that he's going to be released?"

"You don't expect me to answer that."

"All right, then, let's put it this way. How much do you know about the circumstances of his arrest and trial?"

She turned her glass around on the table. "A little."

"He was convinced some of the information against him came from his wife. That there was some sort of arrangement between her and the police."

"And was there?" Self-consciously, Pam smiled. "I don't expect you to answer that either."

From the adjoining room came the sound of breaking glass, the ironic roar of approval, applause.

"Look," Pam said, "I don't know where we're going to go with this. Anything that passed between my client and me, that's confidential." She lifted her spritzer, thought better of it and set it back down. "I don't know what I'm doing here."

"You came."

"Go and meet him, my boss said. A favour to me. Hear what he's got to say." She looked sideways at Resnick and then away. "I thought what else I might be doing, decided it wasn't so important, and came." She blinked her eyes closed and pushed one hand up through the side of her hair. "I'm not so sure it was a good idea."

Resnick tried a little more of the wine. "What else would you have been doing?" he said.

"Tonight? Warm bath, hot as I can stand, glass of wine . . ." Her fingers drummed lightly on the cover of the paperback. "A book."

Resnick's turn to smile. "Everything except the bath."

Pam pulled her shoulders back, making her posture more professional. "All I can do, Inspector, is listen to whatever it is you want to tell me. I can't promise it's going to affect my actions one way or another."

"All right," Resnick said, "it's this. Remarks Prior made, at the trial and after, they were heavily vindictive. The most frequent, the most violent, were directed towards his wife. I'm concerned that after his release he might try to carry those threats out."

Pam was looking at him evenly, paying little attention to whatever was happening around her. "Prior's wife," she said, "do you know where she's living?"

Resnick shook his head. "No."

"It could be anywhere?"

"It could be."

Pam finished most of her drink and opted to leave the rest. When she was on her feet, Resnick pushed back his chair and followed suit and it occurred to her that he was being clumsily polite.

"When you were talking to him," Resnick said, for a moment his hand resting on her arm, "did he mention his wife? Give some indication of how he feels about her?"

What Prior had said was: "Last thing I wanted was her traipsing out here, week after week, another of those poor bloody prisoners' wives. Not that I didn't want to see her, mind. But, look at it this way, ten years minimum, just not on. Best never to start than have it get less and less, once a week, once a fortnight, once a month. Then again, if we'd had kids, might've been different. No, what Ruth had to do, live a life of her own."

"I've told you," Pam said, "anything that passed between my client and myself . . ."

"But he did talk about her?" Resnick persisted.

Pam's mouth was feeling suddenly, oddly dry. All those people. The tobacco smoke. The wine. "A little," she said. "And when he did he was very calm, very reasonable. Now I do have to go."

Resnick nodded and stepped back. Beyond the far curve of the bar, a group started to sing "Happy Birthday." He stayed on his feet to watch Pam Van Allen walk away, the final glint of her hair silver as she passed through the light.

38

Lorna hadn't spent as much time in front of the mirror since she was fourteen and worried about spots. Five times she had changed her entire outfit, five times, everything from those little blue bikini pants she'd bought on sale at Knickerbox to the vaguely see-through cream blouse from Dorothy Perkins. And makeup! She'd put it on, wiped it off, finally decided on a little light eyeliner, a touch of blusher, the new lipstick she'd bought at Boots last Saturday, South Sea Coral.

Of course, she ought to have run round with the Hoover before getting herself all clarted up, but first things first and anyway it wasn't like her mother making one of her scheduled visits. Kevin Naylor wasn't going to be lifting up the glass Dalmatian on the mantelshelf to see if she'd moved it when she was dusting, or surreptitiously running his finger along the top of the cupboard in the bathroom.

"Doing anything special tonight?" Marjorie had asked when they were cashing up.

"No, I don't think so. Probably stay in, watch telly, get an early night."

She wished!

She'd nipped out in her lunch hour and bought a few nibbles—pistachio nuts and bacon-flavoured crisps—which she'd emptied into cereal bowls and left casually around.

The most difficult decision had been about what to drink. Kevin, she thought, was probably a beer man, but, for all that, there was something nice about the idea of sitting on her freshly plumped-up settee with a bottle of wine. In the end, she'd gone to the corner shop, four cans of lager cooling in the fridge and a bottle of that red wine they were always advertising, the one where these old men go off into the fields at daylight to check on the grapes. She hoped it would be all right. She'd had half a mind to ask Becca's advice, Becca not being above dropping the names of fancy restaurants she'd been taken to—"Dinky little portions, so beautifully presented!"—but in the end she'd decided against it. Another patronising lecture from Becca about the last thing she could cope with.

Lorna looked at her watch, checked it with the clock over the oven, peeked between the living-room curtains down into the street, slipped her tape of Lionel Richie's greatest hits out of its box and into place and slotted it into the machine.

She was ready.

Maybe, Resnick thought, Pam Van Allen was right about Prior. Prison had calmed him, all those hours alone with four walls had helped him to see things in their true proportion, rationalise. Maybe whatever grudge he'd had about Ruth had faded into relative insignificance. Out of sight, out of mind, wasn't that the way things worked?

He had stayed in the wine bar long enough to finish his glass of house red, okay, he supposed, but what it had given him a thirst for was a real drink, which was why he was sitting at the bar in the Polish Club, his second bison grass vodka of the night on the point of disappearing.

What probably happened, Resnick thought, was the more you brooded on things, the more significant they became. Of course, he didn't know what it had been like for Prior, spending all that time inside. Except, he guessed, the last thing he would want to do was get back in again. Resnick remembered, as clearly as if it had been days and not years, the look on Prior's face when they had stood, the pair of them, face to face in that garage: the look in Prior's eyes. Fear that had locked Resnick's muscles, knotted his stomach. The only time in his life he had been threatened with a gun. And Prior, thinking more clearly, pragmatic, weighing up the odds. The sounds of other officers outside. The way he had reversed the weapon and handed it across the roof of the car, what might almost have been a smile lighting up his eyes.

Resnick downed his vodka and pushed away the glass: there had to be a risk the prison review committee and the parole board had erred in their judgement, that Pam Van Allen, however experienced, had had the wool pulled over her eyes. It was a risk he had to minimise.

He slipped a coin into the phone box in the hall and dialled Lynn Kellogg's number from memory.

Lorna had opened the bottle half an hour back, eaten half the nuts. The crumblings of cork that had gone into the glass she had picked out with her fingernail, sliding them over the rim. She drank it without concern for the taste, gulping it down as if it were cherryade. No way he was coming now. She was midway through her second glass when the doorbell rang and she jumped, startled, spilling it onto her hand and arm, tiny splashes across the front of her cream top.

Damn!

Kevin Naylor stood on the top step in a dark suit, pale blue shirt, maroon and grey striped tie, an apologetic look upon his face. "Work," he said. "Last moment, something came up. Sorry I'm late."

He wasn't about to confess to sitting round the corner in the car the best part of twenty minutes wrestling ineffectively with his conscience.

"That's okay." Lorna smiled, reaching for his arm as if afraid he might run away. "Come on inside."

The room was warm and comfortable-looking, two small lamps burning, knickknacks that Lorna had been attracted to dotted around on odd surfaces, a pair of stuffed yellow bears pushed together on a low bookshelf in the alcove.

"Don't sit there," Lorna said as Naylor began to lower himself into the one armchair. "This is a lot more comfortable." Patting the cushions of the settee. "I was just having a drink," she said. "What can I get you?"

"No, it's okay, thanks."

"There's wine or beer. Cold lager in the fridge." Standing in the kitchen doorway, Lorna smiled at him and wished now she'd stuck with her new button-through skirt instead of the black trousers she was sure emphasised her hips.

"Lager's fine," Naylor said.

Lynn pulled into the car park at the front of the Polish Club moments before Resnick extricated himself from a one-sided conversation with a committee member and stepped through the door.

"Hope I'm not dragging you away from anything important," Resnick said as the car slowed for the roundabout at the foot of Sherwood Rise.

"Writing to my mum," Lynn said with a resigned smile. "Been putting it off for over a week. Another day or so's hardly going to matter."

"How are things?" Resnick asked. "Your dad any better?"

Lynn shook her head. "Still not sleeping. Fretting himself half to death about his chickens. Mum keeps trying to get him to go to the doctor but he refuses. Claims there's nothing wrong with him."

"Any chance he's right?"

"Lost nearly two stone in four months. He wasn't big to begin with."

"Maybe you should take some time off? Go home."

"Yes, I expect you're right." She lost her patience with the driver in front and swung wide to overtake before the lights. "That's what my mum says, anyhow."

"So how many times is it you've seen him?" Kevin Naylor asked. He was leaning back against one arm of the settee, Lorna facing him, one leg tucked beneath her, the other one inches away from brushing his own.

"Four or five," she said. "That at least."

"And that's definite? I mean, each occasion, you're positive it was him? The same bloke came into the office that afternoon?"

"I'm not going to forget that in a hurry, am I?"

"No, I suppose not."

"That poor old boy, the way he got hit round the head."

"When you've seen him," Naylor asked, "he hasn't, well, he hasn't threatened you in any way?"

"No, but you see that's what I don't like about it. Not that I want him to, you know, threaten me or anything. But it's the way he looks at me, this sort of grin, as though there was some big secret between us and I knew what it was."

Naylor lifted the can from the table and realised it was empty.

"I'll get you another."

"No, you're all right."

But she was already on her way, hand smoothing along his shoulder as she squeezed between the edge of the settee and the low table.

"The worst thing is," Lorna said, coming back into the room, "I get this feeling he's watching me, other times as well. Even here, in the flat."

"Inside?"

She shook her head. "Out there, I suppose. Like he's watching me come in and out."

"But you've not seen him? Hanging around?"

"Only at work, nearby."

Naylor smiled reassuringly. "Likely you're getting all worked up over nothing."

"Am I?" Lorna handed him the can, fingers accidentally pressing against his.

She sat on the arm of the settee and he shifted along but not far. Through the thin material of her trousers, he could feel the warmth of her leg against his side.

"Kevin?"

"Um?"

"Your wife, what time's she expecting you home?"

"She isn't."

Lorna reached for his hand, width of her fingers easily masking his ring.

Rylands had been down in the cellar when Resnick and Lynn Kellogg had arrived; someone had told him that old copies of music papers were selling for a pound a throw down in London and he was sorting through his copies of *Melody Maker* and the *NME,* thinking to make an accurate list of exactly what he had. He led Resnick and Lynn into the kitchen and made a pot of tea.

"This matter we talked about before," Resnick said.

"Which one?"

"Ruth first."

"I still don't know anything definite."

Resnick wasn't sure if he was telling the truth or hoping

to bargain. "Prior's a lot closer to getting out. Could be any time."

Rylands half-turned. "I'll do what I can."

"Your son," Lynn Kellogg said, "you do want us to do what we can to help him?"

"Yes, of course. Like I said, he's not really a bad lad, it's more . . ."

"You've spoken to him?" Lynn pressed. "You know he's willing to cooperate?"

"Not in so many words, no. Not exactly."

Resnick was quickly to his feet, Lynn following suit. "If you don't want him back inside, Keith, I shouldn't waste a lot more time. If he goes down again . . ."

Resnick moved towards the door, letting the sentence hang.

"Thanks for the tea," Lynn said.

They were at the end of the narrow hall before Rylands called them back. "About Ruth, I did hear something. Just a whisper. Nothing definite."

Resnick felt himself relax; he was close to smiling as he turned. "Check it out. Be sure. You know the deal. I get to Ruth in time, we'll go easy as we can on your Keith. Just as long as he's prepared to talk to us."

"Yes." Rylands nodded. "I know."

"D.C. Kellogg here," Resnick said, "that's who Keith will be dealing with." Lynn reached out and opened the front door. "Twenty-four hours," Resnick said. "I think that's all we can afford."

39

"Hey up, kid!" Divine exclaimed the moment Naylor entered the office. "You look shagged out, you."

"Give over, Mark," Naylor said. "Just for once."

"Didn't know you and your Debbie were back together again," Divine said, grinning.

"We're not."

"Oh, hey. Clocked that, everybody? Our Kev's been getting his leg over in the line of duty. Not."

"Leave it alone, Mark," Lynn Kellogg sang out from the far side of the room.

"Who was she?" Divine goaded, leaning over Naylor, who had that second slumped behind his desk. "That bird you were taking a statement from? Right tasty that. Shouldn't mind having a go at that meself. Two's up, eh?"

Naylor's chair went flying as he sprang to his feet, squaring up to Divine, ready for all the world to take a swing at him then and there and to hell with the consequences.

"Come on then," Divine said, stepping back to give himself room. "Any time you reckon you're man enough to try it."

"Try what?" Millington asked from the doorway, freezing the action before it had started. "Well? Kevin? Mark?"

Naylor shook his head and sat back down, leaving Divine with his fists clenched, adrenaline pumped and nowhere to go.

"Get down the health club last night?" Millington asked him.

"Yes, Sarge," Divine said.

"Anything useful? New?"

"I think so. Maybe."

"Good. On account the super wants to see us, ten minutes sharp. Any notes you've got, best make sure they're to the point. He'll not thank us for wasting his time."

Divine nodded and headed back to his desk. Millington waited until he was settled before bending close to his ear. "I don't know who started that little lot—"

"All I did was—"

"Don't know and don't want to know. But hark to this: what you're doing, walking a very thin line. There's them as'd be well-pleased to see you fall off it. Carry on the way you're going, likely they'll get their wish. Right?"

Without looking round at the sergeant, Divine nodded.

"Understood?"

"Yes, Sarge."

"Good." Millington straightened. "Nine minutes and counting. Buckle to."

Naylor kept his head down, accepted the mug of tea Lynn Kellogg offered with a nod; he'd tried to get this incident report filled out three times now and still couldn't get past the first few lines. One of those days it was difficult to spell your own name. Three o'clock when finally he'd got back last night. Who was he kidding? It had been a lot closer to four. And then he'd scarce been able to sleep.

Roaming round the house, rolling the breadth of that empty bed. "Stay," Lorna had said. "What's the point in going home now?" He'd tried to explain without even himself knowing why. "You've said your wife's stopping over at her mum's. So who's to know?" What he hadn't told her, his wife had been stopping over at her mum's the best part of a year.

Light of six this morning, he'd been in the kitchen mashing tea, eating toast with raspberry jam; replaying the night over and over in his mind. My God! One thing he'd always thought, Debbie and himself, their sex life had been pretty good, up till she'd fallen for the baby at least. What he now realised was how much, in their ignorance, they'd been missing. Or maybe it had just been him who'd known no better—his experience hadn't exactly amounted to much. Red-faced fumblings upstairs at the Savoy; tussles in the car park up the street from Madison's and once on a patch of grass in Wollaton Park overlooked by a small herd of grazing deer. Debbie had been the first woman he'd slept with, the first he properly made love to, just as he'd been the first for her.

He hung his head and sighed.

Most likely Debbie did know a lot more about it than him, all those articles in magazines, orgasms, arousal—what was it? G-spots? Maybe she'd lain there night after night, waiting for him to do stuff he'd barely thought of; wanting him to but too shy to ask.

Unlike Lorna: an education in herself.

And nice. The way she said nothing about his inexperience, though it must have been obvious enough. Funny, too. Stories she'd told him about the people at work.

Why, then, had he left there thinking of Debbie, more so, more seriously than in a long time? He'd made his gesture a long while back, left a message asking her to call, and he hadn't heard a thing. What if Divine was right and it was really over, had been for months though neither of them was admitting it? But then they weren't denying it either; they weren't even talking.

He screwed the form into a ball and dropped it in the bin, pulled another one towards him. If he and Debbie no longer had a marriage, why the guilt that he'd been feeling creeping home? How much did that guilt bring to the excitement of what he'd done?

"Now then, Charlie," Skelton said. He was retying the lace of his Nike Air Tech shoes, the ones with pockets of inert gas in the soles to help with shock absorption. Nigh on a hundred pounds and worth every penny. "Seems these lads of yours might be on to something. Whispers young Divine's been picking up about some kind of French involvement in these robberies, didn't look to be panning out at first. Sight too fanciful, aside from anything else. But rechecking passenger flight lists into East Midlands, back from Birmingham, could be something to it."

Resnick nodded, increasingly conscious that mayonnaise was beginning to seep through the brown paper bag in his hand.

"Thought we might let the pair of them fly over, Paris. Little gentle fraternisation. See if they can tie things together."

"Millington and Divine?" Resnick said with vague incredulity.

"Bound to happen more and more. Just wait till that bloody tunnel's up and running."

"Even so."

Skelton decided to do a little gentle limbering up on the spot. "They'll cope right enough. Besides, Graham Millington, got a bit of a thing for languages, hasn't he?"

"I think that's his wife."

"Oh, well, he's no fool. He'll cope."

Resnick transferred the sandwich from one hand to another; set it down on the ground and Skelton was likely to land one of his size tens on it. "I was more concerned about Divine. My guess, he travels about as well as the average English soccer fan. Out of his head before the plane's started circling Orly Airport."

Skelton was bracing himself against the wall, stretching his hamstrings. "He's the one put in all the spade work, Charlie. Credit where credit's due."

Resnick shrugged and stepped back. "Your decision, sir, not mine."

"Yes, well, I'll give some thought to what you say. Any movement on this other business you've got yourself stuck on? Prior, is it?"

Resnick nodded. "Due out any day. I'm keeping an eye."

Skelton lifted first one foot, then the other, hard against his buttocks. "Bit of a sideshow, isn't it, Charlie? My way of thinking. Wouldn't want to explain away too many man-hours boxing with shadows. Chasing old ghosts. Eh, Charlie?"

The superintendent moved off with a sprightly step, leaving Resnick to walk heavily up the stairs towards his office. As Resnick knew, ghosts could be real enough and you ignored them at your peril.

"Wondered if you'd spoken with your Pam Van Allen?" Resnick said when he'd raised Neil Park on the phone. "Since she and I had a chat."

"Only briefly." Something about the connection made it sound as if the senior probation officer were standing in a deep hole. "I got the impression she resented the degree to which you were putting her under pressure."

"I didn't think that's what I was doing at all."

"Come on, Charlie. You're male, more experienced, high-ranking, used to telling people what to do and expecting them to do it. Other ways of applying pressure than waving a big stick."

"It wasn't what I intended," Resnick said.

"I daresay. All I'm saying is, whatever you were hoping for, you might just have pushed her the wrong way."

"It shouldn't be to do with any of that," Resnick said. "All I want is for her to be aware of the risks . . ."

"What you want is for Prior to stay locked away."

"It'd make life a lot easier all round."

"But not for him, eh, Charlie? Not for Prior."

"Look . . ."

"Sorry, Charlie. Rushed off my feet. Got to go." The voice fell lower into the pit and finally disappeared, leaving Resnick staring at a dead telephone and a half-eaten chicken salad and Jarlsberg sandwich.

Kevin Naylor had walked around in his lunch break, window-shopping in Saxone's and the Camera Exchange and what had once been Horne Brothers but was now a bizarre floating market offering T-shirts, three for five pounds, assorted CDs £2.99 each. When he finally convinced himself to make the call, he was so worked up, the coins fell between his fingers and rolled across the floor.

"Debbie?"

He knew if her mother answered he was sunk and the pleasure at hearing his wife's voice would have been hard to fake.

"Kevin?"

Debbie was surprised to hear his voice at all, never mind the tone; surprised to the point where she came close to seeming pleased herself. "I don't think it's such a good idea, though," she interrupted him, "you coming round."

"That wasn't what I meant," Kevin said, taking the bit between his teeth. "What I thought was, you could ask your mum to look after the baby, I'm sure she wouldn't mind. Meet me in the city. Go somewhere for a meal. Somewhere nice."

There was a silence at the other end of the line and Kevin braced himself for the worst, but "All right," Debbie said, still sounding doubtful. "I'll have to check with Mum, though."

"I'll meet you in Yates's," Kevin said, quick before she could change her mind. "That upstairs bar. You know, looking out over the square. Debbie? Okay?"

"Yes, I suppose . . ."

"Eight o'clock. See you. Bye."

He rung off before she had a chance to say anything more. In the small rectangle of glass at the centre of the box, he could see his eyes were unusually bright and there was perspiration on his skin. He knew, without having to look, that his hands were shaking.

40

Something about the Citroën DS had always rated Keith's attention. Not that there was anything special about the performance; plenty of run-of-the-mill motors would whip you along the fast lane of the motorway in half the time. It was more the look of it, that smooth front which helped to make the whole machine seem longer than it really was. And the suspension. Keith had read up on it once, a wet afternoon going through the motoring magazines in the library on Angel Row. What had it been now? Hydrophonic? No. Hydromatic? Anyway, hydro-something, one of those. Nitrogen gas and fluid, he remembered that. Like riding on air.

He'd come close to nicking one before, this great DS 23 Pallas, right-hand drive, five-speed manual gearbox; he'd spotted it gliding off the ramp from the NCP car park at the top of Barker Gate. Practically wet himself, hadn't he? Hung out there morning and afternoon the next five days, hoping to get close to it again. No such stinking luck.

But today, sheltering by the bus stops below the Broad Marsh from a sudden shower, he'd seen another, black with whitewall tyres, queuing to get into the multistorey opposite. DS 21, fuel injection, semiautomatic. High on the top floor, sandwiched between a Fiat Uno and a Metro, that was where he found it. Smooth to the touch. Half an hour and the floor would be full, few motors driving in and out. Keith gave it a quick kiss on the roof for luck and scurried away to the stairs to wait.

All Darren could do that morning, sitting across from Keith in the West End Arcade, not to tell him to fuck off out of his life and have done with it. Keith, fussing around with the ketchup bottle, jinking little dollops of it over the inside of his sausage cob, forever trying to talk him out of it. Too risky. Too close to the last time. Too likely to end up getting caught. That was what Keith was pissing his pants about, getting sent back inside. Knowing they'd be after his arse the moment his feet hit the floor. Miserable little bastard, days like this, Darren was forced to think it served him right. Days like this he thought he should have let Keith go ahead and hang himself, no great loss to the world.

Finally, Darren had had enough. "Listen," he'd said, grabbing Keith by the front of his jumper, "half-two, top of King Street, you be there."

"With a motor?"

"No, what d'you think, going to give me a piggy-back, all the way to Bestwood?"

"Where you going now?" Keith had asked, almost plaintively, watching Darren heading for the exit.

"Never you mind, I've got things to do. Just do your side, right? And this time, don't be late."

One of the things Darren had to do, collect a few supplies. The assistant had been too preoccupied in trying out some new computer game to pay him much attention. Little green men who either changed into trees or else were eaten by dragons, zapped by spears.

"Hey, mate!" Darren had finally called. "You work here or what?"

The name on his tag read Robert, pinned to the front of his navy-blue long-sleeved sweater. From the look on his face, Darren was more of a nuisance than anything else.

"You remember hearing about that robbery?" Darren asked, casual as you like, choosing to ignore the salesman's indifference. "Where they all wore those Mickey Mouse masks, like, sort of disguise?"

"Oh," the assistant said, already bored, "happens all the time."

"Yeh? Well, you got any like that? Here?"

"Life-size masks?"

"Yes."

Stifling a yawn, Robert wandered off, to come back some minutes later with a selection that ranged from an over-jolly Friar Tuck to Cruella De Vill. "This the sort of thing?"

Darren slipped Catwoman over his close-cropped hair and adjusted it so that he could focus through the slotted eyes.

"How about guns?" Darren asked, having to shout through the mask to make himself heard.

"What kind?"

"Pistols. Something that looks pretty life-like."

Robert brought him a black plastic Colt .45 and a metallic grey snub-nosed .38 with NYPD in relief on the butt.

"Okay," said Darren, taking hold of the Colt and pointing it at him. "Empty the till into one of these bags."

"What is this? Some kind of joke? You know as well as I do that's just a toy gun."

Darren reversed it and slashed him hard across the face, cracking the plastic and tearing the skin alongside the eye. In seconds he was reaching over the till, loosening the cash drawer, grabbing bank notes, fives and twenties and tens, from beneath the roller clips that held them down.

The assistant called out and made a grab for Darren's leg. Swivelling on the ball of one foot, Darren kicked him in the throat. "Like you say, Robert," Darren said, voice muffled through his Catwoman mask, "this kind of thing happens all the time."

When he ran past the baked-potato salesman, the newspaper seller advertising *Viz,* the old boy playing "K-K-K-Katie" on his harmonica, back up the steps that took him towards the Playhouse and the old General Hospital, nobody as much as looked twice.

"Where the hell d'you get this?" Darren asked, throwing himself into the front seat.

"Broad Marsh, why?"

"If you wanted to advertise, wonder you didn't hijack one of them buses with slogans all over the sides."

"It's a DS," Keith said, striving for the proper respect. "Collector's item. Give an arm and a leg for one of these."

Darren gave him a quick flash of the Colt .45. "Let's hope it don't come to that." He grinned.

The building society office was close to a cinema whose final programme had been a double bill of Jerry Lewis in *The Bellboy* and Elvis Presley as a half-breed American Indian in *Flaming Star.* Since then it had been a cut-price furniture store, a Quik-Save supermarket and a Fast-Fit tyre centre. Now it was standing empty, boarded up. Keith swung the Citroën smoothly onto the forecourt, applied the hand brake and left the engine running. So quiet, it was like listening to a CD between the tracks.

"Don't go anywhere," Darren said.

"Sure you don't want me to come with you?" Keith asked, hoping the answer would be no. He was enjoying this less and less.

"After last time?" Darren laughed. He had the mask stuffed inside his zipped-up jacket, the broken handle of the toy gun poking out of his trouser belt. "Second you see me come back out that door, that's when you move. Right?"

Nervously, Keith nodded.

There were two people queuing inside the building society, a man in plasterer's overalls and a woman with a shopping trolley, waiting in front of a video monitor that was entertaining them with a tape loop testifying to the virtues of borrowing to your credit limit. Own a yacht. A time-share in the Scottish Highlands.

At the counter an Afro-Caribbean woman was checking that her wages had been credited to her account that month. Darren waited until she moved away and slipped into her place, circumventing the queue.

"Hey up!" said the plasterer. "Think we've stood here for us health?"

"There is a queue, sir," said the clerk. It was only when she looked up properly she realised the person who had pushed to the front was wearing some kind of mask.

"All the cash you've got," Darren said. "Hand it over."

"What?" the clerk said, looking perplexed. Through the mask, she hadn't clearly heard what Darren had said.

"Here!" The plasterer made a move forwards and Darren pulled the pistol from his belt and waved it in the man's face.

"Oh, dear God!" the woman with the shopping trolley exclaimed and wavered sideways, colliding with the television set and knocking it from its stand onto the floor.

"Eunice," Darren said, reading her name from the badge attached to the apricot uniform blouse, "don't bother counting it, just push it through here. The lot."

Another employee came through from the back, wondering what all the commotion was about. A quick look and he ducked back from sight.

"That's not a real gun," the plasterer exclaimed. "It's only a chuffing toy!"

"Eunice," Darren said, seizing the last bundle of fifties

and stuffing them into his pocket, "anyone ever told you you're a darling?"

Later on, giving her account to the reporter from "East Midlands Today," Eunice had to giggle; the last time she'd been called darling had been by a mechanical parrot at Goose Fair. Made her jump half out of her skin it had. "D'you know," she confided in the camera, "gave me more of a turn than what happened this afternoon."

Keith saw Darren dart through the door and eased his foot onto the accelerator. "What on earth you wearing that for?" he asked as Darren sat there, chuckling to himself beneath the mask.

"Video cameras," Darren said.

"What?"

Darren pulled the mask over his head and pushed it under the seat. "Video cameras. On the ceiling. Got them in that branch, haven't they?" He laughed. "What d'you reckon, I want to see myself like a fool, face plastered all over every TV in the country, next edition of 'Crime-watch'?"

Sweating more than a little, Keith bit gently into the inside of his lower lip as he tested the engine's acceleration along a clear stretch of the ring road.

"Know what?" Darren said happily, counting the notes into his lap. "Lot more here'n I bargained for." Reaching across, he gave Keith's leg an enthusiastic squeeze. "Our luck holds, soon be able to buy yourself one of these."

41

Jeans? Debbie used to say how much she liked him in jeans; about the only time you don't look like a policeman. Trouble was, he never really felt comfortable in them. Not the pair he was wearing now, Levi Silver Tabs he'd bought eighteen months back at Bankrupt Clothing Company, nor the ones he'd got in the Gap sale. Simply, they didn't feel right. Like going out on an undercover and being spotted within the first few minutes. He pulled them off and draped them over the back of the chair. Where were those beige jobs he'd worn to the last police smoker? Those and that dark jacket, the blazer, at least he felt smart in that without being dressed up like a dog's dinner. All that was left now was the tie, yes or no, finally deciding no, much too formal, definitely not, then slipping it into his side pocket in case he felt like changing his mind.

Any minute now the taxi would be here.

Watch, credit card, cash, keys.

Kevin hesitated by the bathroom door; the aftershave with a tang of lime—was that the one brought Debbie out in a rash or not?

Divine had stopped off at W. H. Smith no more than ten minutes before closing. "These tapes," he'd asked, pointing towards a boxed set of *French in Five Easy Stages,* "they any good?"

The assistant thought Divine looked more the type for Club Med, somewhere with a beach and sun enough to show off a good body. "We do sell a lot," she said hopefully.

"Yes, but do they work?"

She giggled lightly. Not bad, Divine thought, take away the crossed front teeth and surplus facial hair, fair pair of tits though, wouldn't mind giving it a pull.

"See, I'm off to Paris. Pretty soon. Business."

"Oh. Well, there is this one here, two double-length cassettes or one CD and accompanying booklet. See? 'Eurospeak Languages for Today's Businessman.' That might be more the kind of thing."

"Thing I'm looking for," Divine confided, leaning a well-muscled arm on the top of her counter, "something more personal. You know, relaxing after hours. Hard day's graft. Can't enjoy the nightlife, no point in going. Stay here and get legless at the Black Orchid, eh?"

"Miss Armitage," the supervisor sang out like frost in summer, "let's see you cashing up now."

"What d'you reckon, then?" The picture on the box showed a girl with a long blond ponytail and a black beret pointing excitedly up at the Eiffel Tower. "Biggest one she's ever seen."

Maybe he wasn't cut out for Club Med after all, the assistant thought. Works outing to Skegness, more his kind of thing. "I'm sorry," she said, "but we are closing now."

Divine settled for a pocket phrase book and a paperback visitor's guide to Paris, thumbing through the latter as he stepped out on the pedestrian precinct, stopping short at the picture of a girl in a scarlet G-string from the Crazy Horse Saloon. A mother with a pushchair ran into the back of him and most of the child's Mr. Whippy ice cream slid down his leg.

"What the chuffin' heck d'you think you're doing?" Divine bellowed.

"It's you, you great lummox!" the woman shouted back. "Parking your great backside right in front of us without a by-your-leave. What've you got in that head of yours for brains, sawdust or what?"

And she swung the pushchair and wailing child around him, leaving Divine to wipe away the ice cream that was still slithering down his second-best pair of trousers.

Naylor stood close by the plate-glass front of the upstairs, looking out at the groups who were beginning to swarm the square. Down the hill from the Concert Hall and the Theatre Royal, along St. James Street and past the Bell opposite; from the right past the cinemas, the Odeon and Cannon, spreading the length of the old Market Square itself, past the fountains and the lions to the underground lavatories and the mobile stall selling hot pork rolls and beefburgers with glistening onions. Pushing and shoving and laughing. Bouncers in dinner suits at the entrance to every pub. The police dog van alongside the bus stop. Listening to the plods in the canteen, it got worse week by week, month by month, but Naylor remembered Resnick saying that when he'd been out there in uniform twenty years ago, there'd been trouble Friday, Saturday nights just the same.

He wondered about finishing his half and going back into the bar to fetch another, maybe get one for Debbie too, save queuing later when she turned up. If she turned up. He was rehearsing her excuses in his head—my mother, the baby—when he saw her alighting from a double-decker over on Beast Market Hill. Dark blue skirt or dress, silvery top, thin blue jacket, leather bag slung over one arm. Forehead pressed against the inside of the glass, he waited for her to look up and, stepping off the crossing onto the broad curve of pavement below, and smiling with surprise at her own pleasure, that was what she did.

Keith knew chances were if he simply dumped the Citroën, abandoned it, it would get trashed before it was found. Normally that was part of the point, only this was not a normal car. Gliding along the A52 on his way back into the city, engine close to silent, suspension like feathers, Keith thought he'd died and gone to heaven.

He knew it was a risk, but for the first time ever, he was determined to return the motor to the exact spot where he'd found it.

Our luck holds, Darren had said, you'll be able to buy one of your own. Keith chewed at a hangnail on the little finger of his right hand. Mixture of his luck and Darren's stupidity and he could see himself ending up back in court. Back in prison. Just thinking about it was enough to turn his bowels to water. Never in his miserable life had he been as serious as when he'd tried to top himself in that cell. And Darren, hollering for help, unfastening the sheet and lifting him down. What for? So that he'd have someone to boss around the rest of his life? Someone to look up to him, run errands, steal cars, drive him from one increasingly risky robbery to another.

Hear him running off at the mouth before Keith had dropped him off. About how he was going to trade up from that pathetic toy pistol to a real one; how he was going to walk in on that Lorna Solomon and show it to her, see the look on her face, do the thing right.

Keith had felt grateful to him for saving his life, in a way at least: each day now he was less and less sure. Turning with the traffic in front of the big MGM nightclub, Keith indicated that he was moving across into the inside lane, looking to park.

"Where are we going?" Debbie asked as Kevin Naylor took her arm and steered her around a group of young white males in short-sleeved white shirts.

"You'll see." He grinned. "Surprise."

The restaurant was quite dimly lit, tasteful, round tables with a single flower in a white vase at its centre; the menus were padded and thick and pages long.

"What d'you think?" Kevin said, looking round. He'd asked Graham Millington, who went out for a meal with his wife first Friday after payday, regular as clockwork, Lynn Kellogg too. The consensus seemed to be, of all the Chinese restaurants in the city, this was probably the best.

"It's nice," Debbie admitted. "Only . . ."

"Only what?"

Only you know I'm not all that keen on Chinese food was what she'd been going to say, but instead she shook her head and gave him a quick smile and said, "Oh, nothing."

He had looked nice standing up there in Yates's, waiting for her, really nice, and although talking at first had been a bit of a strain, now they were both beginning to feel more relaxed.

"You watch out for him," her mum had said, "got to be after something, you mark my words." Then she'd got that look on her face, the one she'd paraded when Debbie had first told her she was moving back home, smug and prophetic. "I wouldn't mind betting he's found himself somebody else, that's what this is all about. Wanting to talk you into one of those do-it-yourself divorces. You see if he isn't."

If that were the case, Debbie thought, he'd hardly be

sitting there, wedding ring shining from the back of his hand. Without warning, she thought she might be about to cry, so she picked up her bag and excused herself, went to the Ladies, leaving Kevin to order.

Keith phoned his mum and his stepfather answered, so he hung up; his dad was still hauling bundles of old papers and magazines up from the cellar, sorting through and arranging them in piles all over the front-room floor.

Keith made himself baked beans on toast and ate it watching TV. If there was a tape player in the first-floor room he'd taken over as his own, he would have gone up there and listened to some Luther Ingram or some David Peaston, Galliano or Dream Warriors, except that he didn't have the tapes either, they were still back at his mum's. Truth was he didn't know what on earth he did want to do.

When his dad stuck his head round the door and asked if he fancied lending him a hand, Keith shrugged and said, "Why not?"

It turned out to be simple enough. Check through the pages to make sure they were all there, nothing torn out or otherwise missing; if it was all okay, write down the date and issue number.

"What's all this in aid of?" Keith asked.

"Making a few bob."

"For this old crap?"

When his dad explained it to him, Keith was really surprised. Though he knew youths who'd lash out just about everything they had on some comic or other; ten pounds for one in Japanese and then you couldn't read the words. No accounting for some people's taste.

"Fancy a beer?" Rylands asked after they'd been working half an hour or so.

"I thought you'd given it up?"

"Doesn't mean you've got to. I'm having tea myself."

"Tea's fine."

While they were drinking it, Rylands sounded Keith out on his idea of hiring a stall in the market, Fridays and Saturdays at first, selling back numbers of the *NME* and stuff like that, jazz magazines—kids were supposed to be interested in jazz, weren't they?—maybe other things. He'd wandered into one of the secondhand bookshops on the Mansfield road and come across a couple of hundred mixed film magazines, copies of *Picture Post* as well, made an offer for the lot. Bloke was holding them for him till the Monday. Him and Keith trawled round a few car boot sales and the like, they'd soon pick up more stock.

"So," Rylands said, sitting cross-legged, leaning back against the wall. "What d'you think? Reckon it'd work?"

"Might."

"You're interested, then?"

"Me?"

"Why not? What else you got to do?"

Keith shrugged and made a face.

"Thought, you know, we could run it together."

"I'd lose my dole."

"Not necessarily. Depends how we work it. And anyway, what d'you want, be on the dole the rest of your life?"

"No."

"Well, then. Why not give it a try?"

Keith shook his head. "I don't know."

Rylands finished his tea and pushed himself to his feet. "Best got on. Plenty of time for you to think about it. Might be a bit of fun, though. Laugh if nothing else."

"What about Darren?" Keith asked, staring at the front page of a *Melody Maker* from 1959: *Emile Ford and the Checkmates to Headline Moss Empires Tour.*

"What about Darren?"

"He'll expect me to be with him."

"Don't you worry about Darren," Rylands said, bending to take Keith's empty cup from his hands. "I've got ideas how to deal with him."

"It tasted different somehow," Debbie said.

They were standing inside the hallway of the starter home she and Kevin had first moved into, the one where he still lived.

"Least come in and have some coffee," Kevin had said as the taxi that was meant to be dropping him off drew close. "You can always get another cab in a bit."

They'd got inside the front door and not much further; hadn't as much as switched on the hall light.

"What tastes different?" Kevin said, kissing her again.

When they moved their mouths apart minutes later, she could sense him grinning at her in the dark. "Not this," she said.

"What, then?"

"The meal. Chinese meal. Find it so salty as a rule."

"Ah," Kevin said, grin widening, "that's because I asked them to hold back the monosodium glutamate, I expect."

"I didn't know you could do that."

"Oh, yes. Just a matter of knowing what to ask."

She laughed and reached inside his jacket, tickling him, and they ended up on the floor.

"Kevin, no." Though there was something specially exciting, Debbie thought, about being there, so close to the front door.

"No, we can't." The only place she and Kevin had ever made love was in bed, their own or a bed and breakfast.

"Kevin!"

His hand was high on her tights, ball of his thumb starting to apply pressure . . .

"No!"

"What?"

She smoothed down her skirt and drew her knees towards her chest.

"We are still married, you know."

"I know."

"So?"

"Kevin, switch on the light."

"You're angry, aren't you?"

"No. No, I'm not." She reached for his hand and held it. "Really, I'm not."

"What is it, then?"

Even though it was dark and she could see little more than the outline of his face, Debbie looked away. "I'm not on the Pill anymore. There didn't seem to be any point."

"So?"

"I don't suppose you've got anything with you. Any, you know, protection."

"There's a twenty-four-hour garage not far. They're bound to sell them. I could nip and—"

"Kevin, no. Maybe it's not such a good idea this time anyway." He sighed and she gave his hand a squeeze. "I'm not rejecting you, you know."

"No? Well, that's what it feels like."

Debbie laughed and deftly moved her other hand. "No, Kevin, *that's* what it feels like."

He laughed, surprised, and reached for her again, but she was quickly to her feet and they were both blinking in the sudden light. "What about that coffee?" she said. "While you're getting the kettle on, I'll order a taxi."

"You could stay."

"I know. I will. One step at a time, hmm?"

Kevin grinned and kissed her on her forehead and alongside her ear and, quickly, at the corner of her mouth and, still grinning, walked off into the kitchen.

42

"The hostel we spoke about," Pam Van Allen said, "it's all fixed up."

She waited for Prior to respond but, of course, that wasn't necessarily what he did. Most people, ordinary people, the kind you bump into at parties, supermarkets, dentists' waiting rooms, make a remark like that and they react. "Oh, really?" Or "That's good." A grunt even. Something that helps the conversation along.

Whereas Prior . . .

It was enough for him today to continue to stare at her, not threatening exactly, nothing sexual the way it would be with a lot of men, locked away without the benefits of conjugal visits. Prior simply stared. And waited. Okay, you're here, doing what you're paid to do, now say what you have to say.

Pam crossed one leg over the other, automatically smoothing her skirt past her knee. "Big, old Victorian house over by Alexandra Park. Really nice." She paused. "I don't know whether you know it round there?"

This time there was a grunt of kinds, not expressive

enough for Pam to tell if it meant yes or no. Perhaps he'd simply been clearing his throat.

"Anyway, like I say, it is very nice. Kept up better than a number of hostels we use, I'd have to say that." She saw his eyes shift focus towards her hands and realised that she'd been fidgetting with the silver ring she wore on the little finger of her right hand. "You will be sharing, a room I mean. Did I mention that before?"

Prior shook his head.

"Sorry, thought I had. Two of you most likely. It's the only thing about the rooms being so big. All the usual regulations, pretty much what you'd expect. No alcohol, no drugs. Restrictions about visitors, too. Up into the bedrooms, that is." What was the matter with her? Why was she chattering on? She uncrossed her legs and eased back in the chair; held, for several seconds, her breath and returned his stare.

"As soon as you're released, we'll help you to look for work and accommodation, like I've said. Things like making sure you're on the housing list. Those flats above the Victoria Centre, they fall vacant pretty often. And then there are always the housing associations. They'll look sympathetically on your application as a matter of principle."

The air inside the room seemed to be getting thinner and thinner. Pam wanted to dart a glance towards her watch, but didn't like to try. She seemed to have been talking for ages now, a barely assisted monologue. Prior listening, not caring; as if none of this had anything to do with him. As if she were making plans for somebody else.

"Your wife . . ." The words were out before she could stop them.

"Ruth," Prior said.

"Yes."

"What about her?"

"I was just, I suppose, wondering, well, if you'd thought any more about maybe trying to get in touch with her."

"Should I?"

Pam gestured vaguely with both hands. "I don't know. I mean, no. I don't think there's any should about it. It's not a case, I mean, of obligation."

Now he was staring again, feeling the pressure she had put herself under, enjoying it.

"Sometimes," Pam said carefully, finding her way, "especially when couples haven't seen one another for a long time, there's a sense of—what shall I say?—unfinished business. Things that have gone unsaid for too long. A lot of stuff that has to be cleared away before people can get on with their lives."

"People?"

"Yes."

"Ruthie and me."

"Yes. I mean, I suppose . . . I just thought . . ."

"No," Prior said. "I don't think so. Like I said, that was all a long time ago."

Pam got to her feet; she was feeling shaky but she would have found it hard to have said exactly why.

"Besides," Prior said, "I don't even know where she is."

"I'll see you again," Pam said, "on the day of your release. After that, it will need to be weekly. You can make an appointment to come to the office, regular, that will be best."

Prior nodded agreement and got to his feet, once again offering her his hand, cool and callused and dry.

Resnick was at home when the call came. One thing and another he'd earned himself an hour or two off. For some time he'd employed a woman from up the road to come in one afternoon a week and keep the place clean, hoover and dust. Until Dizzy had nipped her ankle for the third week in succession, it had worked out fine. Now there he was, lugging the old-fashioned Hoover up and down stairs, halfheartedly rubbing lavender furniture polish into the table in the dining room, working a balding squeezy mop over the kitchen floor.

Cat hairs everywhere.

He made it more palatable by playing music loud enough to be heard throughout the house. Eddie "Lockjaw" Davis was rabble-rousing in front of the Basie Band when the phone started ringing, and he didn't hear it until the first solo was over and the sound had diminished down to the sparse notes of the Count's piano.

He almost tripped over a distressed Bud, who'd been catnapping on the landing, one paw folded over his eyes. Still mumbling apologies, Resnick lifted the receiver just in time.

"Said at the station you were there," Rylands said. "Thought they must've got it wrong."

"Hang on a minute," Resnick said. "Let me turn this record down."

"Atomic Mister Basie," Rylands said when Resnick arrived back at the phone. "Great record. I remember the first time—"

"What do you want?" Resnick asked.

"That arrangement we spoke of . . ." Rylands's voice was lower now, as though there were someone in the house he didn't want to overhear.

"What about it?"

"I think he'd be willing to talk, to that young woman, like we said."

"Good. And the other matter?"

A slight pause and then, "I'm not sure now, can't be positive, but, yes, I reckon I know where she might be."

Lynn had picked Keith up several blocks away, close to the Portland Leisure Centre, where she sometimes went for a morning swim, days it opened at seven-thirty, do your lengths in freedom before the first of the school parties arrived. She'd driven round onto the embankment and parked, Keith's response when she suggested walking little more than an inclination of the head. In the end, she had got out of the car and he had followed, the same as he had when she'd set off towards Wilford Bridge.

Now and again teams of rowers went past them, water splashing up in their wake, voices of the coxs clear and sharp as they urged them on. Asian families sat on the sloping grass, women together in brightly coloured saris, children playing in their midst; the men sat off to the side, dealing cards onto a rug.

She was surprised how small he was, how young his face: it was like walking with a shame-faced younger brother, a recalcitrant nephew. A son. A child, certainly. And yet she had seen his record, knew the time he had spent in YOIs. She had read the report of his attempted suicide. *A feeble and misguided cry for help.*

"What's it like," Lynn asked, "living with your dad?"

"'S'all right."

"Better than living with your mum?"

"S'pose so."

"When I was still living at home," Lynn said, "my mum, she always meant well, but she was forever fussing at me, why don't you do this, why don't you do that?" Lynn laughed, taking Keith by surprise. "There I was, twenty years old, standing in her kitchen, taller than her by half a head, and she's still wetting the corner of her handkerchief with her tongue and aiming to wipe away this bit of dirt I've got on my face. Got so I couldn't stand it at all."

"Yes," Keith said. "I know what you mean."

"Listen," Lynn said, stopping to look back the way they'd come, "why don't we walk back there to the Memorial Gardens and sit down. Not too many people as a rule. Might be easier to talk."

Except that the whole place was under the thrall of a mono-lithic tribute to Queen Victoria, it was a public garden like many another: beds of flowers carefully tended by council workmen, assorted trees and banks of shrubs, patches of lawn interrupted by gravel paths.

"You realise," Lynn said, "nothing that I've said's an absolute promise?"

"I'll not go back inside," Keith said. "I'll kill myself first."

She laid her hand on the bare skin of his forearm and he flinched.

"Like I said, we'll do what we can. I'll do everything I can. I promise you that." She waited until, for a second, his eyes flickered towards her face. "As long as you keep your side of the bargain."

"I've told you . . ."

"I know. But I have to be sure."

Without difficulty, Keith conjured up Darren's face. That look in his eyes, that blue-grey brightness becoming brighter still as he toyed with the pistol in his hand. Next time, Keith knew, it was going to be real.

"It's okay," Keith said quietly, staring at the ground. "Long as you play straight with me, you'll get what you want. No mistake."

43

He and Elaine had taken holidays here, Northumberland, a succession of rented cottages close to the coast—north from Amble and Alnmouth Bay, through Seahouses and Bamburgh to Berwick-upon-Tweed. The first had been the worst. The flat itself, upper floor of a small-holder's cottage, had been right enough; where it had fallen down was the panoramic view. An undisturbed vision of caravans at the rear; to the front, cabbage fields as far as the eye could follow. Somewhere beyond those acres of darkening green lay soft dunes and broad beaches, the slow roll of the North Sea.

"Take it on trust," the owner had said. "Me and the missus have for years. In't we, pet?"

Resnick and Elaine had returned to other locations. The sands were largely deserted, topped breathtakingly by castles, impressive in their decay. They had taken a boat out to the Farne Islands to see the puffins and sea birds; had walked the causeway over to Holy Island and had to run full into the wind on the way back so as not to be trapped by the tide.

They had made love in hired beds, often spurred on by a visit to the local pub, a meal eaten in unspoken anticipation. In part, it was what holidays were for.

It was difficult for Resnick, as he turned east off the main road and headed towards the coast, to recall these things with pleasure.

The road narrowed and soon he was facing a T-junction with no sign to suggest which way to turn. Stopping to use the map, nevertheless he made the wrong choice and got lost twice more before he found himself driving down the gentle hill with the sea to his left, into the village where Ruth now lived.

Fishermen's cottages had been built around a green, making three sides of a square; a low wall dividing land from the beach made the fourth. The buildings were uniform, painted white. He guessed that for the most part now they functioned as holiday accommodations, folk who wanted a week or two away from it all. At the rear end of the square there was a small pub, across from that a shop that seemed to be long closed. There were cars parked outside some of the cottages, but not most. It was far enough into the day for lights to be showing faintly at some of the windows. Smoke trailed upwards from several chimneys. Resnick locked the car and stretched his legs and back: it had been a long enough drive.

For a few moments he stood near the wicker lobster pots stacked high to one end of the seawall. South, it was just possible to see Dunstanborough Castle outlined against a darkly reddening sky.

Ruth's cottage was at the northern corner, the first passed entering the village. There were neither lights nor smoke. Resnick began to walk towards it. No answer when he rattled at the letter box, knocked on the door. He would ask in the pub.

———

Ruth was sitting in the far corner of the bar, her feet resting on another chair and a book open against the table. There was a glass by her right arm, a half of bitter it looked like, three-quarters down; a cigarette burned in an ashtray to her left. She scarcely looked up as Resnick came in.

The dog, a large pale retriever that lay curled beneath the table, raised his head and kept Resnick in his sights. When he walked towards the table, a glass of Worthington White Shield in his hand, the dog growled.

As soon as Ruth reached down and touched the dog gently between the ears, he stopped.

"Mind if I join you?" Resnick said.

"What happens if I say yes?"

Her face had become leaner still, sucked in at the cheeks; the flesh around the eyes seemed somehow to have peeled back. There was barely a trace of red in her hair now; what there were, here and there, were white hairs, startlingly strong and thick.

Resnick pulled round a chair and sat down.

Ruth continued to read. Charles Dickens. *Hard Times.* "Decided a bit late in life to get myself an education."

Resnick took a long swallow at his beer and waited till she'd reached the end of her chapter. A torn beer mat marked her place.

"You showing up here like this," Ruth said. "No accident."

"He's getting parole. Matter of days. I didn't know if you'd heard."

Ruth took a drag from her cigarette, finished her beer and held the empty glass for a moment in the air. The barman fetched her over a fresh one, took the old away.

"Not so many customers this time of year," Ruth said. "Get treated like royalty." She laughed low in her throat. "Not ours, someone else's. No," she said after taking a drink, "I didn't know."

"Does he know where you are?"

Ruth shrugged. "What difference? You found me, didn't you? And don't tell me it's your job. He's got ways of pressurising people most of your lot only dream about."

"You could move on," Resnick said.

"Run?"

"You came here."

"That was a fair time back. I like it here. Most people, one week, two, they're in and out, gone. No one knows who I am, what I was, what I was married to. Those as know bits and pieces, none of their business, they don't care."

"He said a lot of nasty things, at the trial."

"He was always saying nasty things. Doing 'em, too. He can't scare me. Not anymore. And even if he could, I've stopped running." She swung her feet to the floor and the dog shifted position. "He tried anything now," she said, stroking the animal's fur, "this one'd let him know what for. Wouldn't you, darlin'?"

The dog twisted his head to lick her hand.

"He threatened to get even."

"What for? Ten years? He thinks that was down to me? That was never down to me. You had evidence, witnesses— that sorry bastard Churchill turning grass. Christ, you had him cold with a gun in his bloody hands. What did it need me for?"

Resnick didn't answer; the truth was, in detail, he didn't know. How much Rains had wheedled out of the bitter wife, how much from other sources?

"You must take it serious, driving all the way up here."

Resnick nodded. "I do."

Ruth laughed again, breaking off midway into a racking cough. "What you going to do," she said once she'd controlled herself again, "stick around? Be my personal bodyguard?"

"No. Just wanted you to know, that's all."

She nodded towards his glass. "Now you'll want to be getting back. Duty tomorrow, most likely."

Resnick took a quick drink before pushing the glass aside. "Always sediment at the bottom; no matter how carefully you pour it."

"Yeh," Ruth said. "Bit like life, eh?" She laughed. "Christ, hark at me. Not through one Dickens and I'm talking in symbols."

Resnick got to his feet and once more the dog growled, low in his throat. "One thing," he said.

"Do I still sing?"

"When did you last see Rains?"

What colour she had drained from her face. "Not since he dumped me. Best part of ten years. Best part's been not seeing his lying face."

Resnick placed a card with his name and number on the cover of her book. "Any reason. Any time. The station can always raise me."

Ruth looked up at him with a raised eyebrow. "Regular Lazarus, eh? Something in the air, all these blokes coming back from the dead."

By the time Resnick had reached the door, she had her feet up and was back reading. A few more of the windows were showing lights and a wind had got up from the northeast. He turned his collar up as he crossed the green towards his car. He would stop at the first place on the main road and get coffee; traffic should be relatively light and it shouldn't be too long before he was home. Though to the cats who were waiting to be fed, it would seem an age.

The headlights of Resnick's car raked across the whitewash of the cottages as he swung round, but failed to pick out the figure standing deep in the shadows beside the seawall, biding his own time.

44

Millington had been so chipper that morning, the idea had flirted across his wife's mind that he might be having an affair. It was partly the sparkle in his eye, partly the appetite with which he'd wolfed down his muesli and dried fruit without as much as a pulled face or an offhand reference to the tastelessness of skimmed milk. He had rinsed his bowl, brought her a second cup of tea without being asked, brushed her cheek with a kiss that was forceful enough to make clear he'd trimmed his moustache that morning.

When she wandered out into the hall, he was brushing the shoulders of his jacket on its hanger and whistling what sounded suspiciously like "Love Is a Many-Splendoured Thing."

"See that James Last's on at Concert Hall again this summer," Millington said. "Maybe I should get us a couple of tickets?"

"After last time, Graham, I should hardly thought you'd have wanted to go again."

Last time, the woman behind had tapped Millington's wife on the shoulder and asked her in quite a loud voice if there wasn't something she could do about her husband's snoring.

"Oh, aye, restful, though, weren't it?" He slipped on his coat and headed for the front door. "Possible, bit on the late side tonight. Pint or three after work. Business, like."

"Yes, Graham," she said, "whatever you say."

Blimey, Millington thought, getting into the car, what's eating her? Face like one of them frozen dinners before it sees the inside of the microwave.

He was in the CID room, close to the door of Resnick's office before his superior arrived, loitering with intent.

"All right, Kevin"—ten minutes later Resnick's voice audible from the stairs—"first things first. Let's take a look at last night's files."

"Sir."

"Morning, Graham. Bright and early."

Naylor had been in since before seven, the early shift, one of his tasks to organise all messages received during the night into national or local, another to ensure the log showing the movement of prisoners was up to date. He carried these files over towards Resnick's office now and Millington held out his hand.

"I'll take those in, lad. You could do worse than set tea to mash. Okay?"

Naylor shrugged and did as he was told.

Millington placed the files on Resnick's desk, then closed the door by leaning his back against it.

"On to something, Graham?" Resnick asked with a grin. His sergeant could hang on to a secret about as long as a small boy could harbour a fifty-pence piece.

"This chap I've been meeting for the odd pint down in Sneinton. Strictly small time, like I've said, but knows a few of the bigger boys. Or likes to let on as he does."

"Which is it?" Resnick asked. Up to the present he'd

found it hard to take either Millington's low-grade grass or Mark Divine's high-flown theories about Eurovillains too seriously.

"Got a bit cheesed off last night, he were standing there scoring drinks out of me left, right and centre, and what he'd offered, so much hot air. I told him, come up with something new, something we can use, or he could find someone else to do his drinking with."

"And?" Resnick prompted. Sitting behind his desk and watching Millington's face, he could taste the anticipation.

"Rains," Millington said, unable to prevent himself from smiling.

"He put up his name?"

"Along of one or two others."

"No doubt about it?"

By now Millington's face was positively beatific. "D.C. Rains, late of this parish."

"D.C. no longer."

"A long way from it, so it seems."

Initial elation over, Resnick's mind was racing. "I thought he was abroad?"

"So he was. Still is, by all accounts. Northern Spain, well away from your hoi polloi. According to my friend, he isn't above flying over to take care of a little business."

"What business is he in these days, our ex-colleague?"

Millington was enjoying this enormously. "Much the same as before, apparently, only from, what would you say, a different perspective."

Resnick was on his feet. "Do we know this is anything more than malicious gossip? After all, easy to spread stories about someone a thousand or so miles away."

"What made it gel for me," Millington said, "remember that blagger was mixed up with Prior? More than a passing interest in armed robbery himself, though he played that down at the trial. Did his best to set it all at Prior's doorstep, planning, shotgun, the lot."

"Churchill?" Resnick said.

"Frank Churchill."

"He's in this as well?"

"According to what I was told last night, him and Rains've stayed in touch more or less ever since."

Darren had wasted half the day looking for Keith. First off, he'd waited for him at the usual café, but Keith never showed; the best part of an hour hanging around the square, wandering in and out of various amusement arcades. When finally he'd rung his old man to find out what the hell Keith was playing at, Rylands had told him he had no idea where Keith was, he had left the house about half-nine or ten, never saying a word.

Well, okay. He'd get this done on his own.

The shop was up Carlton Hill, one of those places piled floor to ceiling with stuff people have no further use for—toasters, radios, steam irons, manual typewriters, video recorders that would neither record nor play. The pavement outside boasted refrigerators and electric fires, cookers with rust-encrusted rings, a wheelchair that was chained to the wall to prevent the local kids from commandeering it for joyrides down the hill.

The owner was a sixty-eight-year-old woman called Rose, whose sister had scarcely been out of the wheelchair the last four years of her life. She viewed Darren with a proper suspicion, uncertain if he was going to try to sell her something stolen or order her to empty the till.

Darren picked up an antique Teasmade and gave it an exploratory shake. The matron at the home had boasted of owning one of those, though he'd never seen it. There'd been other lads, older and bolder, who claimed they had.

"You want to buy that?" Rose asked.

"What I want to buy," said Darren, "is a shooter."

"How's that?"

"You know. A gun?"

The woman opened her arms and pointed around. "Find one amongst that lot, duck, sell it you with pleasure."

Darren reached into his trouser pocket and pulled out a thick pile of twenties and tens. "What I was told, anyone wanted something like that, you could arrange it. What's it called? On commission."

Rose pushed her hands down into her apron and sucked her top plate back against the roof of her mouth. "I'll have to make one or two calls. You come back here in an hour or two."

Resnick and Millington were in Skelton's office. The elements had decided to turn the screw a little and after an oddly humid, muggy morning, rain was now rattling the windowpanes.

"What degree of involvement are we talking about here?" Skelton asked. He was standing with his back to the weather, the industrial landscape beyond his shoulders disappearing into mist. "How actively involved are we saying Rains might be? Is he planning these robberies? Difficult if he's spending more time out of the country than in. Are we meant to assume he's actually taking part? What?"

Resnick looked over at Graham Millington.

"Er, afraid he's not too clear as yet . . ."

"Your informant?"

"Yes, sir. So far he's not gone into a lot of detail."

"You think he might?"

Millington took his time in answering. "It's possible, sir."

"So, presumably, is the supposition that since you were pushing him hard for a name, he pulled one out of the hat? One he knew it would be difficult for us to check."

Millington fidgetted on his chair. "Yes, sir. It could be, only . . ."

"This informant," Skelton said, "you've used him before?"

"Once or twice."

"And the quality of the information?"

Millington shrugged. "Fair to middling, I suppose you'd say."

Skelton resumed his seat. "I'd prefer to say something a lot more positive than that, Graham, if I'm to stand behind this as a new line of enquiry."

What had started out as a cracking day, Millington thought, was losing its sparkle by the minute.

"What happens if we haul him in, this bloke?" Resnick asked. "Lean on him?"

"Might yield something. Then again, might send him back into his shell."

All three men fell silent and there were only the muted footfalls from other parts of the building, the hiccup of telephones and the swirling beat of the rain.

"The original investigation, Charlie"—Skelton was moving paper clips around his desk blotter with the precision of a war room general—"when Prior and Churchill were brought to book, let me see if I'm remembering straight. A lot of the preparation of evidence for the DPP, testimony and the like, Rains was responsible for that."

Resnick nodded. It had been Rains who had come up with the dates and places that had shaken Prior's alibi; Rains who had dramatically produced details of planning meetings that had taken place in Prior's house.

"And his connection with Churchill? Enough to imagine some kind of relationship might have been formed between them then?"

"Rains visited Churchill a number of times in prison, when he was on parole. That was when Churchill agreed to corroborate allegations that were still pretty much up in the air."

"And bought himself a light sentence in return."

Resnick nodded. Six years to Prior's fifteen, released after less than three. Yes, Churchill had good reason to think cooperating with Rains was beneficial. Question was, how far had that benefit become mutual?

Skelton was on his feet again, pacing the room. Resnick responded to Millington's wordless question with a light shrug of the shoulders and a quick sigh.

"You knew him, Charlie. Rains. Worked with him. You were a lot closer to him at the time than either Graham or I. Serious armed robbery—do you see him being involved in that?"

Resnick leaned forward in his chair. "The thing about Rains, one above all others, he was never afraid of pushing hard where others—myself included—would tend to hang back. No matter what else, I always had a grudging sort of respect for that." Resnick sat back. "About the only thing I did have respect for. Find a weakness, use people, dump them—that was Rains."

"So if he's yet to dump Churchill?"

"He's still using him."

"And robbery, heavily armed," Skelton probed, "he'd have no compunction about that?"

"If ever he reckoned the gains worth the risk, I don't think the thing's been invented Rains'd have one pennyworth of compunction about."

The rain drummed and drummed and Skelton rested his head against the upturned fingers of his hand. Millington, sensing the way the wind was turning, allowed himself the beginnings of a smile.

"Okay," Skelton said, hands now flat on his desk, "Graham, lean on this informant of yours just as far as you think you safely can, your own judgement. Meantime, we'll chase Churchill up on the computer, last known addresses, whatever we can. Contact Interpol and the Spanish police and see if they can locate Rains, be nice to know where he is. If he's been travelling here regularly, it's possible he's been using an assumed name, in which case it might be the one he's living under over there. Divine's been checking the flight manifests for this French caper of his; much of the information we want should either be on file or, better still, on disc." He looked from one to the other. "Gentlemen, let's keep this pretty much to ourselves for the time being, but meantime why don't we run with it as far as we can?"

Both Resnick and Millington got to their feet and turned to leave.

"Graham," Skelton said, calling him back. "Good work. Much more of this, we'll run out of excuses to keep you where you are."

Millington was so chuffed, he came close to colliding with the door on the way out.

45

When Darren had arrived back at the shop, Rose told him he would have to wait a couple of days. Darren couldn't believe it. No wonder private enterprise was going to the dogs if you couldn't get hold of a shooter without going through a lot of red tape and standing in line. It was nearly as bad as signing on for the dole.

"No," he said. "No way. Not two days. I want it now."

"Fine," Rose said, "there's somewhere else you can get the same, good luck to you."

But Darren didn't know anywhere else.

"Look," Rose said, lowering her voice to avoid being overheard by a couple who were mulling over the purchase of a gas fire. "Look, don't be a stupid boy. What's so important it has to be done the next couple of days? Eh? Someone's slipping your girlfriend a little something on the side and you want to catch them at it, don't you think he's still going to be at it the day after tomorrow? There's a post office you've got your eye on, a betting shop perhaps, it'll still be there, believe me."

Darren felt like whacking her around the head for suggesting that he was stupid, but she patted him on the arm as if he were a recalcitrant child. "You come by, oh, not too early, eleven, eleven-thirty, I'll have it all arranged. Okay?"

Darren had grunted that it was okay.

"Good boy!" And she patted his trouser pocket with a laugh. "You keep tight hold of it now. Don't go spending it on all the wrong things."

Now Darren was waiting on a patch of disused land close by the canal, across from a disused warehouse from which the letters spelling out BRITISH WATERWAYS were steadily peeling. Pigeons bunched on the sills of broken windows, launching themselves without warning into sudden flurries of flight. Darren tightened his hand around the iron bar beneath his jacket for comfort. Half-ten the meeting had been set for and his watch had passed that nearly fifteen minutes ago.

Not far from his feet the water lapped gently and above his head the moon slipped in and out of cloud. If Rose was setting him up, he'd go back to the shop and turn her face to mush.

Even as he had that thought, he heard the car engine slowing on the road, the crunch of gravel as it turned towards him. A moment later he was caught in the uneven circle of dipped headlights and the car was slurring to a halt.

One man was black, the other white. Lethal weapon's right, Darren thought with a nervous grin. Wearing short jackets and jeans, one with Converse basketball boots, the other tan deck shoes, neither of them looked that much older than he was himself.

"Got the money?" the white bloke asked.

Darren nodded: yes.

"Show."

Darren had a fleeting thought that they were going to mug him and drive off, pitch him into the canal.

"I've got it," Darren said, "you don't have to worry."

"Okay," the young black man said, turning back towards the car, "we wasting our time."

"No." Darren lifted the roll of notes from his pocket and held it for them to see.

The men exchanged looks and made their decision. The boot of the car was unlocked and snapped open. Resting on the spare wheel was a canvas duffle bag and it was this that the black man unfastened and reached inside.

There were two guns in thick polythene, bound at each end with wide brown tape. The tape was prised loose from one end and pulled back, the weapons shaken out onto the bag.

"Pistols, right? That's what you said?"

"Yeh."

"Okay, this one . . ." Lifting it for inspection. "Browning. Like new, hardly been fired. Well good. This—PPK, nothing better. Here, cop a feel."

Darren took first one, then the other weapon into his hand; they felt alien, cold, heavier than he'd expected. He didn't want them to know this was his first time, but there was no way they couldn't tell and their eyes found each other in the dark and shared their amusement at his expense. The white man lit a cigarette and the smoke from it showed light upon the air.

Darren liked the heft of the PPK in the palm of his hand. "How much?"

"Seven hundred."

"You're joking."

The black one held out his hand for the pistol. "Joking," his companion said, "not something we do a lot of."

The PPK was replaced carefully inside its polythene sheath.

"The other one, then," Darren said. "What was it? Browning, yeh. How much for that? That can't be as much, right?"

The pistols were already out of sight.

"What we were told," he said, closing the boot, "you were serious. Must've been a mistake."

"Six hundred," Darren blurted. "I can manage six hundred."

The white man in the deck shoes had the driver's door open. "Six and a half."

"Ammunition. I'm going to need—"

"Half a dozen shells." He was back in front of Darren, holding out his hand. Behind him, the boot door popped up and the duffle bag reappeared.

"You won't regret it," the man said, counting out the notes. "Will he?"

"No," his mate said, shaking six shells loose from a cardboard box. "I doubt it."

"This is it?" Prior said, staring up at the house.

Pam Van Allen nodded. "This is it."

A large building originally, it looked as if extra rooms and sections of roof had been added piecemeal, to accommodate unexpected children or, more likely, a live-in gardener, an under-maid. Ivy clung to the face, thick around the windows and above the polished oak door. At any one time there were a dozen ex-prisoners housed there, occasionally more.

Pam walked with Prior into a high, wide entrance hall with the original patterned tiling still on the floor. The staircase would have allowed four people to ascend it side by side without touching.

"You're lucky, you've got the room at the back. There's a really nice view."

One of the two beds was already occupied, though not at that moment; the covers had been carelessly pulled back and there were clothes bunched on it in small piles, shirts and socks, a pair of jeans.

A transistor radio had been left playing and Pam walked over and switched it off. "See what I mean?" she said, pointing out over a ragged patchwork of allotment gardens and unclaimed land, down towards the centre of the city.

But Prior had already blocked her out. He was sitting on the other bed, hunched forward, rolling himself a cigarette.

Darren had picked up the girl at Madisons. Outside, actually. She had been leaning up against the brick wall opposite the stage door of the Theatre Royal, forehead pressed down against one hand, while with the other she fumbled for a tissue inside her bag. She was wearing a blue dress with a high neck but a deep V slashed out of it that gave Darren a good view of her breasts.

I've seen her around somewhere, Darren thought, and as she realised he was watching her and stood away from the wall, ready to challenge him, he remembered where.

"How about," Darren said with a grin, "a meat feast with extra cheese, garlic bread with mozzarella and a large Coke?"

"Do I know you?" The girl blinked. It wasn't long since she'd stopped crying and her makeup had smeared.

"Della, right?" Darren said, moving in closer. "Pizza Hut. Manageress."

"Trainee," Della said, close to a smile.

"Not for long, I'll bet."

Aware that he was staring down the front of her dress, Della pulled the gap together with her hand.

"How come you're out here?" Darren said. "What's up?"

"My boyfriend's in there dancing with somebody else, that's what I'm doing out here."

"Wants his head seeing to."

"You think so?"

"I know so."

Della blew her nose into a tissue and dabbed at her eyes. "Well, I might as well be going."

"No." Darren smiled, shifting his balance enough to set himself in her path. "'S'early yet. Why don't we go over the Café Royal? Have a drink?"

"I'm not stopping long," Della said, turning on her low heels to look round the room. It reminded her of boarding houses she'd been to stay in with her parents when she was younger, Southport or Filey or places like that. It didn't look like a room in which somebody actually lived.

"How many sugars?" Darren called from the shared kitchen.

"One," Della said.

Darren appeared in the doorway with a mug in either hand.

"I shall have to be going soon," Della said, taking one of the mugs and standing in the centre of the room. Last mistake she was about to make, go over there and sit on the bed.

"'S'okay," said Darren. "Lot to do myself tomorrow as it is. Tell you what, though . . ." Sitting back on the bed himself. "'Fore you go, you won't believe what it is I've got to show you."

46

Millington wanted to get out of the car and give his legs a stretch; he wanted to take a pee and not into the plastic bottle which he'd swiped before his wife could put it away for recycling, fresh orange juice it said on the label, produce of more than one country. He wondered if he weren't getting a bit long in the tooth for this kind of obs, all right for youngsters like Naylor, sitting alongside him, working his way through an old issue of *The Puzzler*.

"Hey, up!" Naylor said as a car nosed into the street from the far end.

Both men sat tense as the maroon Datsun drove towards them at a regulation thirty; when they were certain it was going to turn into the drive of number eleven, it continued blithely on past.

Naylor sighed and shook his head. Millington reached into the glove compartment for another Bounty bar, dark chocolate covering, not the milk. Kevin Naylor shook his head and popped a Polo into his mouth. It was coming up to three-thirty in the afternoon and they had been in position since morning.

"Tell me something, Kevin," Millington said, screwing

up his Bounty wrapper and transferring it to his jacket pocket. "If you were pulling down one big score after another, all that cash split—what?—five, six ways?—would you elect to live in Mansfield? In a semi three streets away from your mother?"

"Long as it wasn't Debbie's mother, I don't know as I'd mind."

"But Mansfield . . ."

"I don't know. It's not so bad. We nearly bought a place out here, actually. When we were getting married. Starter homes on one of them small estates, lot cheaper than in the city."

"So why didn't you?"

"It were Debbie. Didn't feel right, moving so far away from her mum."

"Her and Frank Churchill, then—lot in common."

No matter how much he tried, Naylor could never stop himself from breaking the mint with his teeth before it was as much as half gone. If they had set up home up here, he was thinking, things might have gone a sight more smoothly for them. Without Debbie being able to nip round to her mum's every time any little thing went wrong, they'd have had to work things out for themselves more.

"How is it going now?" Millington asked. He'd heard the rumours, same as everyone else. "You and Debbie."

"Not so bad," Naylor said. "Pretty good, in fact. Thanks, Sarge, yes. Looking up." They had spent two evenings together now, met for lunch one day at Jallans and Naylor had been certain Debbie wanted to go back to bed after, but he was on duty and she was due to see someone about a part-time job.

This time the car was a Granada, six months old, and the driver signalled his intentions to turn into number eleven some forty yards away. He had his head turned aside as the car swung onto the drive; the gap between the driveway and the door was no more than twenty feet and he didn't stand around to watch the roses grow, but Millington and Naylor saw enough to be convinced that this was their man.

Frank Chambers. Frank Church. Frank Churchill.

Probably back from visiting his dear old mum.

Lynn Kellogg had been out of the office when Keith first called and he'd refused either to leave his name or speak to anyone else. When he tried an hour and a half later, ringing from the only unvandalised box in the Bridgeway Centre, Lynn was on her way back in with her arms full of files.

"Hello? D.C. Kellogg."

His voice was so faint, she couldn't make it out, but guessed anyway. "Keith, that you?"

They met back in the Memorial Gardens, walking round and round between the beds, all that Keith could do to remain there at all, never mind sitting down.

"And you are positive?" Lynn asked. "About the gun?"

"He showed it to me."

What Darren had actually done was slide the PPK beneath the table in the café and jab it against Keith's balls, not so hard as to make him cry out, but hard enough for him to reach down and find out what it was. It had been almost enough to make Keith wet himself then and there, something he hadn't done since he'd been shut away in Glen Parva.

"How can you be positive it isn't a replica?"

"We got into the lift in the Trinity Square car park and stopped it between floors. He showed me. Ammo, too. No way it's anything but the real thing."

When they'd got the lift going again, Darren had walked along the roof as far as the edge and leaned against the parapet, aiming the pistol at people walking along the street outside Jessops and the Stakis Hotel, taking careful aim and pretending to fire, making clicking sounds with his tongue and laughing. "There. See that? Right between the fucking eyes!"

"And when did you say he'd told you to steal the car?"

"Wasn't definite. Just be ready, be ready. Don't let me have to come looking for you and not find you, that's all."

"Okay," Lynn said, "just do as he says. Get back to me as soon as he's contacted you. That way we'll have plenty of time to get into position."

Keith stopped alongside a small rockery with pink and purple flowers. "What'll happen?" he asked.

"Happen? We'll disarm him, take him away fast. Lock him up out of harm's way. Your way, too. It's all right, Keith, you're doing the right thing. There's nothing for you to worry about."

Now I know how it feels, Lynn thought as they walked towards the embankment, lying to my hind teeth.

Skelton had decided it was time to go public. It seemed as though, after nearly nine months, Operation Kingfisher was showing signs of coming home to roost. Most of the officers involved in the enquiry were present: aside from Resnick's team, Malcolm Grafton, Helen Siddons and Reg Cossall were looking over the newly circulated reports, waiting for the superintendent to spell out the next stages.

What Skelton did was to signal twice with nods of the head, once towards the lights, once the projector. A slide showing a man standing inside a walled garden, snow-capped mountains behind him, flicked into view, to be followed by a medium shot, head and shoulders, finally a close-up, slightly blurred by the necessary use of the zoom lens.

"Rainsy." Reg Cossall breathed. "As I live and breathe."

"Former D.C. Rains," Skelton confirmed, "taken in the grounds of the villa where's he's been living these past six years. About seventy miles north of the town of Leon in the

Cantabrian Mountains." Skelton looked around the darkened room. "Since these pictures were taken, Rains has disappeared. If he's flown, especially using a British passport, it must have been under an assumed name."

"What about other modes of transport, Superintendent?" asked Helen Siddons.

"The car registered to him is still garaged at the villa, but, of course, that means nothing. The Spanish police have promised a thorough check of car hire firms in the area, but so far nothing's materialised."

"Too busy enjoying their siesta," suggested Cossall in a stage whisper.

"It's not so far to the French border," Malcolm Grafton pointed out. "Pick up one of those TGVs, you're talking getting on two hundred miles an hour. Ferry across the Channel, here in no time."

"If *here* is where's he's heading, Malcolm," Reg Cossall pointed out.

"If we're not working on that possibility, Reg," said Helen Siddons, "I don't know what we're doing here at all."

Cossall sat back glowering. Reg! What did that jumped-up tart think she was at, having the bollocking temerity to call him Reg?

Skelton signalled and the slide disappeared, the lights came back on. "There are still a lot of ifs. If Rains has been travelling to and from this country with any frequency, we've yet to establish proof of this. If he's been in this area, you might think it strange there doesn't appear to have been one sighting of him, not one solitary rumour that he was here—until the one floated by Graham's informant. Having noted all of that, what interests me most is the supposed Churchill-Rains connection. It's Charlie's opinion they could have been close; the informant's busy telling us they've become closer. And one thing we know for certain, though we've been short of a great deal that's provable in court, Churchill is a long-term villain, a professional robber with likely half a dozen scores to his name since he came out of Parkhurst in 'eighty-seven."

"Time the bastard was back," someone said to murmurs of agreement.

"We're keeping him under surveillance," Skelton said. "Round the clock. Either Rains contacts him or vice versa, we should know."

"Have we got a tap on his phones?" Helen Siddons asked.

"What we have is an outstanding application to monitor all calls."

A low moan ran round the room.

"One thing," asked Malcolm Grafton, "how does this affect the status of the French enquiries?"

"Continuing, Malcolm. Possibly a little closer to the back burner, that's all."

"What that bugger wants to know for," Cossall said to Resnick, who was sitting close to one side, "reckons he's on to a Parisian bloody holiday, doesn't he? All expenses paid. Taxpayers' money to spend his nights down the Folies Bergère. Waste, eh, Charlie? Going to send anyone, down to you and me."

In the event it was to be none of them. Skelton passed the news to Resnick at the end of the meeting and it was his duty to impart the decision to Divine, who was entertaining the CID room with his impersonation of Maurice Chevalier performing a particularly lewd version of "Thank Heaven for Little Girls."

"Mark, my office a minute."

Divine stood inside the closed door, hands clasped at his back.

"The, er, French connection you've been working on . . ."

Divine's eyes began to shine.

"I'm afraid it's been decided there's a need to send a more senior officer. Someone fluent in the language and of a rank which would enable them to . . ." The rest didn't need saying. The change in Divine's expression made it clear how well he understood. "D.I. Siddons will be the liaison officer travelling over; seems she's more or less bilingual."

There was a day when Divine would have tried to make a joke out of that, but this wasn't it.

"Sorry, Mark," Resnick said, surprising himself by actually meaning it.

"Thanks, boss," Divine said gloomily.

Instead of going back to his desk, he walked through the CID room and out at the far end without saying another word. In either language.

47

Ruth padded across the tiled floor in bare feet. Why hadn't she been surprised when Resnick had walked into the pub? Recognising him instantly from the trial and earlier—standing in the side door of the house, Rains behind her, watching Resnick and her husband face to face. Watching her husband's face, the gun; knowing that he was playing the percentages inside his head. How much do they know? How much can they prove? How much time am I going to get? She remembered how close Rains had stood to her, warmth of his breath against the side of her neck; even then, his hand reaching out for her, touching her back.

She poured nearly boiling water into the pot and swished it round as she took it to the sink and poured it down. One tea bag and one for luck. Digestive biscuits in the tin on the shelf. She poured on the water and replaced the lid, left the tea to brew.

The dog watching her all the while, clear eyes following her every move. A ritual like many others. One which Resnick's visit had left undisturbed. A couple of halves in the pub, few chapters of whichever book, back to the cottage for a cup of tea and while that was standing, she would feed the dog. Afterwards, walk him on the beach. Well, she would walk, the dog would run. Then home for a little telly, maybe the radio, another early night, the dog curled on the rug at the bed's foot.

Ruth stood with both hands to her face, pressing deep. Resnick had walked into the pub and told her what she had always known, sooner or later, would be the case: he's coming out. *I'll get you, Ruthie. Get even with you. Pay you back, you double-crossing bastard. Cunt. You bitch.* There had been a photograph of her, front page in most of the papers, little black dress, descending the steps outside the court. Pale face. There behind her, smart in his suit, that handsome smiling face, hands raised and spread to ward photographers and press away.

Mrs. Prior will be making a statement later through her solicitor.

Pleased, course I'm pleased. We got a good result.

Prior's release, so long coming, she had ceased to fear it long since. What would come would come and who was she to say she didn't deserve it? *Grassing up your old man, you slag, you don't deserve to live.* Rumour was his mum had hired some tearaway to teach her a lesson, throw acid in her face. Ruth hid herself away, down London, abroad, a spell in Glasgow, back for a while to the city, then here.

You can walk but you can't run.

She liked it here. The quiet. All those early years in front of speakers jacked up so high she was lucky not to have permanent damage to her ears. In Glasgow once this journalist had recognised her, a stringer for the *NME*. Begged her to let him do her story. Not talking a magazine piece here, I mean the real thing. A book. Built around you. The history of British Rhythm and Blues.

She hadn't told that story or any other. Not even after the trial when they'd all been round her like flies round the honeypot. The *Sun*. The *News of the World*. Money she'd been offered. My Life with a Villain. My Life with a Face.

Some tart who reckoned she'd screwed him silly in her scabby little bed-sit had sold this yarn about champagne and foursomes and how Prior hadn't been able to get enough. Well, after all the years of virtual abstinence he'd practised with her, maybe that was the only part Ruth had believed.

It was late. The dog had finished his food and was waiting, bemused, by the door. The tea was cold and stewed. Ruth changed her shoes, buttoned up her coat.

The roll of the sea as it folds back against the sand. If Prior walked up to me now, out of this long dark, Ruth thought, what would I say or do?

Returning, as she neared the seawall, she heard the quick scratch of a match and, moments later, saw the soft glow of a cigarette. Just kids, she thought, doing some cold courting.

Resnick's card was still in the pocket of her skirt and she dropped it onto the kitchen table as she walked through. For fifteen, twenty minutes she sat with her feet up, listening to Radio Two: Brian Matthew more relaxing than another bout of Gradgrind.

"Come on," she said, and with his usual enthusiasm the dog trailed her up the stairs to bed.

On the outer edge of the city, nights before, travelling back, Resnick had pulled across to the side of the road and cut the engine. Lights splayed out before him like a net. A feeling, not quite pain, had caught low in his throat. His instinct had been to slip a fresh cassette into place but inside his head Lester was already playing "Ghost of a Chance."

unseen, not quite unbidden,
someone has just slipped in.

Ruth was vaguely aware of the dog padding off downstairs, but it was such a familiar sound she never really woke: what did wake her was the sharp, sudden sound of tearing close to her head.

"What's that?" Jumping up with a start, blinking into the near-dark.

"That," the familiar voice said, "was the sound of your dog's throat being cut."

"Bastard!" she sobbed, reaching sideways for the light.

Beside the bed, Rains smiled down. "Don't worry, Ruthie. It was only this." One of her shirts which she'd left hanging over a chair was dangling from his hand, ripped from tail to neck.

"The dog! Where's . . . ?"

"Downstairs sleeping, not to fret."

"He wouldn't . . ."

"Hungry. Gave him a little something to eat."

"If you've . . ."

"Just a few hours. He'll be right as rain." Rains smiled. "Funny that, isn't it? Always makes me smile. What's so right about rain?" Never taking his eyes from her, he sat on the side of the bed. "Always when you least expect it. Forgot the umbrella, raincoat in the car." He laughed, smiling with his eyes. "Good to see you, Ruthie. You look like shit."

He scarcely looked older; what age there was, if anything, had made him even better-looking. Too handsome for other people's good.

"No sense pretending we parted on the best of terms, is there? Even so—I thought some things were all agreed. No true confessions, no stories. No talking out of turn."

"How did you get here? How did you find me?"

"Ruthie! Used to be a detective, remember?"

"I know what you used to be."

Rains leaned one hand against the covers, close to her

leg. "Followed him. Charlie. Heard he'd had the feelers out, asking questions, and I followed him."

Ruth glanced away and when she looked back his expression had changed.

"You thought shutting yourself out here would stop people finding you; thought getting that dog would protect you if they did. Well, now you know better. And I know you won't forget." His hand moved fast and he had hold of her jaw, fingers pressing hard against the bone. "One thing, when he comes to see you, Prior; if he wants to know what went on between us, if I used you to fit him up, you don't tell him a thing. Don't as much as mention my name." Leaning quickly forward, he kissed her on the mouth. "Life's good, Ruthie. Too much so to have it fucked up by some jealous bastard, fresh out of prison, harbouring a grudge."

She stayed there for a long time after Rains had gone, allowing the warmth gradually to seep back into her skin. Only then did she put on her dressing gown and go downstairs and kneel beside the dog, unconscious on the kitchen floor; sit, with his head resting in her lap, until he stirred with the first light glinted off the sea.

48

Resnick woke at two to the sound of breathing: lay there for second after second, aware of the heart pumping against his ribs, that the fevered breathing that had woken him had been his own. He was layered with sweat. The fear was not his own.

a tideswell like moving bone

Like Monk fingering "These Foolish Things"
from broken glass

He got up and didn't switch on the light. The cat, knowing it was too early, recircled himself at the foot of the bed and closed his eyes. Because the fear was not for himself, it was no less real. He stood beneath the shower and the sound that he heard was water dragging back across the shore. He knew that Ruth had no phone: knew that he could phone the pub and rouse the landlord, call the constabulary in the nearest town. Knew, without knowing why, without questioning, that whatever had happened, that part of it, was through.

Deliberately, he dressed, made coffee, buttered bread, broke cheese. Some of the coffee he drank, the remainder he poured into a flask. If he drove fast he would beat daybreak. His headlights cut channels across brick and stone. The only fear now was what he would find.

Ruth had stayed in the kitchen with the dog, cradling him, until, at last, his eyes rolled open and, moments later, he shuffled unsteadily to his feet. Now the animal lay curled on the battered settee in the living room and Ruth sat, trying to read, with her umpteenth cup of tea.

It snagged at the back of her mind, like a hangnail, that she should slip on her shoes and find her purse, walk the few yards towards the seashore and dial the number Resnick had left her. She was loathe to admit to herself that part of the reason she didn't do this was she was afraid to take that first step outside the house.

Yet why?

If it were Rains that she feared most, he had proved to her how easy it was for him to magic himself inside her house. If he had wanted to do her physical harm, he could; if he wanted to harm her in the future, he could again. She had no doubt of this.

But maybe Rains was not the one she really feared.

She would call Resnick and say what? This friend of yours was here threatening me. What did he do? He tore one of my old shirts. Ruth smiled. Resnick and Rains, had they been friends? It seemed unlikely. She thought that to Rains, admitting to a friend would have been a sign of weakness, strictly to be discouraged. Friendship meant give and take and life, for Rains, was all in the taking.

She was back in the kitchen, refilling the kettle, when she heard the car approaching.

"Do you always act on your hunches?" Ruth asked. They had walked up away from the beach, onto a green knoll that never seemed to reach its peak. Off to the west woods became fields and fields became lost in hazy mist. Squinting along the shoreline into the early light, they could see the silhouettes of castles, bulked against the sky.

"Not always," Resnick said. "Usually."

"Doesn't it ever get you into trouble?"

"Doesn't everything?"

They walked on until the land seemed suddenly about to fall before them, tumbling sharply down to a narrow cleft, a stream of grey-green water that wound snakelike towards the sea.

Ruth patted her pockets, found and lit a cigarette, smoke from it quickly lost in the air. "So what did you expect?" she asked. "To find me dead?"

"I wasn't sure."

"But that was one of the possibilities?"

"I suppose so."

She almost smiled. "You weren't disappointed?"

Resnick shook his head.

"But Rains," Ruth said, "you didn't think it would be Rains?"

"No. I mean, I didn't know. But, no, I don't think so."

"He's out, then?" Ruth said, moments later. They both knew she meant Prior.

"Yes."

"And you're watching him?"

"No."

"Expect me to believe that?"

Resnick shook his head. "We haven't the reason, haven't the resources. He'll be expected to report to his probation officer once a week."

Ruth snorted.

"D'you want to start walking back?" Resnick said.

"All right," Ruth said, but neither of them moved.

"What you have to understand," Ruth said several moments later, "no one had looked at me like that in so long I swear I'd forgotten what it meant. No one had touched me, wanted to touch me. It was as if, early, stupidly bloody early, that part of my life had just stopped.

"And then there was that bastard, hands all over me, like he couldn't get enough." She finished her cigarette, nipped the end between finger and thumb and opened the last of the paper, scattering shards of tobacco towards the ground. "I knew he was using me, though, of course, he denied it. Knew and I never cared. I thought, Prior's going down for a long time and what that means to me he doesn't care, he doesn't give a shit. I'm just this thing that he's lived with and used to cook and clean and wipe between his legs. I felt *that* low." She looked at Resnick and made a gesture with her hand as if she were holding something minute. "And what Rains did, he stopped me feeling like that. Oh, Christ alone knows, not for long. But when he did . . ."

Ruth began to walk and Resnick moved into step beside her. All the while she had been talking he'd shut out the constant roll of the sea and now that she was quiet it came back the more strongly, accompanying them home.

"You haven't got any coffee," Resnick called from the kitchen. The past five minutes he'd been through every drawer, every cupboard.

"That's right."

He made more tea.

"What I've got," Ruth said, wandering in followed by a still dazed-looking dog, "is a stomach lining I'm going to leave to medical science. They'll use X rays of it in years to come, illustrating the dangers of tannin."

For all the jokes, she still looked lined and drawn, still jumped at the first strange sound.

They sat at the table, the dog beneath it, asleep again, snoring faintly.

"Rains," Resnick said, "he didn't give any indication of where he was staying, anything like that?"

Ruth shook her head. "You'd go and talk to him? I mean, officially?"

"I daresay."

"What for? What could you prove?" She drank some tea. "What did he do, aside, I suppose, from breaking in?"

Resnick leaned towards her. "There's more."

"With Rains?"

"Yes."

"What sort of more?"

"We're not sure, but . . . one or two things, we think he might be involved."

"What kind of things?"

Resnick leaned back. "When you were seeing him, did he ever talk about Frank Churchill?"

"Only questions. The usual things. Meetings, places and times. All the usual things."

"He didn't give the impression they might be close?"

"Rains and Churchill!" Ruth gave a derisory laugh. "Fine bloody couple they'd make! Only person Frank Churchill's ever been close to's his mother. Rains'd never get that sort of close to anything unless it was a mirror. Anyhow, why d'you want to know?"

Resnick's turn to shake his head. "Doesn't matter."

"No? That's what Rains'd say. Every time. We'd be lying there, you know, after making love, I'd be waiting and sure enough they'd come, the questions, on and on, and if either I wouldn't answer or ask him why he wanted to know, that's what he'd say—doesn't matter. Ten, fifteen minutes later, he'd be asking the same thing." She reached out abruptly and caught hold of Resnick's arm. "One thing I never done, knowingly, give that bastard anything that'd push my husband deeper into the shit. Never. And if that's what Rains was saying, to you lot or anyone else, he was lying. He was covering up." She released his arm and the marks of her fingers were left, pale, on Resnick's skin. "Maybe what you were suggesting was right, maybe he did have something going with Churchill, more than was thought. As far as jobs was concerned, I shouldn't think there was anything I knew as Frank Churchill didn't. Less." She got up and carried the two mugs, hers and Resnick's, to the sink.

"I ought to be going," Resnick said, looking at his watch.

"Thanks," Ruth said.

"What for?"

"Being bothered. Coming."

"Just one thing," Resnick said.

"What's that?"

"Why did you stop singing?"

"Fuck right off," Ruth said, grinning.

49

Darren pressed his finger full-force against the bell and kept it there until Rylands, flushed in the face with anger, threw it open.

"What in God's name d'you think you're at?" Rylands demanded.

"Keith," Darren said, ignoring his reaction. "He in?"

"Out."

"Out where? Been walking all over the city centre past couple of hours, looking for him."

"He went to the job centre," Rylands said.

"Job centre!" Darren was incredulous. "What the fuck's he want to go there for?"

"Here you go, Sarge," Naylor said, shutting the car door with a clean thunk. "Jumbo sausage and chips."

Millington's eyes lit up. Go anywhere near his wife with a jumbo sausage and you risked a lecture on harmful additives and carcinogenics. "Get the mustard?" he asked.

Naylor fished a sachet containing a vibrant yellow from his breast pocket.

"Good lad!"

Naylor had fetched himself cod and chips. Or was it haddock? For the best part of fifteen minutes both men ate, neither spoke.

Millington was dipping the last few inches of his sausage into the puddle of mustard when the door to number eleven opened and Frank Churchill came out. Without looking around, he unlocked the door of the Granada and climbed in.

"Probably off to see his mum," Naylor suggested.

"Goes there," Millington said, screwing up the wrappings of his lunch, "he walks."

"Maybe he's taking her for a drive?"

"And maybe I've just been eating prime beef."

Naylor fired the engine and waited while Churchill backed out across the road and headed away from them at a good speed.

"Just make sure you don't get too close," Millington said. "Last thing we need, him spotting us."

Naylor nodded, indicated right and changed down for the bend.

"Where the fuck've you been?" Darren grabbed hold of Keith by the shoulder, swinging him round so fast that Keith lost his balance and ended up on his knees.

"Get up, you prick! You look fucking pathetic!"

Keith scrambled to his feet, aware that several passersby were looking round at him and sniggering. That's it, lady, laugh your tossing head off, why don't you? He shook Darren's hand clear and said nothing.

"You avoiding me or what?" Darren demanded.

"Leave him alone, you great bully!" called an old woman with what looked like a year's supply of papers in a pram. "He's only little."

"Sod off, Granny!" Darren yelled back.

"Yeh," said Keith, "sod off."

They walked together across the road, ignoring the traffic, forcing it to stop or swerve around them.

"Gum?" Keith said, holding out a pack of Wrigley's.

"Yeh, ta."

They sat on the wall near the gents' toilets, kicking their heels against brickwork that was covered in graffiti and pigeon shit.

"Your old man said you was down the job centre."

"'S'right."

"Anything there?"

"Don't bloody joke."

"This car," Darren said.

"Which one?"

"The one you're going to nick."

"What about it?"

"Friday."

"Why Friday?"

"'Cause more people take money out Fridays, birdbrain. Lot more cash there waiting."

"We going to do another building society?" Keith asked.

"Yes," Darren said. "And this time we're going to do it fucking right!"

"On the M1, boss. Heading north." Divine was monitoring Millington and Naylor's progress as they followed Churchill's Ford Granada. "Reckon he's heading for a meet with Rains?"

"Any luck," Resnick said, "he's doing exactly that. Keep me in the picture."

"Right."

Resnick went into his office and dialled a number, asked to speak to Pam Van Allen.

Frank Churchill was sticking to the outside lane, keeping the speedometer between seventy-five and eighty, moving over only when some salesman, flogging his company car, came fast up behind him, flashing his lights.

Naylor kept several vehicles between himself and their quarry, alternately moving up and falling back, doing everything he could to make sure his wouldn't be the vehicle Churchill habitually saw in his rearview mirror.

"He's slowing down," Millington said. "Pulling over."

Naylor had noticed already, dropped behind a lorry carrying pharmaceutical goods north from the Continent.

"Service station," Millington said. "Just up ahead."

Naylor checked in his own mirror and signalled to leave the motorway.

"I don't want you to think," Resnick said into the phone, "that I'm pestering you about this. . . ."

There was a silence, out of which Pam Van Allen said: "I'm trying hard not to."

"I was interested to know how you think he's taking to being out, settling into the hostel, whatever."

"Pretty much the way you'd expect somebody to do when they've been excluded from society for ten years. He's tense, apprehensive . . ."

"Angry?"

"I didn't say that."

"I know. But I'm concerned. . . ."

"For his wife's safety."

"Yes."

There was another pause, longer, and Resnick could almost hear the probation officer thinking. Through the glass at the top of his door he could see Divine's head, bobbing a little as he spoke into the telephone.

"After what you said," Pam Van Allen said cautiously, "I talked to him about his wife, his feelings towards her.

Everything he said suggested he sees that relationship as being very much in the past. He showed no inclination to open it up again, get back in touch. Certainly he expressed nothing like anger towards her."

"And you believed him?"

"Yes. Yes, I did."

"Good."

"Good-bye, Inspector." Resnick had a sudden image of her as she set down the receiver, one hand pushing up through her cap of silver-grey hair, the other pinching the bridge of her nose as she closed her eyes.

"Boss!"

Alerted by Divine's shout, Resnick hurried into the main office.

"Graham," Divine explained, holding out the phone. "Wants to talk to you."

Resnick identified himself down what was clearly a wavery connection.

"Good news is, it's Rains right enough. No mistaking him anywhere. Standing in line in the cafeteria waiting for Churchill to join him over chicken, chips and peas."

"What's the bad?" Resnick said.

"Where they've sat themselves, bang in the middle of the place, can't get near 'em without getting spotted. Tried getting Kevin at the table behind, but what with all the chatter and the background bloody Muzak and the cutlery, you'd need to be leaning over them with a hearing trumpet to know what they were talking about."

"Lynn's on her way in a car. Rendezvous outside. When they leave, you take Rains, let her tag along with Churchill."

"What if she don't get here?"

"Stick to the plan, follow Rains."

"Right," Millington said and then quickly, "They're moving, got to go."

———

Naylor walked down the steps from the cafeteria, and ahead of him Rains and Churchill separated, neither one of them in any obvious hurry to go back to their vehicles. Churchill browsed through the magazines in the shop; Rains spent a pound or so on the games machines near the exit. Churchill went into the gents and locked himself into a cubicle. Millington didn't think they'd been spotted, though there was no way of knowing for sure. What they were observing could simply be careful practice, nothing more. At least, it gave Lynn Kellogg more time to arrive. He had no way of knowing the northbound carriageway had been temporarily blocked by an accident involving a lorry and a fifteen-year-old youth joyriding in a stolen Fiesta.

Suddenly Churchill was hurrying across the parking area towards his Granada and that diversion was enough to give Rains a vital start back up the steps towards the bridge linking the two sides of the motorway.

Three blue saloons left the service area heading south in a virtual convoy and between them Millington and Naylor got the registration of one and a half. And they couldn't be sure which of the three Rains had been driving.

Frank Churchill, meanwhile, had continued his journey northwards and they could only hope that a sense of filial duty would take him back to Mansfield so that they could pick up his trail again.

"A balls-up, Charlie. A regular balls-up, I don't know what else to call it," Skelton said after Resnick had made his report.

Alone in the CID room, smarting still, Graham Millington thought after that day's work he'd be fortunate to retain his sergeant's stripes, never mind promotion.

50

Lorna didn't know why it was, but ever since Kevin Naylor had stopped returning her calls, something appalling had happened to her appetite. Instead of settling down to watch "Neighbours" with a Linda McCartney low-calorie broccoli and cheese bake, she found herself reaching for the telephone and waiting, tummy impatiently rumbling, until the Perfect Pizza delivery man appeared on her doorstep. Her lunch had progressed from two crispbreads and a piece of celery to lasagne and chips at the local pub. Breakfast was no longer a single shredded wheat, it was porridge with maple-type syrup and cream, several slices of toast and marmalade and instant coffee with two spoonfuls of sugar.

She had overheard Becca yesterday whispering to Marjorie in a voice that could have been heard up and down the street, "You don't suppose, do you, that our Lorna's got herself pregnant?"

Fat chance!

"I'm sorry," Kevin Naylor had said when she'd finally raised him on the phone, "but there's another officer handling that now. I've been shifted onto something else."

Shifted back to his wife, Lorna thought. She still hadn't

forgotten that in the midst of their one and only night of passion, Kevin had etched a particular moment forever on her mind by digging his fingers sharply into her shoulders and shouting, "Yes, Debbie! Yes, Debbie! Yes, Debbie, yes!"

Lorna ran her finger round the inside of her breakfast bowl, scooping up the last of the syrup and cream, before rinsing it under the tap. Oh God, she thought, next thing I'll be running out of things I can wear, having to go out and buy myself a whole new wardrobe. The one saving grace was the example of Marjorie, huffing and puffing and perspiring her way through every working day. The minute Lorna found herself rivalling Marjorie, she was enrolling in Weight Watchers, withdrawing her savings and booking two weeks on a health farm.

In the bathroom she cleaned her teeth with care, applied the finishing touches to her makeup. At least it was Friday, another week nearly over. Maybe tonight she'd go down the Black Orchid, let her hair down; dance enough she might even lose a few pounds.

The senior officers involved in Kingfisher had been in closed session ever since Jack Skelton came back from his early-morning run. The consensus was this: Rains was back in circulation and his meeting with Churchill was enough to suggest that Millington's information had at least a patina of truth. Rains, moreover, was aware of the possibility that he and Churchill might be being watched. There was no certain way of knowing whether their tail had actually been spotted or if they were merely taking precautions. But then, as Reg Cossall suggested, you don't waste time fiddling around with a condom if all you're interested in's a quick wank. Even as he said it, Cossall thought he might get an earful from Helen Siddons, but all she did was compliment him on his awareness of the need for safe sex. All you need do, darling, Cossall thought, is carry on looking like that. What he did was smile and keep his mouth shut.

Finally it was agreed that they would maintain a careful watch on Churchill for another day, Frank having obligingly returned to his Mansfield home in time for tea. Meantime, extra officers would be assigned to the search for Rains. If nothing had developed within twenty-four hours, Frank Churchill could be brought in for questioning. If they moved quick enough, rattled him enough, they might squeeze some answers out of him before he was able to shelter behind his brief.

"Fetch us another tea, Keith. Make sure it in't stewed, eh? More like gravy, this last cup."

Keith could tell from the tone of Darren's voice that he was seriously on an up. Sitting by the back wall of the Arcade café, finishing his cooked breakfast and looking so sodding full of himself. At least his cropped hair had started to grow out a little, he didn't look so weird anymore. Like one of them skinheads you saw sometimes round the city centre, lace-up Doc Martens and Levi's and swastika tattoos.

"Better treat yourself to something more than that," Darren said, watching Keith with his two of toast.

"How come?"

Darren winked. "Big day today, can't afford for you to be feeling queasy."

"What's on, then?"

"What's on? Day trip to Skeggy, what d'you think? You and me, we've got some unfinished business to do, right?"

Keith looked at him sharply, the unnatural gleam in his too blue eyes. "You're not serious? I mean, not after what happened last time, it's not . . . ?"

"Jesus Christ!" Darren had one of Keith's hands tight inside his own and was squeezing hard. "You know what, I reckon I'd've done us both a favour if instead of cutting you down inside that cell, I'd let you swing. You're about as much good as a foreskin in a force-ten gale."

Tears were forming in the corners of Keith's eyes as his face grimaced with pain.

"All you got to do, be out front with the car, ready to get us out of there. I'll go in on my own." He snorted with derision. "Worked a bloody sight better without you last time, why not this?" And he gave Keith's hand a final squeeze before letting it go. "Now don't take too long," Darren said, "it's time we were out of here."

Keith pushed half a slice of half-cold toast into his mouth and almost choked.

"No word from young Rylands?" Resnick said, pausing by Lynn Kellogg's desk.

Lynn shook her head. "Not as yet."

"See if you can raise Mark or Kevin for me, will you? Maybe something's happening on the Churchill front."

It was Divine whom Resnick eventually spoke to. The most exciting thing that had taken place was Churchill mouthing off at an old man with an orange delivery bag over his shoulder, cluttering up the place with useless leaflets not worth the paper they were printed on. Chop down half a sodding forest just to keep you walking the streets.

Better kind of villain, Resnick thought, setting down the phone, not only is he nice to his mum, he's worried about the ozone layer and the state of the planet.

Shivering in the call box and not from the cold, Keith was having difficulty getting his coins into the slot, pressing the correct buttons for the number.

"Oh, Miss Solomon," Becca piped in her shrill little voice, "could you come and help here, please?"

Lorna pushed aside the computer printouts she'd been checking, query from an account holder about the regularity with which her salary had been paid in, and got to her feet, automatically smoothing down her skirt as she stood.

What all the fuss was about, she didn't know. There were no more than three people waiting, pretty average for this time of the day; she didn't see why Becca couldn't cope on her own till Marjorie got back from her coffee break.

"Thank you, Miss Solomon." Becca smiled as Lorna took a seat alongside her. "Mustn't keep the customers waiting."

Ever since she had started putting on a little weight herself, Lorna couldn't help but notice how skinny Becca really was. Like a couple of twigs in American tan tights.

"Yes, sir," Lorna said, looking up through the glass. "How may I help you?" And then thinking, Oh, no; oh, Christ!

"Hello, Lorna." Darren grinned. "Remember me?"

"Becca," Lorna started, "I think—"

"Never mind about no one else," said Darren, "this is between you and me. Now here . . ." And he pushed a green bin liner through beneath the glass. "Get that filled and don't piss me about."

Lorna froze.

Becca spotted the bin liner from the corner of her eye and screamed.

Darren reached towards the waistband of his jeans and pulled out the gun.

A middle-aged man wearing decorator's overalls began to move towards the exit and Darren yelled for him to stop, levelling the pistol at his head. The man stopped.

"Lie down!" Darren ordered. "All of you. Flat down with your hands over your heads." He'd seen them made to do that the other night in some film and it had looked pretty good.

"Okay," he said, swinging the PPK round until once again it was pointing towards Lorna. "Lorna, what you have to do, all that cash, in the bag. And Lorna, nothing clever like you tried before, none of that business with alarms." He tapped on the glass with the barrel end of the gun. "Reinforced or not," he said, smiling, "once I press this trigger, this isn't going to be worth shit."

Becca had doubled forward, head towards her knees, praying for it all to go away. Lorna, scarcely taking her eyes off Darren and the pistol, was dropping handfuls of money down into the bag.

Stretched across the floor like sardines, none of the customers moved.

"Come on, come on!" Darren urged. "Be quick!"

Lorna held up the green bin liner for him to see. "That's all there is."

"You wouldn't be holding out on me?"

There wasn't a patch of colour anywhere in Lorna's face.

"No, I suppose not." He gestured with the gun. "Back over here."

Reaching up to retrieve the bag and the money, Darren had his face close to hers. "Have to come round and see you some time. Easy now I know where you live." He grinned and winked and blew her a kiss.

"Everyone stays where they are!" he called out at the door. "Less they want to get hurt."

Pushing the pistol down from sight and switching the bin liner to the other hand, he pushed his way through the door to where Keith was waiting in the car.

Except that Keith wasn't waiting and nor was the car.

"Armed police," said an amplified voice. "Put your

hands behind your head and get down on the ground. Do it now."

Darren could see four vehicles, angled across the road; behind each one were men in blue overalls, arms outstretched, weapons at the ends of those arms all pointing at him.

"Keith!" Darren screamed in anguish. "Keith!"

From the safety of the car where he was sitting with Resnick and Lynn Kellogg, a block away from the building society, Keith heard Darren's voice calling his name and brought up both hands to his ears.

"Armed police," the voice repeated. "You are surrounded. Raise your hands above your head now and then clasp them behind your neck. This is your final warning."

Darren reached inside his jacket and pulled clear the pistol, bringing it round until it was held out in front of him, aiming in the direction of the nearest car.

The sergeant in charge of the tactical response team gave the order and Darren was hurled back, swayed like an off-balance skater, before falling forward with nothing to break his fall.

He had been hit once in the neck, twice in the chest and, to all intents and purposes, was dead before he struck the ground. The crash team from the ambulance did what they had to do but really it was for show. The officer who retrieved the unfired 9-mm Walther PPK would testify in court that the safety catch was still on.

Inside the unmarked car at the far side of the disused home improvements store, Keith Rylands sobbed against Lynn's shoulder till his throat was sore, while Resnick stared through the windscreen and tried to blot out the sound.

51

The media thought it was Christmas come early: a young man, albeit armed and potentially dangerous, being shot down and killed by the police on an unremarkable city street in broad daylight was still an unusual enough occurrence not to pass unremarked. The assistant chief constable gave a press conference and went into the news studios of both independent television and the BBC. The legal officer of Liberty issued a statement condemning the use of firearms in a public area as questionable and the police response as being excessive. The only one of the marksmen who had fired who could be persuaded to comment publicly, said he had simply done what he was trained to do. The dead man had aimed a weapon in his direction and he had felt that his own life and those of his colleagues were in danger.

Not only the local but the national newspapers cleared the headlines, published photographs of both Darren and Keith; there were illustrators' reconstructions of the events and several pictures showing the blood on the pavement as a dark, blurry newsprint mass, akin to an abstract painting.

Local radio spoke at length to Lorna Solomon—"brave

and resourceful"—and Rebecca Astley—"cool and elegant under pressure." Keith Rylands's father—"former rock star with hit records to his name"—said that his son was under sedation and too distressed to comment.

In everything but the *Express* it was newsworthy enough to drive the constitutional problems caused by the rift between the Prince and Princess of Wales onto page 2.

Resnick and Lynn Kellogg finished the afternoon at the market coffee stall, drinking strong espresso and saying very little. Earlier, Resnick had phoned Rylands to make sure that Keith was okay, given what assurances he could that, in the circumstances, Keith was unlikely to be charged.

He accepted a lift home from Lynn, eschewed his usual shower and soaked in a hot bath until it was hot no longer. He was in the kitchen feeding the cats and beginning to wonder what he was going to feed himself when the front doorbell rang.

Afraid it might be a reporter chancing his arm, Resnick opened up cautiously; of all the people it was least likely to be, his visitor was in the top two or three.

"Now then, Charlie. Big day, eh?"

It was Rains.

Sitting across from him in the living room, watching him drink the beer he'd asked for and got, Resnick was surprised how little Rains had changed. The face was fleshier perhaps, especially around the jaw; his body generally was thicker, all in all he'd probably put on ten or twelve pounds, but he was still fit. Resnick guessed he played the occasional game of tennis or squash, swam, worked out. But then he also drank and smoked.

He lit up now, asking first as a matter of course and taking Resnick's shrug as a yes.

"Anything to do with you, Charlie? That business today?"

"Something." What the hell are you doing here? Resnick was thinking. Why have you come?

"Things've changed a bit, eh? Hardly open a paper nowadays without some poor bastard's got himself shot by one of our lot. Your lot. Not before time, my way of thinking. That kid today, for instance, bit of a cowboy, wasn't he? Not a real pro. Nothing to get worked up about." Rains took a long swallow from his glass. "Not a bad drop of beer that, Charlie. What did you say was, German?"

"Czech."

"Good anyway."

Get to the point, Resnick thought; if there is a point.

"We used to put a few pints away, eh, Charlie? Back when we were mates."

"We were never that."

"What? I've closed more pubs and clubs with you and Reg Cossall than any of us'd like to remember."

"We were never mates."

Rains cocked his head to one side. "Have it your way."

"What do you want?" Resnick asked, impatient with waiting.

"What?"

"You heard, what do you—"

"What do I want? Fine question, Charlie. Not seen hide nor hair of you in what? Eight, nine years. What's wrong with a social call?"

"After this time?"

"Not been around, Charlie. Been living abroad."

"I know."

Rains grinned and set down his glass. "Better get me an ashtray, Charlie, or this is going to go all over the carpet."

"Let it."

"Elaine would never've let you get away with that."

"Keep her out of it."

"Like you did?"

Resnick was on his feet and for a moment Rains thought he was going to take a swing at him; he thought he might enjoy that. Instead Resnick walked past him to the square bay of the window and looked out through the partly drawn curtains into the shadows of the front garden.

"How much do you know, Charlie?"

Resnick turned slowly. Rains was lolling back in the comfortable chair, the one Resnick usually sat in himself, alone there in the evenings, thinking, listening to music. He hated the way Rains had arched his knee onto one of the arms of the chair; hated the smug expression on Rains's face.

"Most of it," he said.

"Such as?"

"I know that you and Churchill had a meeting yesterday; that, one way or another, the two of you have been associates since you persuaded him to grass up Prior."

"Is that what I did?"

"Didn't you?"

Rains smirked. "Maybe."

"You got inside information from Churchill, enough to send Prior down for a long time, and so as to keep him in the clear, let on you'd got it from Prior's wife.

"You wanted Churchill still smelling sweet because if his colleagues thought he was a grass, they'd freeze him out, never work with him again, and that wouldn't suit you because you wanted Churchill back in action passing on a share of the take.

"You wanted Prior out of the way because you were having an affair with his wife, probably because you hoped you'd get information out of her as well, but maybe because you genuinely liked her, fancied her at least."

Rains made a sound which meant don't be a fool. "That was work, Charlie. Diddling that slag, that was work. You don't think I could have feelings for a woman like that?"

Resnick moved away from the window, closer to where Rains was sitting. "I don't think you could have feelings for anyone outside of yourself."

"No?" Rains laughed. "Never mind, eh, Charlie. Feelings enough for the both of us, you've got. Regular bleeding heart. Always were and I daresay you've got worse."

"This is your last chance," Resnick said. "Say what you've got to say and get going."

"Told you, Charlie, needed to know if you really had anything or if you were just fishing. Thought if I came to you and asked straight, you'd find it hard to lie." Rains smiled. "Not in your nature, never was."

"I'm grateful."

"Yes," said Rains, getting to his feet. "For once, so am I."

"What makes you think you can just walk out of here?" Resnick asked. "How do you know I won't stop you?"

"Arrest me?"

"Why not?"

"What charge?"

Rains moved towards the living-room door and Resnick set himself in his way. More than anything else, what Resnick wanted to do was tear the smirk from Rains's face, do so with his own hands. He stepped to one side and allowed Rains to walk by. Heard the front door open and close. He stayed there, without moving, for a long time; until it was quite dark around him and the muscles of his legs were numb.

Perhaps the most pernicious thing about people like Rains was they had the power to make you behave like them.

52

The first thing Ruth saw when she looked through the window that morning was the car she had heard drive up, parked now down by the seawall, close to the first of the lobster nets. One of those removable signs on the passenger door, a mini-cab, car and driver for hire.

Ruth threw a coat over her shoulders, told the dog to stay where he was. "You didn't come all this way by taxi?"

Prior gestured, palms of his hands outwards. "I don't have a licence, Ruthie, don't own a car. What else was I to do?"

Stay away? Ruth thought, the words catching on her lips. Christ, she thought, I would hardly have recognised him. For the first time she had some insight into what it must have been like for him inside, locked away all those years.

Prior stood before her, almost sheepish. "Aren't we supposed to kiss or something?"

Despite herself, Ruth smiled. "Why break the habit of a lifetime?" she said.

Prior smiled back with his eyes. He wasn't going to hurt

her, she could tell that. "Why don't you come inside?" she asked. "I'll make some tea."

Prior looked off towards the sea. "If it's all the same to you, I'd sooner stay out here."

"Fancy a walk, then?"

"Why not?"

"Wait a second," Ruth said, turning back towards the house. "If I leave the dog behind, he won't understand."

She waited until they were on the hard, damp sand, heading south, before telling him of Resnick's visit, telling him about Rains, the way he had got into her room at night, half-frightened her to death. Pretended to have killed the dog.

"Bastard!" Prior whispered.

"Rains," Ruth said, "there's more."

"You don't have to tell me. I don't want to know."

"Yes, you do," Ruth said. "It's why you're here."

When she had felt married to him, living with him, imprisoned by him, Ruth had never been able to talk to him; now she had seen him again, this stranger, she could tell him anything.

She did: anything and everything.

Prior listened without interruption; said nothing for a long time. When he spoke it was almost wistful, distant—"Makes you think, what happened to you, me, Rains running free." There was no disguising the hurt and anger in his eyes.

"D'you want to turn back?" Ruth asked when they reached a point where the dunes came down closer towards the sea. "We've come a long way."

"Yes, all right. Best think about the taxi fare, eh?"

Several times walking back towards the cottages, Prior picked up a piece of driftwood, bleached white, and threw it for the dog to chase. At the seawall, Ruth turned quickly towards him, kissed him on the face and hurried across the green, just managing not to run, not looking back until she was inside and the car was pulling away on its long journey home.

Too late to cry now.

Prior remembered Churchill's mum, how she always maintained he was a good son. When Prior called on her, out of the blue, she was pleased to see him, invited him in.

"Frank never told me you was out."

"Could be he doesn't know."

"He'll be round soon. Always comes by of an evening when he can, likes to know I'm all right. Well, you can see I am. Come on in the lounge and put your feet up, some dreadful rubbish on telly, never mind. He'll be right pleased to see you, will Frank."

He was so pleased he tried a runner, but Prior had him by the throat, face pressed hard against the paintwork of his mum's lounge door. "I always knew you weren't worth the paper I shat on, Frank. Just give me where I can find Rains, that's all I want with you. And don't you try and warn him or I might be back."

"Thanks, Mrs. Churchill," Prior said at the rear door. "Nice to see you looking so well."

Rains had more or less finished his business here, one more plan to okay, another investment to be made on his way back through London, currency to be transferred into his bank in Spain as pesetas. It was as well he come out to talk to Frank himself, convince him of the wisdom of riding their luck less hard. When you'd kept a good thing going this long, criminal to see it come down, all because of a little local greed. But he was happy now. Frank would pass along the word, see it all dated. Tomorrow he'd be back on the plane, leaving Resnick and the rest of his former colleagues still floundering.

Rains took the brandy bottle over to the bed, poured a good measure into the glass and slid between the sheets. He had bought a Jeffrey Archer at the airport coming over and he read a couple more chapters now before finishing his drink and switching out the light.

In less than ten minutes he was asleep.

He was still asleep when a hand clamped across his mouth and a voice he failed to recognise spoke his name. Suddenly awake, he wriggled against the weight that was holding him down.

"Rains?"

The only reply was muffled, angry. What the hell was going on?

"It's me. Prior. This is for me. And my wife. In a way it's from Frank, too."

It was the old coal hammer that had stood by Frank's mum's hearth more than twenty years. When her late husband had worked down the pit, she'd got free coal and she'd kept the hammer there, handy, for breaking up the larger chunks. Prior lifted it above his head and brought it down between Rains's eyes as hard as he could.

Likely that blow was enough to kill him, but Prior didn't stop until the greater part of Rains's once handsome face was spread across the pillow and beyond.

He dropped the hammer down and wiped his hands upon the sheet, wiped splashes of blood from the bottle and gulped down some brandy, neat. There was a telephone in the next room and he used that to make the call.

"Hello? Who is this?" The voice was faltering, heavy with sleep.

"Is that Pam? Pam Van Allen?"

"Who is this?"

"It's me, Prior."

"Why are you ringing me at home, and at this time?"

"You gave me your number."

"Yes, for emergencies."

"Right," Prior said, "that's what this is."

Resnick waited a week. Prior was back inside, awaiting trial for murder. True to form, Frank Churchill had grassed on all and sundry in order to save his own hide; six men were on remand, facing five counts each of armed robbery, including Churchill himself. Ruth stayed put in her cottage and Debbie Naylor had moved back in with Kevin and the baby, though she left some of her things at her mother's just in case. Lorna Solomon applied for a job in the principal office of the Abbey National Building Society in Sheffield and got it. Mark Divine went to France for a weekend by Hovercraft and was sick both ways. Resnick waited a week before dialling the probation office number and asking to speak to Pam Van Allen.

"I suppose you're calling to crow," she said when she knew who it was.

"What over?"

"Prior, of course."

"Why? You were right. You said he had no antagonism towards his wife and you were right."

There was an uneasy pause and then Pam said, "Look, I'm sorry, but I'm really busy. . . ."

"What would you think about meeting me some time?" Resnick asked. "A drink or something. After work."

He imagined her staring at the phone, surprised, maybe slightly embarrassed, maybe pushing one hand up through her silver-grey hair.

"I don't know," she said finally. "I'll have to think about it. I'll let you know." And she hung up.

Resnick replaced the receiver and went out into the CID room, hoping not too many people would notice the smile beginning to form on his face.